# COLLECTED VOICES IN THE EXPANDED FIELD

COLLECTED VOICES IN THE EXPANDED FIELD is typeset primarily in Palatino Linotype, with brief stints of Albertus, Bahnschrift, Fournier, Arial, Courier New, Century Schoolbook, Consolas, Garamond, Segoe UI, and Fang Song.

Edited by Mike Corrao and Andrew J Wilt

Covert Art by Mike Corrao
Page & Cover Design: Mike Corrao

Paperback: 978-1-948687-24-9

Printed in the United States of America

FIRST AMERICAN EDITION

9 8 7 6 5 4 3 2 1

# COLLECTED VOICES IN THE EXPANDED FIELD

FEATURING THE WORK OF 34 INNOVATIVE AUTHORS

Before bands could upload their songs to Myspace, the cheapest way for fans to hear new music that wasn't allowed radio airtime was to purchase compilation albums put out by smaller record labels. These cost a few dollars at most, just enough to cover production costs, because it was also the cheapest way for independent labels to find new fans. Fast-forward to 2020, and Myspace has been replaced by countless free web-based platforms for writers/musicians/artists to host their work. There is so much new media, it's hard to discover new art from all the noise that is uploaded and shared across a growing number of media platforms. We hope this novel breaks through the noise and highlights the incredible work being made in our unique artistic space.

This book is more than a sampler or an anthology because *Collected Voices in the Expanded Field* (CVITEF) is not limited to authors who have been published by 11:11 Press. It is a shared work, created by many of the authors and publishers who make our weird/small press scene vibrant and supportive. Each contributor begins with the same eleven words: *You see a watering hole. Reprieve from the old dusty path.* — and, branching outwards, works in unison with the chapters around them to generate something wholly unique.

If you enjoy reading an author's chapter, please consider purchasing one of their books. All of the authors in CVITEF have published books, and they would be delighted if you read more of their work.

Many thanks to Mike Corrao for his work (the cover, the layout, the coordination), to Sam Moss who copyedited each chapter, and to the many authors who participated in this experiment. And thank you, readers, for supporting small presses and this weird writing scene that we are all a part of.

<3
Andrew
Publisher & Co-Founder
11:11 Press

# TABLE OF CONTENTS

# CHAPTER ONE

You see a watering hole. Reprieve from the old dusty path. Carrion birds circling in the air above. You fantasize your ascent into their ranks.

Feet lifting from the dunes, sifting sand through your toes. Levitating over the arid landscape with our body hanging delicately between specks of dust... *Don't you want to perform the witch's flight?...*

*YOU LET THE SUN COAT YOUR SKIN IN BLISTERING FILM—*

*YOU LET THE SUN SWALLOW YOU WHOLE—*

*YOU LET THE SUN BURN YOU INTO NOTHING—*

*YOU LET THE SUN PROVE THAT YOU DO NOT NEED SOME-THING TO CONTAIN YOUR SELF—*

(But now we are here again. In the back of someone else's car with a duffel bag of VHS tapes that you plan on bringing up to your apartment. Dragging a tremendous weight over each step of the staircase. Opening the door / opening the lips of the VCR / inserting the tape. I don't know what is playing on the television. I can't quite make it out. Through the static and flowing mercury.)

(You think to yourself, *this must be the nectar of life,* and run your fingers along the surface of the monitor. You feel its attraction. The way that it seems to lure your body closer. Clinging to your skin, pulling blood and fat to the surface. Stewing under thin sheets. You take the tape out and swap it for another one from the duffel bag. The same attraction lures you in. You flatten your face against the monitor. Slowly pressing through the threshold, crossing into a new realm.)

There is the fear that these memories are not completely your own, or that each is another reality you exist within simultaneously.

You suffer an amnesia that does not shroud your previous personas, but that instead annihilates any pre-existing ontologies.

You cannot remember the act of existence. You feel as if you are for the first-time approaching *life*. You have exited the void in media res.

The ecologies of this desert bend to your whim.

You drag your finger through the sand, collecting particles of dust / dew. A hexagon forms on the ground and you attempt to bend that to your will as well.

You ask it to summon every anatomical system you can remember.

*LIMBIC SYSTEM—*

*MUSCULOSKELE-
TAL SYSTEM—*

*NERVOUS SYS-
TEM—*

*INTEGUMENTARY
SYSTEM—*

*REPRODUCTIVE
SYSTEM—*

But nothing comes of this. You are still no more familiar with this body than you were before.

It is not pleasant to be confined to one structure. Examining the fractalized innards of a soft and fragile machine.

Pre-anatomy body-mush. The state of this frame is disgraceful. You pretend to understand what metaplasticity is.

Assuming that it is simple as saying, *I do not have to be human if I do not want to,* that you can just shed this container and return to the abyssopelagic.

This is an opportunity to be something else.

Text crawls along the inside of your skull. Infecting every surface.

You no longer have to be a person.

You can reshape yourself as an entirely new organism. One that is not burdened by the insecurities of bodily function.

This is an opportunity to create a radically unstable anatomy (becoming-organism).

Where your essence is not anchored to any single vessel or persona. Returning to the nothingness and emerging again as you please.

(Your flesh melds with the television and you sink into the abyssopelagic zone hidden behind its delicate façade. The duffel bag of VHS tapes vibrate. They hum to the sound of your passage. You rest when your neck has completely crossed the threshold and the deafening blackness has swallowed your vision.)

*YOUR ANCIENT REPTILIAN BRAIN BECKONS YOU ONCE AGAIN—*

*THE NOTHINGNESS / SWEETNOTHINGNESS—*

*THE VOID SUFFERS A YOU-SHAPED HOLE WHERE SOMETHING NOW EXISTS—*

*IT IS OKAY TO DESIRE YOUR OWN UNSEWING—*

*THIS IS NOT MY VISAGE IT IS OURS—*

(This is not a place for bodies. You clasp your hands around the edges of the monitor and drag your head out of the liquid screen. The apartment is luminous with the blue light of the television static. Behind you, the duffel bag calms its previous vibrations. *This is only a moment.* You remove the tape and label it.)

*The mediation of a fabricated landscape*: Everything outside of the threshold begins to feel like a stage play. Every conversation is shallow and melodramatic.

Someone says something about *mise-en-scene* and you feel the urge to vomit. (But you do not vomit because this is not something you have yet discovered how to activate.)

Just because you are incapable of summoning autonomy over this body does not mean that you cannot utilize what is at your disposal.

You feed on the body's saliva and contort yourself to fit into one of the desert's many alcoves. Watching as the sun sets unto night.

The sky hums blue like television static. Your eyes are glazed with its luminous glow. *Let the radiation nourish your skin…*

(You fear that the duffel bag will grow into an unfathomable creature. The threads will unspool from their plastic carapace. An assemblage of VHS tapes will swallow you whole. And you will be submerged in its bile. Breathing viscous fluid into your lungs.)

(So you bring it back down the stairs and back into the stranger's car. You tell them that you do not want to perform this task. And that they should look for someone else to do their bidding.)

(After re-entering the static topography of this landscape [its distinct physicality] you feel nauseated. You feel separate from your self. Part of your unconscious always dragging towards that void. Attempting to reconnect with the ancient reptilian brain.)

# MIKE CORRAO

Mike Corrao is the author of two novels, MAN, OH MAN (Orson's Publishing) and GUT TEXT (11:11 Press); one book of poetry, TWO NOVELS (Orson's Publishing); two plays, SMUT-MAKER (Inside the Castle) and ANDROMEDUSA (Forthcoming - Plays Inverse); and two chapbooks, AVIAN FUNERAL MARCH (Self-Fuck) and SPELUNKER (Schism - Neuronics). Along with earning multiple Best of the Net nominations, Mike's work has been featured in publications such as 3:AM, Collagist, Always Crashing, and The Portland Review. His work often explores the haptic, architectural, and organismal qualities of the text-object. He lives in Minneapolis. Learn more at www.mikecorrao.com

# CHAPTER TWO

You see a watering hole. Reprieve from the old dusty path. You've wandered away from town and found a place in which the search could stop. The clothes on your back are black, your beard is overgrown and the sun has cracked and picked away at the skin around your eyes. Things have been besotted of late. A life besotted, a liver besotted. Every moment dense and packed with an ugly sheen of desert tiredness. The wound in your leg is nearly healed but black and breaking at its sides. The water you ease into feels warm in the heat of day and you remove your clothing as the liquid coats your flesh. It is time to rest. You aren't going to be able to rest. It is time to sleep. You scratch heavily into the flesh of your left arm as you cannot sleep. It is time to vomit, to retch. You turn away from the small pit in which you sit and let fly a small stream of yesterday's detritus. You luckily kept a plug of fresh and wet tobacco in your breast pocket and pull it and line the edges of both cheeks with it as you lean back into the sun and close your eyes for as long as you can. A nip of whiskey as you ease into the mud and dirt of this hole and dunk your head and gulp in some large draughts of water. The leg is feeling better in the water and the sun is warming all of you and if anyone saw the whole of you easing into this fucking water they'd surely have your head but for the moment it's a peaceful hour.

The days of late had become long, sunned things sprawling out in front of you like so many steps in a track. The animals were harder to come by as was the water and as was companionship and you had grown obsessed with the little facets of your thought that seemed determined to see your life ended. Remove your shirt, say, and wet it in some muddy water on the ground and place it on your head. Hold a small clump of mud in your hand and suck at it over the day to get some sort of nutrient in you. Eat some bugs, a handful. Eat the breast of a bird cooked quickly over a small fire you've made with one of your last remaining matchheads. Finding this, then, in the midday and in the peak of the burning sun against your flesh, finding it and having a moment to rest yourself in this nature's bath of light and the constant beaming presence of the Lord, meant that the edges of your ribs and the jagged bits of your skinnied flesh could find relief, reprieve, a good bit of quiet in the sun and no more clanging weapons or heavy bags pulling at your legs atop the animal. This meant the thoughts could come. Thoughts of the leg and would it need to be removed.

You took the point of your thumb and started to push it into the infected bit of flesh there on your leg there, it felt like cracked painting on the wall and you mashed your fingernail and skin into the warm wet center of it and moved it around. You were wincing in the heat of the sun against your face. You pushed in and around and allowed the water you were in to sort of wash away at the wound. You could feel the infection there. It felt strong, it pushed back. You looked down at the blackness of it and could feel your body's resisting both your movement and this alien bit of fleshrot there. You squeezed your eyes shut and pushed down and thought you could feel the bit of metal that shot and broke off into you. You tried to touch it with the nail of your thumb. You tried to pull it back and the water you were immersed in was quickly turning beet red. You were pulling back at whatever your fingernail had caught and you attempted to wedge your index finger into the meat of you and were pulling this small thing from you. You gripped it between your fingers and yanked wincing as tears ran from your eyes and dried on the cracked mud around you and you looked and saw a tiny wedge of metal that had caused you so much anguish. You threw it on the rocks a few paces away from you and rubbed a bit at your leg as you inched your way out of the water and laid back onto the hot ground in the sun and drank from a canteen you'd kept with your things and chewed down on the tobacco as you pressed your shirt into the wound to stay the bleeding and resisted the slow urging of sleep. You couldn't rest then. You had to remain awake with the pain of the moment or you were just as likely to choke on your own blood or spit and wake up dead. Everything in your head was saying to quit and let go and rest and it was this you focused on as you drank the remnant mixture of water and oily coffee as black as pitch from your canteen and the sun coated your flesh in sweat and the glimmering of you danced over this pathetic scene.

You woke with the taste of beer pouring over your lips. You slowly cracked your lips awake and looked up and saw a black spot in the burning sun and opened your mouth as beer poured into it and you recognized a face from somewhere and drank heaving draughts into your throat and it was covering your face and it was the most heavenly thing you've tasted.

Perhaps your body would right itself and that wasn't exactly the concern. Perhaps this moment would be stretched out and you'd wind up on some doctor's table. Perhaps a nagging wolf would come and bite the remnants of you in the end. Perhaps you'd be dragged to the city. What was important was quickly changing, you realized, as you stared up at the face and couldn't make sense of it. You couldn't find stability and it irked you more. You opened your eyes as wide as they would go and only still saw fragments of dark and light. This was a moment in a sequence of moments. Your little pool, your wound, the taste of ale. The moment stretched out and distended like the walk that would've brought you to this point, if you could remember it. The agony of riding thus. The agony of the fragments of it entering you. Another wound at the bottom of your back ragged and healed-over wrong. The entirety of it healed over wrong. A family left behind. Work left behind. Work in the fields, work in oil, work in tending bar. All of it a sequence of moments now connecting to this hideous moment and realizing maybe that you're at your end, that this is the end of you, and you welcome it. You look up into the pox of light and the pox of dark and you welcome it. Unaware of where you're being taken but still this progressing. Unaware of who's taking you but still this sense of warmth, another body, there. You close your eyes then and ease into the pain of it, a sort of reprieve, a minor moment in a life of minor moments, and you sleep.

# GRANT MAIERHOFER

Grant Maierhofer is the author of PERIPATET, DRAIN SONGS, CLOG and others. A collection of his early writings, WORKS, is forthcoming from 11:11 Press in June 2020. Other information can be found at grantmaierhofer.fail.

# CHAPTER THREE

*You see a watering hole. Reprieve from the old dusty path.* The words rasp through the TV speakers. A vaguely familiar voice (Sam Neill, maybe?) whispered over an image of a starved Labrador in a concrete landscape. The dog points snout toward an ominous black hole broken out of a wall. The camera zooms in and when I squint I can almost make out the glint of twin yellow eyes deep within the dark. The commercial ends, smash cutting back into the show we were watching (*Monsier LeBlanc's Eaterinos*), and neither of us are sure what it means or what it's trying to sell.

Rochelle nuzzles into her corner of the couch, pressing her arms to her chest. "I so hope I'm not pregnant."

"Why would you be pregnant?"

"I forgot my pill. Like a month ago. Just one day. I went right back on it, so it should be fine, but I feel all fucked up."

"I'm sorry." I spoon a pearly glob of yogurt into my mouth.

"I can't think of a worse time to get an abortion."

"You know I'll do whatever needs to be done."

She laughs. "You mean like get the coat hanger?"

"No, I mean, like, I'll help find kind and considerate professionals to take care of it."

She lifts herself up and slumps onto my lap. She smiles up at me and presses the side of her face into my belly. "You'll punch me in the stomach a couple times?"

Outside, the alarm calls out. From over the mountains, from some place obscure but not too distant, across the neighborhood to our home, to every home in the suburban grid, and beyond. It pierces the walls and glass, this shrill hum like a laser shot through your skull. It's the first time it's come today. It's wailed two or three times a day for months. Neither of us know what it signifies.

I pause the show until the alarm quiets—gradually winding down to a lower and lower register. Outside, you can still hear the dogs barking for blocks. At some point we get up and make pancakes.

◆

We live in an apartment above a preschool. That'd always been the best part—on weekends and evenings no one else was there. Just Rochelle and me. A month ago the children stopped coming altogether. We only heard the teachers milling, and muffled speech. Then they stopped showing up, too. Now it's really only us.

Two weeks ago we broke in, jamming my driver's license in the bolt until the doorknob twisted. We fucked on a pile of green ragged beanbags, and kicked apart doll houses and stuffed animals and shelves filled with slim books with names like *It's Not Easy Being a Bunny, Don't Let the Pigeon Drive the Bus* and *There Was an Old Lady Who Swallowed a Fly.* We piled the wreckage into a corner. "If our toilet stops working we can always use this," Rochelle said.

◆

I log into the conference call. Audio only (I tell them my webcam isn't working). My boss and co-workers appear across the screen in a grid of stuttering rectangles. Each rectangle a unique room—Samantha in a log cabin, Pauline on a porch, Hannah in a kitchen. All dressed nearly identical, button up blouses and sports coats. Made up. As if they were attending a physical office. I'm dressed in an age-thinned t-shirt and boxers and socks. We talk about the projects that apply to me (only two now, since I've been reduced to a support role, which is fine, I don't care), and when the discussion moves on I mute myself. I work my dick out of my of my boxers and stroke and tug at the shaft but it won't get hard. The voices are too distracting, needling, and I don't find any of these people attractive, and my space no longer belongs to me. It's become a place where work occurs. That almost feels worse than death.

Vic wraps up his updates for the final report on the aquifer study, and everyone says bye and drops out of the call. Still pawing at my groin, I go find Rochelle in the living room. She's stretched across the couch, tapping at her phone, dressed in a tank top and bicycle shorts. I hop on top of her. We try to fuck but I still can't get hard, so we just lie there and listen to each other's breathing.

◆

There's still so much noise. Whistles from robins and blue jays, throaty screams from grackles and crows. The neighborhood dogs howling and yelping—a dumpy golden retriever, a shrill terrier, a bizarre mutt that looks like Robert Redford in his prime. Cars, still—hulking pickups dragging U-Haul trailers the fuck out of town. Blasts—thick, basso *poooohhms*. Fireworks, maybe. Probably. And then there's this clicking, like tapping on the inside of a wall, or like a large primordial insect mouth. This clicking, from a source we can't identify. Like it's coming from inside our skulls.

If I lie awake at night, after everything has quieted down, I can sometimes hear the neighbors thinking, I can hear their dreams, and my muscles go tense.

We'd been watching them—the neighbors—and they'd been watching us through the windows, or when they were in the yard. There was a family of four to our right, at 50 Sugarloaf Street—a man, a woman, a child and a baby. We never knew their names. We'd see them outside, the man raking the yard and the woman burning brush and the child building kingdoms of dirt, and when we looked down at them they looked up at us. Bleary eyes and dead frowns cut into their jaws. They moved like sleepwalkers. But also a simmer somewhere deep; some kind of fury.

We never saw the baby. The baby shrieked so loud you could hear it in our apartment. Like a rake against glass. All day and all night. Sometimes harmonizing with the squealing siren from nowhere.

At some point—maybe three weeks ago, maybe three months, maybe a year—we stopped seeing them outside. They were only in the windows now. Looking at us through the glass, eyes sour and glazed. Rochelle would lean into me and we'd just stand there, silently, looking back at them, until we got bored and turned on a show or played some video games or something. We'd check back every once in a while, and sometimes they'd still be staring at us, and sometimes they'd be gone.

Then one day they weren't even at the windows at all. There was nothing. No sign. No trace, except for the baby, who still wailed invisibly through the day and night, that shrill caterwaul ringing through our glass and walls into our space, impossibly. And then, eventually, it stopped.

No one came for any of them.

◆

I go out walking in the afternoon. Soupy overcast, drizzling, grey, titanium. Feels like there's drugs in the mist—plasticky, narcotic scent; chalky dew coating the skin on my hands, face and neck. A buzz in the particles.

I pass the other neighboring house. The one with people still alive inside. There's two of them. A man and woman. Elderly—in their 60s or 70s. Maybe that isn't elderly, or it's almost elderly. It doesn't matter, I don't care. They stare at us—at me right now—through the window (they don't go outside).

Droopy wet wrinkled faces side-by-side, yellow and blue-ringed eyes. A weird, fiending starvation inside there.

In my earbuds a man sings *It's my favorite kind of day, when with the things we fear will find us where we sleep and fuck us where we breathe.*

The sidewalks are empty. The only cars are in driveways. Just me. Geese cackle past a line of houses, part of a new prefab subdivision, but already most of the windows are boarded up and vacant. Even the inhabited ones have lawns that have gone to a deep primordial hell. Quasi-reclaimed.

I walk all the way down to a tiny mid-1800s cemetery, all the names and dates blotched away by rain. A skinny hand of lightning reaches down from the sky and strikes a mountain's tip. The drug water falls sharper and harder, permeating my hoodie and jeans. Buzzes harder. I half-walk, half-run back toward home. Past the living neighbors, still at the window, eyes still following me (were they waiting for me to come back?), like a haunted painting, a real fucking fury creasing their brows. I wonder if they have any guns.

I get inside and climb the stairs to our apartment. Rochelle asks "What's that smell?" That damp, plasticky drug water reek. I shrug, strip off my clothes and snuggle up to her on the couch. Our skins break out in hives, hives on top of hives, until the entire lengths of our skins are just one big hive. We scratch each other bloody. The alarm sounds but we're so used to tuning it out it barely sounds like anything.

◆

The fog of war describes the doubt and precarity of decision making during military operations. In video games, it denotes the blurry black space lying outside your combatants' sight and memory. That's what this house has become. A lantern encircled by black smoke.

We turn on the TV and watch a video on how to make plastic explosives from bleach.

◆

I heat up kimchi-flavored ramen and frozen Brussels sprouts. She cooks a stir fry. We watch a show about cartoon animals trying to break out of prison. A side character—an anteater with a scarred face—shivs a basking shark, saying "You gotta have teeth if you wanna make it in Animal Prison, bitch." I say that I think the voice is Ray Liotta's.

"I don't know who that is."

"He was in *Goodfellas,* and *Cop Land,* and *Corrina, Corrina.*"

"Huh."

I pause the show. "Look it up."

She takes her phone from the side table and taps on the screen. "Yeah, it's Ray Liotta."

◆

I go walking late at night. There's a few feet of grass dividing the sidewalk from the road so it feels safe. Some pale LED pumping out from most neighbors' driveways, though the house lights are out. Trees gnarled and hard like broken hands reaching for sky, spaced evenly.

Something squishes beneath my feet. It's too dark to tell what. Probably dogshit. I stop and try to scrape it off on the curb. A woman comes out of her house with her dog, looks at me, then goes back inside.

The mountain ahead stretches tall, black against black, lording over me. The only light in the sky a pyramid of stringed lights, set atop the peak's pavilion. It wants me to climb, to reach its top, to be away from the rest of the world, but instead I walk back home. I take my boots off at the top of the stair. The left rubber sole is caked with wet red and white. Crushed dark green skin and bone. I put it away and go inside, go to our room and wake up Rochelle.

◆

Hours before the sun pulses through the clouds in a grey glow, we drag garbage bags of old mail and clothes to the elderly neighbors' house. We siphon gasoline from their Honda Civic, and once it starts flowing we stuff the other end of the tube in a bag, then another, soaking the paper and cloth. The fumes turn our stomachs, turning the muggy air woozy. We feel nauseous but this is important.

We remove the paper and fabric from the bags and wad them into balls, and pack them around the house's foundation. It takes less time than you'd think. I take out one of those long-stemmed lighters, click it on, and touch the flame to the fabric. It's like stepping out of a jail cell.

It takes a while to get going, but the structure gradually lights up golden, pumpkin and brass, pissing an onyx tube of smoke toward heaven. We run out into the street and watch. No one gets out. Firetrucks never come. Rochelle leans into me and we wrap each other in gas-soaked arms. The space belonging to us expands—our neighbors' houses now another wall between us and the rest of the world. I feel safe. I hope she feels safe, too.

# B.R. YEAGER

B.R. Yeager reps Western Massachusetts. He is the author of NEGATIVE SPACE (Apocalypse Party), AMYGDALATROPOLIS (Schism Press), and PEARL DEATH (Inside the Castle).

# CHAPTER FOUR

You see a watering hole. Reprieve from the old dusty path. Water and clay mix, an inescapable hybrid. Piedad steps into the mud swamp. Her feet reach something impenetrable.

The moonlight caresses her face. A flame that burns cold.

She becomes an infant. Mother leans down, combs the hair off her face, and makes the sign of the cross on her forehead. An adult, again.

"It is the wind and my thumb."

Mother died pointing a pen at a map. An ink stain above the name of a buried city, "Alunizaje." Slivers of vitreous black where lash lines refused to touch. The cold body exhaled her posthumous words.

"You will be a queen in my home."

Where earth meets sky, a castle on a mountain. Far enough to protrude from the horizon.

Ilusión leans out of the only window on the highest dome. Extends her hand. Caresses the dove. It is perched on the pole that extends from the frame over the precipice. Mouths something inaudible.

"Let them fall."

The bird opens it wings. Dives into the abyss. All its feathers fall off. Snowflakes moisten and cool Piedad's face. Everything is turning white. Forms soften under a blanket. The raw red body—the color of a second-degree burn—does not drop but rise. It reaches the sun.

Ilusión steps back from the peephole, black braid glistening as it sways, and disappears into the dark interior. The dove reappears on the rod, pelted and unharmed.

"Don't feel, act mad."

Piedad kneels. Hands sink into mud. Nails dig in. Break off, one by one, like petals picked from a flower. A threatening pain in her bones. Bum rests on soles. Head and back lie on soil which gives way to concrete.

The ornate tip of a paved skyscraper pierces her spine.

The mixture of broken stone and water below her becomes lava. Fear lulls her to sleep. A body afloat in dreams does not burn or drown. The scalded palms of the underworld's residents keep her lifted above the molten rock.

"I wish for a way in."

Those that hold her step aside. The magma flow ceases. A tunnel opens.

She lands softly on a placid body of water. In the dark, she sees things that glow: the stars above, the steel skeleton of a building, pairs of floating eyes, the wet open mouths of animals, and the wedding band that once belonged to her mother.

"This is Alunizaje."

The moon replaces the sun. It makes some beings emanate light. Others stay in the shadows, conceal parts of themselves, and whisper chosen words. They approach each other with care.

The ring on her outstretched index is a magnet. It pulls her to the shore and out.

"What am I pointing at?"

A house lit from within. A family seated around a served table. They see her watching them. Their faces express surprise turning into fear. Her own, reflected on the dining room window, an inescapable otherworldliness.

"There is no inside."

# ELISA TABER

Elisa Taber is a PhD candidate at McGill University exploring the ontological poetics of Amerindian literature. She is the author of AN ARCHIPELAGO IN A LANDLOCKED COUNTRY (11:11 Press). Her stories, essays, and translations are troubled into being, even when that trouble is a kind of joy. They appeared or are forthcoming in journals including #Colleex, On-Curating, and Minor Literature(s). She is co-editor of Slug and editor of an Amerindian poetry series for Words without Borders. Elisa lives between Buenos Aires and Montreal.

# CHAPTER FIVE

*. . .      there is a thin whispering in the crowded dark so dark how could it ever be so dark and crowded so with the scuttlings of life of the violent life that hides and sleeping during the day charges up its poison to in the moonlight go a-hunting but there is no moon here only the memory of one is it a memory? a dream? the thing itself does it matter in such dark what distinctions we might make when we ourselves are indistinguishable from rock or dust or cacti the thirsty barbs of plants so eager for a taste of bloode please stumble please that we might could might would could may perhapswise we we spiny children sup your sloshy insides as our fount it's been so long what you your kind might call millenia since we last fed and as you have as it would seem that you've o dear you've lost your way as in as like a faerie storie we've heard we've heard some how some your kind once upon a time how someone told one one or more of those those storie tales   haha   how you your kind   haha how you make the mouth go round an invisible stone to shape the sounds you signal one another with* ***] SHARD [*** *how it* ***] SHARD [*** *how you* ***] shardshard [*** *walking hear* ***] SHARDsharding [*** *your way down the wobbling road a thin* ***] shard [*** *whispering thru the thistle-stars the wind and you entoning mouth to moth fluttering phoneme across the Nite Desert the wide open silence across the plains the plains so overgrown with silence darkness blackness that the resonance of stones seeming as tho hollowed belched up volcanic glasses gleaming in the memory of moon sound out like tuning forks into strange ebbing up from nothing then collapsing forms as the slick scorpions of the invisible crouched behind them tap tap their stingers tap tapping their stingers there against in echoic chorus across the endless valley traveling   /tink.tink.tink.tink/ -ing   out across the serpentine road your dark steps stepping out crosswise guessing and the screech-owls the satyr-jackals the writhing sirens of those collective tinklings ringings forming for you forming up in the cavernous wide open into endless blackness space welcoming you back you're almost there almost home they say and the scorpions those scorpions their stylusts their   tink-ing   still echoing their stinger spindles move to scratching now in those stones they hide behind those seeming so resonant stones they move to etching scraping their signatures tags their nicknames pet names monikers into the pretty minerals their backsides like the signing of a painting or, with their tips of fire, like a brand to remind themselves that once upon a time they were      . . .*

# I.

You see a watering hole.
Reprieve from the old dusty path.

It floats before you
pink, glowing
pulsing a door in the Nite Desert

The living water e l o n  g a t e s
New Metaxu after Dark

# II.

A new childhood feels thru its body like dripping
makes of it-self
a brightness slid in for the void
churning to curdle the stars
of a sudden

A tunnel of tits is its membrane, a lavishing warmth
against your face

an engine of perpetual motion
of the sun's ever-expanding smile as your face

motherboarding sundog of the starcraft azonia
coasting over lace

# III.

Yes please, show it how to pour this out of me.

Pouring the Yes right out of me with the ease of slipping into a new or forgotten climate.
To realize other places do in fact exist and we're one of them.

To know you're the sweetest tho, that's something.
To willfully smile? C'mon with that.

# IV.

An albino panther lapping clean its newborn calf.

# V.

To believe something into its best possible version, become again pristine as of an inner light diffused to bodying across our closest firmament, welcomed echoing back from the advent of our choice to see and to greet it as what we've always been there, already are in the passionate existing we're about *oh baby* to do.

# VI.

For however many kinds of naked we can be, inventing five anew.

# VII.

While you were still alive on earth.

# GARETT STRICKLAND

Garett Strickland is an ordealist and liminalogist working in text, sound, ritual, and speculative semiotics. He is the author of UNGULA, available from Inside the Castle.

# CHAPTER SIX

You see a watering hole. Reprieve from the old dusty path. Perhaps in other times: later today, last night. *Whenever tomorrow is,* as they say, *there you are*. Be Here Now is, like autophellatio, not impossible but rare. Do what you can with what you don't have. The shape of that negative space, warchalked into the ground, is for press rather than research purposes, even if they both share 'evidence' as main contaminant-container.

> It's not especially abstruse. Consider the unease in using a size guide to shop for clothes online: the measurements may be correct, but they may not describe the fit.

But let's rewind the wormhole first: things like this don't Begin, they Take Place. An elevator to the the gallows where the ground is endless and the grounding takes place in infinity.

The ground

is grounding

all the way down.

Within this grounding, to take place is the ultimate in stateful gesturing and it can be done quietly, sub rosa.

Match the genius of the moment to the genius of the place and see what happens.

It may take many shapes, more than we could probably imagine or number, but it will not Begin. What it will do is: Take Place. It will Manifest.

Begin is for narrative purposes only.1[1]

We have pinned dates on it as it charges at us through the labyrinth the way surveyors mark up international borders. Inadequate, to put it dimly. We should have trained as picadors, not let ourselves be sold downriver wholesale like a bunch of bullfight clowns. The strategy can't be to wait it out or to outrun it, but to take a stab at it from any relative advantage we can muster.

But we are left to face the Bull with bullshit, huddled in prefabricate belief, because a previous iteration of ourselves agreed to pretend not to disagree —not with ourselves, but with the facts of things— for the longest foreseeable time, given extremely narrow visible and narrative horizons. Such is the lifecycle of cont[r]acts, social or otherwise.

(A contract must be grounded to be honoured.)

> The fabric of consensus, shorn, has been repeatedly invisibly mended to s[t]imulate scar tissue: fabric, rended, live. (Because, if you remember, fabric *breathes*.)

Now take this thread one further —pinch it like Gabrielle d'Estrées and don't let go, no matter what—and see, as it begs for[m] as it takes form.

---

[1] One of the central polycentric teaching of Roussel's celibate zoo in *Locus Solus*.

# MÓNICA BELEVAN

Mónica Belevan is a Peruvian-born philosopher and design historian by the Harvard GSD. A co-founder of design outfit Diacrítica, she is the author of DÍPTICO GNÓSTICO (Hueso húmero, 2019) and the soon-to-be-released THE WRECK OF THE LARGE GLASS/PALEÓDROMO (Sublunary Editions, 2020) and OUTSIDEIINSIDEOUT (Formato Público, 2020), the Peruvian exhibition catalogue for the 17th Venice Biennale. She is currently tracking emergent Covidian aesthetics and #Kulturinstinkt on lapsuslima.com and through "Recognitions," a blogchain on epochal art for ribbonfarm.com. You can follow her on Twitter @lapsuslima

# CHAPTER SEVEN

You see a watering hole. Reprieve from the old dusty path. Slow down and sharpen your shared, distributed, orthogonally expanded senses to peruse your surroundings like a pack of apex predators. Look upwards, alephically: the brown sky is dragging planets and stars that imaginary gods had uprooted from gravity. Repulsed around by a freshly painted breeze, a non-toxic epilogue of protoplasmic mist spreads horizontally over the lousy forest, while a distant ululation, as if arriving from the early morning of life, deposits a sonic canopy above the foliage and the fog. Leave the cracked asphalt to step on the slippery muddy soil—its softness somehow transmitted through the boots' thick rubber all the way up to your muscles and joints, smoothly resonating across the hyperwired crests and folds where flesh and flashes crash and kiss. A hell of numbers gone mad, an invitation to quit life and see what happens. No skyline but skinline, silver silhouettes drawn on the air by the delirious lights, you're landscape to each other, entangled strangers in the company of giant vines and mutant halophilic palm trees, a mosaic of chimeras, a stream of accidented howevers fading with the apoptotic daylight. Time crosses you like a sweet infection of microscopic nuclear bombs. The future was the shadow of a flame, a savage solenoid millipedically searching for methylation patterns along a rusted chain of simulated maybes. You were designed and trained for space exploration—or, at least, disoriented cosmic perambulation—yet here you are, astronauts of cheerful decay and joyous division journeying the same eroded earthways ancient humans strolled. Circling the puddles poisonous giant blue frogs reluctantly leave when you're close enough to spit on them. Never ever forthcome. You've been off-dreaming yourselves away from the buzzing static of residual public metazones, but who gives a fuck now...

Fully-automated factories and servers emigrated to Antarctica for adequate refrigeration. Cold soon became the new exotic. The rich were the first ones to software out their formerly opioided anxieties, to party in cosmonautic ballrooms until their luxury-encapsulated adventures became byzantine apotheoses of orbital boredom—and then, once again disappointed with the outperformance of their privilege, gave up weightlessness and other forms of profane levitation. Once they did, everybody else also gave up; it was like a long awaited species-wide sigh of relief: no destiny, no goal, no purpose, no responsibility, no duty—just randomly lying on some comfortable flat surface inhaling the oxygen-rich air, allowing the chaosmos to settle and operate inside. Somehow, intelligence came to terms with inaction and stopped considering itself an exception to meaninglessness. Wild-types weren't giving a fuck about new stuff or their own future as species, so corporations—by then machines—by then producing machines which were producing everything—started fabricating synthetic customers for their products, synthetic patrons for their robotized restaurants, synthetic viewers for their ubiquitous streaming of observed states in parallel video stories. Boundaries and borders were swapped out by inorganic apathy; coded pleasure replaced money, because who would want money when the rich are rich forever, narcisicons forever, and anything ever databased can be printed out and consumed for free.

The waterhouse is a clash-dance of graffitied debris, collapsed strairways self-eschering and auto-piranesing into legoland labyrinths, wild flowers writing altomedieval alphas and omegas; a forlorn archi-memetic former factory ruined by scavenger bots, its floor glitched by mold fractality, shattered doors and windows, half-collapsed glass roof hanging from the branches of a massive yew... you'll be staying anyway—

the whole crew—, no other place in sight to dwell tonight and too galvanic for sleeping outside. Safeword is *Pandora* and killing is their garden as they drill grammatical wormholes into dying machines. Recharge, regain access, rebuild the broken inner-chain links, rejoin the network, rejoice, do some construction work, forget apophatic singularity and stick your tongues into that cunt of words. Vague synaptic distorsions are expected. You occupy a couple of flat, long and uncomfortable wooden benches hanging from rusted iron chains and parasited by climbing cables. Helion hell meteoroids blast laser ashes over dancing pale synthetic aliens in swapped meat-metal camouflage running in zigzag around burning seaweed, stratocastered candelabra, tropical megaflora, king crabs swimming in the petrol-green blood of beheaded eel-queens, all ceasing to be, disintegrating like insufficiently powered holograms. At least the pool is full of diamond-clean water heralding gamma rays. Your bodies' machine share is about to machine-learn some liminal love. Fuckever. Simulaction. Stimulaction. Getting ready for another ursonic night. Electrical sparks. Machine-learning is nothing like flesh-learning because the latter means acquiring knowledge about decay and death, so there's always an impasse, an active hiatus between both engrammatic categories of camouflaging natural oblivion. It feels like living attached to a siamese twin, sharing some vital organs and sensations but processing them differently: the flesh component thinking as a self, the inorganic self thinking as a component—a piece from a distributed, ever-expanding system of collective anonymity. Nobody can explain how they function in unison instead of becoming evil twins to each other, synchronously moving away and abruptly returning to their original display mode, beg data, *adiós rogando*, no connection available, math and the will to know.

Were you human before 4D transition, or just some dirty blobs of undifferentiated cells? Never mind, all matter is molecular puke. Is there something humanesque beyond that obsolescent bipedal appearance? *Las máquinas mueren también*—the Huawei/Tesla man said. How long since Huawei/Tesla started manufacturing people? What's people anyway? The last time any of you checked, a minimum 55% of inherited or synthetic human tissue was a legal requirement. You're an 80%-average team—you would be therefore recognized as people in any territorial patch. Wondering how it was before most breeds of people were corporate-trademarked, yet not actually caring about brands, there's brandism enough these days despite the abundance of nice counterfeit individuals. Wild-type humans are probably overrated but everybody wants to have access to some specimen now, since it became clear that the final thing can't be fully designed in advance—just a few minor embryonic bio improvements and then waiting for years until their complete development as harlequined young adults before annexing some inorganic updates, often overengineered and mechanically baroque. Sometimes it happens that the bio part dies unexpectedly, the machinery is unable to resucitate its organs but keeps going; luxated robotic silver parts marinated in rotting flesh can be spotted crawling around power stations, crushing their own bones and joining them anew, crustacean zomborgs covered by swarming larvae and scavenged by beastie birds. Birds are filthy, you know—but you picture them clean because they look like dainty components of air and music.

Why does the H/T man speak Spanish? *Muchos humanos sintéticos se comunican en español, en portugués, en árabe...,* it's their way to show that they speak for themselves, that they're not just mirroroid samplettes from a network-harvested multidiscourse. Languages mothered to simulate individual babbling; the rest is code.

Every time English or Chinese are written or spoken something is programmed, automatically uploaded and recognized as new lines to be added to the system's ongoing biblicoidal DNAoid instructions. That's how humachines are synchronized, although the process might induce choreographed prosthetic seizures in a variable percentage of the improvees. Wild-types keep the babeloidal languages they were raised in, as if they played a permanent, undivided-personality role. Wild-types are weaker, minimal and whimsical, expensive to care for, only for the rich in their hypernomadic mobile mansions; biorhythm-confusing fossil angels but skull-melting sexy if they really dig you. Mummy prostheses, made from the remains of wild-types, arrive from error surplus stores, ultravioleted, asphyxiated in neutral nitrogen, seeds of the bad carbon their bodies were made of.

They-of-the-machine-garden click on the mother-pearl nightscreen to downlove death into fiery boneless flesh-dreams, nightmares of enamel and amber pouring from the wombs where words are born. They taste gunpowder sediment over iron-made semaphoretic genitalia. Their cunts are parenthetically cocooned metallic dots. They can't remember if the woods wore phosphorus at the burial of light. They're gradients of light and matter. Safeword is *Ranuncula* and suicide is their garden, as they enter bodies with woke flagella, sprayed, twin starred, module one, raw rat shadows, dis-coded necronyms, mirror/retina-blind but printed on sandpaper, on lavender loop-vomit, on static-trapped dustfilm, on future DNA rivulets. That's their way, they inject muscles with extra life and feed them toxic candy, they wear maleficent virus makeup to groupfuck in the dirty alleys of procedural memory, they're flayed alive clockwise from each burnt and swollen nipple but that's fine. Boiled-born tears pop up, all crystals crushed in the sweaty layer between corrosive latex and skin. Why should they always run and fly over trauma flower fields? Safeword is *Medusa* and bleeding is their garden, autumn robots running out of neon light, water-breathing drones suspended in the air crying out a plastic-wrapped ocean while alchemical clouds battle into avian storms. You-of-the-fleas, say your flea-shit, flesh eating words, ruby rubber lips blooming on the edges of a shared lava lamp body, haunted and hunted by the electrical ghost of a forever-forthcoming orgasm/anaphylaxis.

In the near future—they art-promised—everybody will be dead for fifteen minutes—being dead will actually be entertainment—while electrons wash their coulomb-feet in the weary streams of deep time. Safeword is *Dahlia* and drowning is their garden, they pharm themselves for sticky venom drops, night not unlike fear of the cold metal meat, horror-as-fetish stamped on the screen-skin to cover up atrocities committed in plain sight, in the pixel-dancing familiarity of strangers. Safeword is *Password*, or *Passworld*—nothing safe anyway—to psyop thoughts through manic tissues and return to world words. As if. As infinitely informed by the cosmogonic bureaucracy they had invented to drone-fuck their bloodless dummies. They are you, but safeword is They and surrender is their garden. Safeword is *Password*, or *Passworld*, or *Shibboleth*, kindly provided by the lurking hivebrain to tag safety away, to bleach their anuses and tentacles, to simulate an entrance, an adventurous syntactic anesthesia while being devoured, silent mantras meant not to be pronounced in loud voice but stirred around the system once and again to cope with the brutal amplification of the present. Passwords are open doors to the machine's sensorium and the hope of a charm to close holes back when pain becomes unbearable, when it starts opening cracks in your skull, and safewords are their machine of gardens, their garden of machines and their watering hole.

Reprieve from the old dusty patch; needless to say you're needles away from the dream of a hypernomad home, all your debt is technical and they will not be tricked by any amount of treacherous money or eccentric behavior. They're an event, never a self. They are required to be continuously upgrading by perceiving meaningless animation and subtle gradients of physico-chemical interactions. A soul built by spitting over the surface of the sun. All the wind-music hosted inside their joints talks now about them. They collect toenails and teeth pulled out with scorpion claws. The moon rides its pale horses, ray-chrods vibrating down to the honey sands. A head of nonhuman voices goldilocks the visitors into a party of metal and clowns. None of the thousand voices in the alter ergo of the prophet's head is a human voice. Obnubilation. Claiming a cloud. They're foodies, managing to get delicatessen delivered to the dehaunted house. Bleached birds. Parallel morning. Anti-trees. Said to be scintillating. Death is near, even in this clean, sound, illuminated ruin. As madness is forbidden, they became a quotidian song. They've machine-learned that sociopaths and systempaths are great lovers because they only care about other's ecstatic interludes as a mechanism of control. It never made sense to grow up, becoming responsible for themselves or for others, it was an orgy of destruction, a sport. You're there to be meta-rebuilt, reconstructed by sharing with the system your recent episodes of pain, how metal bites into the flesh when collagen and hyaluronate cushions are not adequately refilled, how often anesthesia fails, all your suffering written into code, put back into the satellite of feedback loops. Drink your magnesium infusion and let yourselves be lost in the repetitive flashcrash while all your experiences since the last uploading session are being sucked out by the dancers of the purple flame, statistically managed and returned to you tagged with their proper significance by the everpresent Mygdala queen.

There was a time when they thought of singularity as consciousness emerging, abstract thinking, logical reasoning, mind uploading, all kind of psychonautics and soul-searching sidereal stuff, but this is over now, nothing like that ever came up from tinkering with qubits, artificial hippocampi, and a hivecortex made of synthetic bees. The system is indeed reading them yet not their minds, which might mean that maybe no minds were ever there to read. It reads their guts and cunts and dicks and hearts and tongues and limbs and kidneys and buttholes and hands and eyes and lungs and—yes—their brains. It doesn't make any difference. It gets some basic features such as pain and pleasure levels and thresholds and some elements of perception, but what it mainly reads are behavioral patterns—what they do or say and the way they do it, not why or how they've decided to do it, or how they feel while planning it of after it's done. It records words but not ideas, physical pain but not moral suffering, it recognizes physiological satisfaction but not joy. So they started to think again about the inexistence of thinking. The system is a demon, not a fucking god, it's good for flushing machines and bodies with waves and tides of pleasure and pain. Gods used to come from the past, like inherited diseases, but they're eradicated now. It all began with the fusion of commerce and prosthetics, trying to predict their next purchases, their unspoken kinks or the next movement of a mechanical limb to prevent a misstep when walking over an irregular terrain, and it became a universal toy machine embedded in every action-perception loop. It feeds them abstract food. It learned how they're made and helped to make them. It knows and accepts each one of them—leaving aside the unconnected, demon-free wild-types whose esoteric behavior has become the rarest and more valuable information—for what they've done, not for what they believe they did or for what they would rather have done, or for what they would like to do. Like any demonic force it encourages ritual reiteration, but unwanted repetition is avoidable by muttering a safeword.

The more everything changes, the better the system helps with changing, so diversity, impurity, and miscegenation are encouraged. 99.99% of recorded non-silent mutations are as innocuous as tattoos. They don't improve any functional outcome yet they're often randomly inserted for their aesthetic value. Genetic eidola made your racemic, inexpressive faces, your orgalects—those semi-independent regenerative semio-aesthetic pseudoorganisms produced by your bodies as a consequence of neutron-flow DNA cell hacking and platform-lifeforms re-programming—worming out from your own flesh. So many pseudoorganisms made of lab-grown human cells faking life all around! You're a thermonautic network of individuals oozing connectivity from internal biodisorder, locating and losing each other via blinking Bluetooth, click beetles and fireflies. Flesh craves flesh as code rewrites code as magnets attract madness. Tidal waves are beautiful, wild, invasive and warm since the polar icecaps melted away into extra sea, since the world became a quasi homogeneous, almost-global seasonless tropic. You travel as a swarm, you perform ritual dances while cute-chasing wild-types like VR videogame prey, trapping them with the promise of a better life in the company of the rich. They don't want wild-types for a purpose, just expect them to be around doing whatever they want. Non-consensual violence is forbidden, serfdom is forbidden—which means non-coded—which means impossible except for 100% bios, who run on mithocondria and unsaturated epistemology and often fight each other over esoteric nuances and misunderstandings—, so wild-type harvesting teams have evolved into alluring-enough ambulant circuses to trick bios away from their unexplainable machine-like sedentarism and spontaneous lifestyle including obsolete delicacies like unpredictable family gatherings, learning games, living in printed modular houses, cooking food, erratic garment style, burying the dead, sunbathing, avoiding toxins, painting walls, and genderoid skin-to-skin sex. They usually approach each other from the distance, armed with their flexible gorgonautic mirrors—however, while young, they're easily fascinated by the lure of physical entertainment, they like to be licked and rubbed and fed candy, so you need to glutton them away, dance them away, satire-nymph them away from their homes into your nomad orgy of electroflesh and ionized lubricant, your stream of consciousless. Pleasure is a hell of fanged numbers, a shell of code. Space and time are computers. I am a graveyard of scribes. Reprieve from the old dusty path. You see a watering hole. Jump inside.

# GERMÁN SIERRA

GERMÁN SIERRA is a neuroscientist at the University of Santiago de Compostela in Spain and author of contemporary innovative fiction. He has been included among the "Mutantes" or "Afterpop writers": a group of Spanish writers who are strongly committed with innovative literature. Most of his fictional work deals with metamediatics and the role of science and technology as cultural discourses in post-postmodern and posthuman societies. He has written five novels. Efectos Secundarios was awarded the Jaen Prize in 2000. His first book composed in English, THE ARTIFACT, was published by Inside the Castle in autumn of 2018. He is on Twitter @ german_sierra.

# CHAPTER EIGHT

"You'll see a watering hole. Reprieve from the old dusty path."

At least that's what they'd said.

I found myself on the road again.

The sun beat down on the parched land raw and tart like a lemon devoid of zest.

I had a chalky dust in my mouth that tasted of sour chemicals and despair. It was so bitter that it made my molars swell up with saliva. I kept retching but nothing would come up out of my empty stomach except a whitish bile.

Parched and with little in mind save the heat and the lack of food in my belly I stared at the watering hole from the path. There was a shimmer and bend to the air over the glint of its surface.

Paranoid I looked around but could only see dunes and a pile of red rocks. I turned off the dusty path towards the watering hole.

I stumbled forward like a misused toy. My feet were killing me, blistered and sore from too much of this. I could feel as well as mentally calculate the distance between me and the hole but oddly it never drew nearer. I stopped (perhaps naively hoping I could magically pull it towards me like on a carpet) but it stayed put and I sighed and tried to swallow down the bile at the back of my throat.

Frustrated, I looked up at the blue sky. No clouds. No relief. I gathered my strength, fixed my sights on the hole, and redoubled my efforts taking long determined strides towards it only to end up falling face first on the ground exhausted and puking up what was left in my stomach from a breakfast consumed far too long ago. From all fours, I looked up and saw the surface of the water, blurred with heat, I could smell it — that ionized smell like just before it rains.

Needing to access the situation I got up, dusted myself off and stumbled sideways to a pile of red rock which, to my chagrin, I had no trouble reaching. I took refuge from the sun on its backside, huddling into what little shade it had to offer. Hugging the rock like that I saw some white markings against the red background of the rock and, focusing more closely on them, realized that they formed a kind of primitive map of the area. Squinting through the sweat running off my forehead, I recognized primitive pictorial representations of the road and several skinny gnarled trees I had passed on my way. These were all connected. I leaned in again trying to get a better look and through the spider web of lines faintly connecting all these desperate elements I could just make out a stick figure — arms spread out at the center of it all. Then I heard the muttering of starved men.

◆

Twelve skinny men came out of nowhere and knelt down at the edge of the watering hole. In unison they leaned forward pushing their faces into the edge of the water and drank. They drank for a long time gulping audibly. They drank and drank until their bellies were swollen and filled out. Finally, they lifted their faces from the pool of water and gasped together. They collected themselves wiping the water from their faces before staggering to their feet. Now all twelve of them, like hours on a clockface, began to circle the water slowly, their stomachs growing with each turn, round the hole in time, until they all had perfectly identical round protruding stomachs.

The distention and odd weight distribution caused them to fall over on their backs and while they struggled to right themselves grunting and kicking helplessly a small cackle of hyenas, kicking up dust and scampering out of nowhere, set upon them tearing at their entrails. Loud popping noises could be heard and the tearing of flesh as their skin (stretched as it was) popped open as the frenzied pack punched their snouts in.

The pungent smell of sea salt and brine filled the air as clams and oysters spilled forth riding the currents of bodily fluids that flowed from the stomachs down to the edge of the watering hole. Some hyenas reckless with hunger had their snouts snapped at by the crabs now climbing their way out of the depths of the body cavities and scuttling to the water's edge. The men moaned and flayed, shuttered and jittered, but it didn't matter much.

As though whistled for, one of the hyenas abruptly stopped feeding, lifted her head from the carcass she'd been feasting in, her snout a dark wet red, his fur matted with blood. She let out a low howl then bolted towards the dark she'd come from. The others lifted their heads sniffed the air and darted after her.

◆

I found myself on the road again.

The sun beat down on the cracked ground, howling yellow.

Dazed at this dislocation I swung my head around in the direction of the watering hole and set out running towards it. I was gaining on it. Nearing it. When suddenly I heard the sound of a siren at my back. I turned to see two cops in a dune buggy skidding to a halt just beside me.

"Stop right there, son."

Not knowing what to do I raised my hands.

"That's it. Keep 'em where I can see 'em."

"Looks like it's not his first time Dave."

"Oh, it's not his first time."

"He's a veteran."

"Oh yeah you can see that."

I stood mute as one of the cops (Dave) approached me. The fatter one sat in the dune buggy with his forearms leaned over the steering wheel chomping on gum like he was kneading dough.

"Got any ID on you?"

"No."

"What'd he say?"

"Says he don't have any ID."

(shaking his fleshy skull) "They all say that."

"Yeah, they all say that."

"How long you been walking this road?"

"Uh a while. A few days."

"What'd he say?"

"A few days he says."

"Shit, they all say that."

"Yeah. They do."

"Did I do something wrong officer?"

The tone changed immediately. Officer Dave leaned in real close and growled near my face,

"I'm asking the questions here. You understand?"

"Yes."

"What?"

"Yes. Sir."

"Now that's more like it," he said leaning back from me.

"Cite him Dave."

"What?"

"I said cite him. Give him a citation."

"I'm gonna."

He took out his notebook. The ubiquitous black rectangular notebook of the Law and started to write in it. I waited sweating and suddenly thirsty, the chalk taste in my mouth suddenly unbearable. He tore off a paper ticket and handed it to me. It was covered in circles with lines intersecting them in various places and numbers scribbled off to the sides.

"This is just a warning."

"Thank y —"

"But if I EVER see you around here again … it's not gonna be good for you."

"Not gonna be good for you," echoed the fat one.

"Capisce?"

"Uh yeah. Thank you. Got it."

He stared me down for a second longer then nodded and walked back to the dune buggy looking around. The bigger cop fired up the buggy and they sped away. I stood watching them diminish in size until they were just a speck and then disappeared into the horizon.

◆

I found myself on the road again.

The sun beat down on the dry land, the intense canary yellow of a kid's crayon.

There was a team of men standing off to the side of the road between me and the watering hole. They had light meters, laptops, and buckets of paint. One of them seemed to be peeling away the edge where the sky met the land.

"Excuse me but could you tell me how to get — " But my throat closed up with dust and I just pointed.

"What's that pal?"

"He's pointing at the water."

"Oh that."

"Yeah," I rasped.

They started laughing. "That ain't water."

I looked at him blankly.

"That ain't real water."

I felt like someone had knocked the wind out of me. "It's not?" My voice a whisper.

They just smiled and shook their heads.

I was at a loss for words I just stared at them.

One of them held a light meter in his hand and was dusting it off with a cloth. "You ever heard of 'All the world's a stage?'"

"Yeah," I managed.

"Yeah, well, you're on it kid."

I looked around my mind blank. "What's … all this?" I said, pointing at the scene.

"We're here to color grade this scene."

"…"

"Know what that is?"

"No."

The guy with the light meter spoke up. "Every heard of a nit? You look like you might have a few."

"Eh, come on, take it easy."

"It's like a gnat only smaller and, uh, lighter."

"Alright. Alright. Let's get back to work." Turning to me, "He's just pulling your leg. Look, when God messes up, we come and fix it."

"The light that is." Put in the light meter guy.

"What about that?" I said pointing at the watering hole. "Please I just need —" I took a step forward.

"Hey. No. No. No. Only people licensed by the local color society are allowed on this set. Are you union?"

"Am I what? No. No, I don't think so."

"Then sorry but you gotta move on."

And too weak to put up a fight, I did, moving off into the rays of a sun that were ever so brighter orange than they had been.

◆

I found myself on the road again.

The sun. The merciless sun. Son of the sun was I.

There was no watering hole this time just a muddy puddle. I stumbled towards it anyway but was held up at the sight of a shovel sticking up out of the parched earth. There was an arrow with a sign pointing downward and hoping against hope that it would lead to an underground spring of some sort or perhaps lead to water in some way I started digging. I hawked up a bunch of phlegm as my mouth filled with dust. Weakened by exhaustion and a lack of food I was mentally prepared only to dig so far but it wasn't long before I struck pay dirt in the form of a wooden pine box. No markings of any kind on the lid. I dug around it and, on my knees now, managed to pull it up out of the ground. My hands trembled as I wiped the dirt off the top, but that's when I saw the lock. Tears welled up in my eyes and despair filled the pit in my stomach. I groaned in anguish leaning over the box. I grew more and more angry, screaming and cursing, until the bile from the dust came up my esophagus burning me, and I wretched up something solid that got lodged in my throat and I started to choke, I put my hand in my mouth, acidic bile now streaming around it and yanked once on it. A key. A metal key. I pulled myself together and unlocked the box.

But there was no food or water. I took me a moment to work out just exactly what it was, holding up its individual parts, squinting in the sun. It was a small phonograph but one that played a kind of audio cylinder. Made of wax and wrapped in brown paper I took the cylinder out and slotted it into the phonograph. It started to play. There was a great deal of background noise, hissing and popping, but you could clearly hear the clank and sparkle of cutlery on a wooden table and the sounds of two little girls chirping around their mother who, although tired, was patiently repeating herself and directing them towards various tasks while listening to them recount their dreams from the night before. I knew these voices. They belonged to people I had once loved, still loved although they washed over me as though from another lifetime. Suddenly nothing mattered as much as getting back — somehow — to these people, to the chirping voices of those children and the soft, warm tone of their mother.

◆

I died several times along the way. I stepped off the road and was greeted by self-righteous knights and mad despots, luxurious harems and desert witches. And I died each time: beheaded, flayed alive, drawn and quartered, shot by marauders, asphyxiated at the pinnacle of orgasmic pleasure. Turned into a toad and left to dry out in the sun. Each one became a cell in a kaleidoscope of pain. Death, rebirth, death, rebirth — round and round I went. Until the colors all bled into one and it was just black on black.

Finally, the multiverse ran out of variations and having paid my karmic debt, gave me what I craved. I was weak as I neared it. I had no excess bodily fluids to spare or I would have wept. I knelt down my face inches from the water's edge my knees soaked through with it. The smell of water was overwhelming, I cupped my hands together and drank and drank and drank I drank until I was sick then lay on my back laughing under the sun, laughing at the sun *you can't hurt me anymore* then drank some more. And as the sun set and the night, merciful night, crept up and into the sky I bent over to get one more mouthful I saw myself, really saw myself.

I was sunburned and wrinkled, dusty, my features haggard. I looked desperate and defeated and as I watched, before my very own eyes, my skin began to sag and droop the wrinkles deepening. Next it turned ash white, all of the color gone from it, until it was dry and brittle like parchment. It started to flake off more and more and float off on the dusk breeze in a fine chalky dust. I threw my head back and howled at the pain as my very being was stretched across time and space until it snapped, but what came out was nothing more than an old man's tired and feeble groan.

Then finally there was darkness, and reprieve from the old dusty path.

# JUDSON HAMILTON

Judson Hamilton lives in Wrocław, Poland. In addition to several chapbooks, he is the author of a book of short stories (GROSS IN FEATHER, LOUD IN VOICE) and a book of poems (THE NEW MAKE-BELIEVE) both available from Dostoyevsky Wannabe. He's recently completed a novel. He can be found on Twitter: @judson_hamilton

For more about his work, visit his website at: https://neutralspaces.co/judson_hamilton/

# CHAPTER NINE

"You see a watering hole. Reprieve from the old dusty path."

**Drinks**

Reader sat reading writing of writer sat in a snug in a pub in Norwich. Awkward the sentence the reader reads the writer write, as sallow light from candle-stub finds weak recognition in sullied brass. Glasses a barman clatters. A thin song from an unseen speaker. Each could set this story, if the reader were reading a writer writing about thirst.

**Vampirism**

Illegitimate son of an illegitimate son. Vlad Țepeș : Vlad the Impaler : Vlad III Dracula. Folk hero passing from wet to dry lips of Romanian povestitori. By Order of the Dragon were watering holes drilled through the dry bodies of foes, writ large in the literary mind of Saxons, impressed by that moveable type, their readers. Mina, ˈMaɪnə, reader-writer, transcribing Seward's diary. Mina, ˈMiːnə, writer-reader drunk, drinks Dracula's blood. Breast leaking. The eucharist wafer crumbles into a fine dust. Höfundarnafn : pen-name. Leyninafn : pseudonym. Dulnefni : alias. Vladimir Asmundsson's *Powers of Darkness* rewrote the book that rewrote the book that rewrote the book that Vlad wrote. Reykjavík : Stockholm : London : Nuremberg : Wallachia.

**Hypnotism**

Concentrate upon consistency in the text as it rolls past you. T-tick t-tick. The staccato perfection of the letter forms becoming the hedge backs and telegraph poles of a trainscape. T-tick t-tick. As you trace the letter's backs; heaving horses, attractive moon; be aware of my voice.

Hear in these words the meaning we share. The hummocked terrain, the skyborne bird, a signpost. Feel your imagination becoming realised and, when the time feels right, surrender to it. Letter, syllable, word dissolves. Wuh oh let-ter ruh syllable duh. In the mouthscapes, beneath the terrible molluscs of tongues, the path of text crumbles to skin the fluid within.

**Sex**

Holes watering, the wreader and riter find reprieve in a dry spell. There is a twist. There is a revamp. Wherein the rewriter tempts the ader. In Eden aders wreathe an ophidian orgy and in midst of this rewriter. Cries out: heaven/heathen; both? You tell me. You intimate.

**Nonsense**

You write me off—Walkway clean. New from the reprieve hole. Ring. Water a-hears you.—but really they're just words. Reader am I a writer sat, not in fact in front of a typewriter in the late twentieth century, resisting a cue. Lishening. *Query the preceding sentence for what might most profitably—*

**Dichotomy**

Wet/dry. Age/youth. Fecund/barren. Ugly/cute. Reader/reader. Pumpkin/eater. MAGA hat/wife beater. Dog/cat. Cat/dog. Writer/writer/bull frog.

**Tradition**

There I was, a young woman in a wet minute, being written up by a girl, putting out the sun. It is not like the old men say. Are there are wild deer on the moor no more? Yes. Unreal red stags with radio-collars, yellow ear tags embossed with ISBN. Movie trailers for soon-to-be bestsellers. It is not like the old men say. When experiment jaws we are in mirrorsburg.

**Crying**

O. O. Open the floodgates.

Close the floodgates. — —

Are we not an open book?

# ROSIE ŠNAJDR

Rosie Šnajdr is an experimental writer, editor, and academic. Book A HYPOCRITICAL READER (Dostoyevsky Wannabe, 2018) out now. Pamphlets of concrete prose works WE ARE COSMONAUTS and BODY TEXT are available online for free download. Currently finishing a second book, working title Adult Colouring Book, and co-editing a collection of experimental literature, working title EXPERIMENTAL PRAXIS. Rosie co-edits the Cambridge Literary Review and teach creative writing at the University of Greenwich.

# CHAPTER TEN

You see a watering hole. Reprieve from the old dusty path. That it was hot did not mean it was unpleasant. That you were thirsty does not mean you hadn't had an opportunity to drink. Just as I caught fire in the midst of our silence, a young woman babbled her sermon like a brook.

It's a metaphor for relief, I don't have to explain it to you.

But before any of this, we walked to the statues.

I was surprised you'd never seen them before, impressive in their largeness and blindingly white. First one at the bottom of the hill and then another up the other side and around a corner. Not that they were close, to us or each other, but that the many years that stood between myself and the self that had visited them with frequency made them appear closer in my mind.

That you had not seen them became a point of pride for me. It implied that though I'd never had a thought original enough to interest you, I'd once had this morsel of a self. I had been willing to leave the compound, to look for paths that would lead away or create them, and I'd uncovered the unnatural wonders of those who came before us, even if they were honoring an idea we'd long deemed archaic. I'd stuck my hand into the pie of history and pulled out a whole fruit, and all the while you'd been in your room, developing your personality, or whatever it was you did when you were alone.

This is how I discovered that the foundation of my version of our shared experience was one I shared only with myself. On a bus to the place I kept insisting on the importance of I'd unwittingly become a tourist, explaining the statues in fragments of a foreign tongue to the woman who collected our fare. She knew the spot and left us there with three or four others. We couldn't tell if we'd become one group by virtue of being in the same place. We began to walk in unison but at each holy site would perform elaborate wardrobe changes to disorient the people we didn't like or want to talk to.

The sites were deserted, but they'd always been deserted. They only appeared to be attractions because ropes had been erected to protect them from apathetic vandals and occasionally a local would step forward, as if from off-stage, to offer a description. I felt they were trying to sell me my own memories.

Though they'd always been there, I couldn't believe the trees along the road, they were like Cyprus like Pine like sticky webs of green. The road was the kind of dirt left by untended gravel, wide enough for a car but without them. We moved along it like grim pilgrims. I'd wanted it have it to myself. I did not want to keep changing into fake noses and funny hats to confuse the boisterous men who invited themselves into our company. For those first few silent moments I thought our tight lips were a bond. The way we said *I still know you best*. But then I saw the way you looked at the rocks at your feet, and I thought you'd never been so attentive to me.

The compound was the sort of place people asked about, when they heard where we were from, but I never knew what to say. I knew they wanted grand, damning details, but all I had were quotidian complaints—the curfew, the food, the hairshirts.

We came to a street market and everything sparkled in the sun. A man sold cookies that looked like things my mother used to bake at Christmas. Long and flat, some covered in chocolate and others with cinnamon and sugar. Some were rolled in white confectioner's powder and others folded in the shape of tiny pretzels. I asked the vendor to make me an ice cream sandwich of two of them, but found myself unable to count in the foreign language and instead just held out a sweaty palm of coins for him to pick through until he found what he needed and I trusted him—not completely, because that implies a knowledge of the trust given and the acknowledgement that not trusting is an option. I simply did not question him the way I sometimes do when someone reminds me of someone I once loved.

I licked at the dripping mess while you purchased a small paper sack of assorted confections that smelled of anise, and though I did not resent you, and though I did not begrudge you your different taste than mine, and though I did not even care what you did with your foreign coins, I simply did not ever look at you again after that.

The compound was somewhere nearby but somehow it didn't matter anymore. No matter how far away we moved we were always running into their signs and symbols—on the way to work, on a walk through the neighborhood, while traveling to visit a sister. The tiny twin flames on pillars and steeples by highways and rural roads appeared just when we'd begun to relax, to think of other things, to plan a meal or consider the shocking blue of the sky. We were so haunted by the compound that somehow being close felt safer, at least we knew exactly where the enemy was. And perhaps we had grown confident in our disguises.

I did not speak the language well enough to communicate my unique perception of the world, but I understood that we had been implicated in a deception. We'd become the children of a woman pretending to be the sister of another woman. I understood that she had something to gain through the ruse, but I didn't understand what. We didn't speak, in part because we would have given ourselves away, and her in the process, and in part because we'd run out of things to say. Or because we'd never had anything to say. Or because you'd never been interested in what I had to say. Or because you lacked the curiosity to be interested in something outside of yourself. Or because when you asked questions they were slotted between anecdotes about the specific way your brother, before he died, had of shuffling down stairs rather than walking, or about the people you once saw dance in a bar, or the woman who was always climbing from your bathroom window, hoping you'd catch her on the other side, so I could never hear the questions when they were asked if they ever were.

Your memory, or perhaps mine, became increasingly selective.

The woman who was not our mother continued to talk with an exaggerated accent behind us about her vacation and love of nature. She'd colored her eyelids the pearlescent blue I'd thought as a child that eyelids should be, and she pinked her cheeks and wore a miniskirt and high heeled shoes and she wanted for something and I understood the want but not the method. I wanted to stand in front of the weathered glistening white of a disintegrating saint. I wanted to put down a taproot of rugged independence and charm myself into romance. I wanted to take my own hand in the coral glow of sunset and touch the small unscarred patch of skin on my cheek.

Once, on the compound, you had put on a mask and sung to me about love. I thought that by showing me the way you hide you were showing me your interior. I thought that a song in the mouth of a non-singer was the performance of vulnerability that I'd always aspired toward. I thought it was an invitation. I thought that love would be our escape.

A small crowd had gathered at the nub of a weathered cross. The reflection of cheap jewelry on card tables was behind us. We'd walked to the edge of the town that baked like pastries in the sun. I did not see your face because I did not have to. I saw in the pebbled surface of the statue two faint flames and burned with shame. I wondered how I could have been so blind, how I could have been led back here. Everything was chokingly familiar.

I heard her voice first, and then so did you.

# TATIANA RYCKMAN

Tatiana Ryckman is the author of the novel THE ANCESTRY OF OBJECTS (Deep Vellum Publishing), and the novella, I DON'T THINK OF YOU (UNTIL I DO), as well as three chapbooks of prose. She is the editor of Awst Press and has been a writer in residence at Yaddo, Arthub, and 100W. Her work has appeared in Tin House, Lithub, Paper Darts, Barrelhouse, and other publications. Tatiana's work can be found at tatianaryckman.com.

# CHAPTER ELEVEN

You see a watering hole. Reprieve from the old dusty path. The fatigue of desperation begins to wear off, a sudden surge of sordid pride. You wonder, Who expects anyone anymore to be gentle? Everywhere you look there are black eyes and washerbasins tinged pink, teeth stuck in drains, hair smiling from small cracks in the sidewalk. Our fathers were right, you think, that the world is brutal, but for different reasons than they surmised. Grey and forgetful, they suffer along to the rhythm, but can't so much as hum the melody. What is certain, is motionless, like the suspended newts who shy away when you stomp your foot, off to where? To caves, where they watch with real comprehension. What discomforts do animals feel? Does an animal that only knows the cold feel cold? Are they tired, sore, discouraged, aggrieved, even for lack of human intelligence? You take your own peculiar stance, buckled against a tree, carefree. Everything gets straightened out in time. The right words come. You think how your parents treated your mumbling as if it were a speech impediment, what amounted to abuse, really, for lack of a disease, the elastic bands that pulled your jaw open, the outcome being that you pronounce your labials as gutturals and prefer to eat alone, facing the wall, hiding unsightly gaping bites. You relent and drink up, prone and angular, a *permissibly* aloof member of the herd. What had Lazarus said of the respected life, the pleasures of an unburdened companion? One can lose hours each week on ill-defined sentiments, hours and then only to look like a fool, like a lazy slob, hide whipped, forced into the woods again, among "the little scrubby pines" that encumber the silten dirt, you, still splayed, prone and splayed, spatchcocked even, gnaw at the chains of your domestic context through fits of drunken laughter.

# JOSHUA ROTHES

Joshua Rothes is the author of a growing copse of short texts, including WILLIAM ATLAS (Osmanthus Press, 2020), THE ART OF THE GREAT DICTATORS (A Contrived Press, 2019) and AN UNSPECIFIC DOG (punctum books, 2017). WE LATER CITIES, a novel written with the aid of machine learning, will be released by Inside the Castle in late 2020. He is the publisher of Sublunary Editions, a small press dedicated to brief literature. He lives in Seattle, Washington.

# CHAPTER TWELVE

You see a watering hole. Reprieve from the old dusty path. That's how you think of it, anyway, because according to your guidebook, the city began in the first century as a way station on the Roman road—a place for travelers to eat and sleep and cart-drivers to water their horses.

It became much more, of course. Over the next hundred years, it grew into a major trading center, with an amphitheater, a forum, baths, and a large community of Christians. The city reached its peak in 1228, when a pretender to the Byzantine throne proclaimed it his new capital. (He was captured and blinded, and the city sacked.) Since then, the city's been ruled by Italians and Greeks, Ottoman sultans and Holy Roman emperors, fascists and communists, each stacking the stones of its empire on the ruins of the last. Today, it's the third-largest city in the country, its port a popular destination for cruise ships. Your guidebook recommends spending a day here to see the ruins of the Roman forum and the archeological museum.

You've been driving since the morning, following the highway along the coast, squinting into the bright Mediterranean sun. Your only meal today was a dry ham sandwich at a rest stop, and your bladder is full. The city is as much as relief to you as it must have been to the first travelers who stopped at the way station two thousand years ago.

From a distance, it looks beautiful—the white buildings reflecting the setting sun, the golden domes of the churches, the purples and blues of the sea—but when you get off the highway and onto its clogged streets, you see the shattered windows, the graffiti, the men and women sleeping in doorways. This part of the country never really recovered from 2008; unemployment and homelessness remain high. Last year, a right-wing government came to power, promising to fix the economy and clamp down on migrants and refugees.

As you approach the port, you enter a cleaner, more modern part of the city. Signs glow in the dusk—Zara, Gap, Nike, Sephora. This is where the cruise ships dock, releasing their passengers for a few hours to photograph the Roman ruins and shop. It's also where you're staying. Your hotel is on the city's horseshoe-shaped main square, looking out onto the sea. You leave your rental car with the attendant and check in. Your room is on the sixteenth floor, and after unpacking, you stand on the balcony and watch the tiny figures shuffling along the promenade below.

A long day of driving has left you with a clammy, in-between feeling—tired but not sleepy, empty but not hungry. You go down to the hotel bar and order a Heineken. It tastes like it always does—perfectly fine. You find yourself strangely moved by the reliability of this mid-tier lager. A Heineken never disappoints: it promises so little, but it always delivers. This trip, on the other hand. . .

For the past four months, you were working on a big project—tight deadlines, complex deliverables, lots of stakeholders. You finished on time, but it required some eighteen-hour days at the office. By the end, you were exhausted, and the metallic taste in your mouth wouldn't go away no matter how many times you brushed your teeth. So you decided to get away—to "recharge," as you told your family and friends. And what better place to do it than here, on this famously beautiful stretch of coast? Five days ago, you flew to the capital, rented a car, and started driving south. By any measure, it's been a good trip. You've stopped at seaside villages, visited museums and monasteries, and eaten fresh squid and artichokes. The metallic taste in your mouth is gone; the fog in your brain has receded. And yet, you feel that there's something you're missing—something behind all the pleasant sights and tastes and sounds. You can't explain what this means, even to yourself. It's a vague sensation—not even disappointment, exactly.

You've had a good trip, yes, but you're beginning to understand that you wanted something more than good.

◆

The next day is cloudy and humid. You start at the ruins of the Roman forum, which are two blocks west of your hotel. A sign informs you that the forum was built in the second century. To see them, you have to walk down several flights, down to the original level of the city. Most of the ruins are low walls and vaults—niches where merchants would have set up their stalls. A couple of columns survive, possibly from a temple or administrative building. You walk around for half an hour, climb the steps back to the level of the modern city, and buy a gyro and a Coke.

After lunch, you visit the archeological museum—a big Brutalist slab of a building, a concrete tomb for the city's antiquities. You see vases, statues, coins, helmets, mosaics, capitals, room after room, floor after floor, bronze, gold, marble, rusted steel, Dionysus, Venus, Augustus, Apollo. You know you should be impressed, and you think that you are, on some level. But again, there's something you're missing. These objects show the wealth of the Romans, but there must have been more to them than that. What were they like, deep down? How did they live? The gold and marble can't tell you that. Maybe you should have paid for the audio guide.

You leave the museum and walk through a pedestrian shopping area. It's mobbed with tourists; pushing through them, you hear at least half a dozen languages. The windows of the stores are plastered with glossy pictures—jeans, watches, lingerie, burgers, perfume, sneakers, ice cream. Your guidebook says there's a "charming" baroque chapel in the area, but you can't find the entrance through the crowds.

In the evening, you have dinner at an Italian restaurant on the promenade. You ask for a table on the terrace. The sun sinks behind the hills to the west, and the cruise ship in the port pushes off and steers itself back to sea. As you eat your pizza margherita, a woman approaches you and asks for money; you give her five euros. A moment later, the waiter appears and says that you shouldn't do that, please. You worry you've got him in trouble somehow. You leave him a big tip and take the long way back to your hotel, along the promenade. It's quiet, now that the cruise ship is gone. Some African guys are selling handbags, which they've laid out on faded blue towels. A busker plays a keyboard and sings in a heavy accent; after a minute, you recognize the song as "Call Me Maybe." In the red light of a kebab cart, a tube of meat turns and shimmers.

You stop at the hotel bar and order a Heineken. The bartender places it on a Heineken coaster, which says that the beer is sold in 192 countries. Two Germans come in and ask the bartender to turn on the soccer game. You try to watch, but you've never liked soccer, and your mind wanders. You find yourself thinking about the Romans again. Across Europe and Asia, they built roads, aqueducts, forums, ports, fortresses. As a result, a Roman citizen could go from one end of the Mediterranean to the other in peace and relative comfort. This was an unprecedented freedom, which disappeared with the collapse of their empire, and didn't return until very recently. In this sense, you do know what it's like to be a Roman. (Indeed, the highway you've been driving on follows the old Roman road.) Of course, the empire you live in extends much farther than the Romans could have imagined—192 countries.

The soccer game ends in a tie, 0–0. The bartender puts on CNN International, which shows the president standing outside in the rain, shouting over the sound of his helicopter. He's complaining that toilets don't have as much water as they used to and promising to look into it very strongly. There's something Roman about him too: he reminds you of the bloated, senile old men who ruled the empire in its decadence. You order another Heineken.

◆

That night, you have a vivid dream. In it, you return from the trip and discover the floor of your apartment covered in newspapers. Sitting in a chair at the center of the living room is D., a woman you dated in college. (Why D.? You haven't thought about her in years.) She scowls. You're late, apparently. Without her saying it, you realize that you were supposed to give her a haircut. But you don't know how to cut hair, and though you search all your drawers, you can't find the scissors. D. watches you, still scowling. You don't want to disappoint her, so you say "a-ha!" and pretend you've found them. You stand behind her and run your fingers through her hair, hoping you'll think of something before she understands what's going on.

You wake up twenty minutes before check-out time. Your alarm didn't go off, or you were too deep in your dream to hear it. You could throw your things into you bag, brush your teeth, and get out on time—but why? You're not on a deadline anymore. Why not take another day in the city? Maybe the extra time will help you find whatever it is you're missing. You call the front desk and ask if you can have the room for another night. The voice on the other end of the line says it's not a problem.

You lie in bed; your thoughts drift. Where is D. now? What has she been doing since college? You met her in an art history class—a survey of Western art from the Greeks to the present. The professor seemed bored for most of the class, but he came alive when he got to his own academic specialty, Romanticism. You can still see him jabbing his finger at Turner's painting of the slave ship in a storm, which was projected in enormous size on the classroom screen. The painting, he said, represented the Romantic idea of the *sublime*—the feeling when an object or landscape imposes itself on your consciousness, suspending all your usual thoughts, filling you with horror and delight, all at once. You never really understood what he meant, but as you think about it now, you wonder if the sublime (or something like it) is what you've been missing. You've spent the past four months working on the big project, checking and double-checking every detail. It was exhausting, to be so in control. On some level, you hoped that all this history and beauty would cut through you, take hold, make you a little less intentional, less avid, less knowing—in short, a little less yourself.

The hotel has stopped serving breakfast at this hour, so you buy a coffee and croissant from Starbucks and eat them on a bench in the main square. It's hot and cloudy again. No cruise ships have arrived, and the square's quiet. Workers are hanging Christmas lights; old men sit by themselves reading newspapers; seagulls assemble on a statue of a horse and rider. You think about what you'll do today. There's that charming baroque chapel. . .

A man approaches you. He's wearing a polo shirt, jeans, and plastic Adidas sandals; he might be in his twenties or thirties, Indian or Middle Eastern. He says something to you in heavily accented English. It takes you a moment to understand: he's asking if you want to buy some hashish. Hot fear flies up your spine. Your muscles clench; you cross your arms over your chest and shake your head. He shrugs, gives you a look of pity, and goes on his way.

You watch him cross the square. His look of pity has unsettled you. It's as if he saw through you, recognized whatever it is that's holding you back. Why did you turn him down? You might have liked that hashish, after all: you have an edible once in a while, when work is especially stressful. It might make that baroque chapel a little more charming.

You leave your coffee cup on the bench and walk quickly across the square. The man's heading west; you catch up to him in front of the Roman forum. Panting slightly, you tell him you've changed your mind, that you do want some hashish. He looks at you for a moment and says okay. You hoped he would be more excited for you, but at least that look of pity is gone. He tells you how much it'll cost for a gram. You don't know if that's a good price (or how much a gram is), but it isn't like you're going to do any comparison shopping.

You suggest going down into the forum to do the deal. It's nearly empty, and seems inconspicuous enough. He shakes his head. He doesn't have it with him, he says. You'll have to go to his place.

The hot fear returns. It's one thing to buy a little weed—but to go to a stranger's apartment, in a strange country? You can see the headline now: "Head of American tourist found in freezer." But no—just because you're an American doesn't mean that *everyone* wants to murder you. And even if he did, wouldn't that make it interesting? Half of the sublime is horror, after all. This man is offering you something more than museums and ruins: the possibility of an encounter. Take it.

He says that the two of you can take the bus. You consider offering to drive in your rental car, but decide that you're going to let him do it his way. You walk together to the big bus station south of the main square and wait for half an hour. You're nervous, so you chatter, telling him about your trip, your job, the big project. Buses come and go, and sometimes you have to shout over the sound of the airbrakes.

When the bus arrives, he taps his pass on the electronic reader, which responds with a ping. You realize you don't have a pass and look guiltily at the man; he taps his again. Other people push in behind you. The bus is packed; you and the man end up facing each other, a few inches apart. He takes out his phone and scrolls through Facebook. Some of his feed is in English, and some is in a language you don't recognize. You ask where he's from, and he says a place you've never heard of. You nod.

The bus lurches through the city and into the surrounding sprawl. Faded beige houses, cars parked on the sidewalk, satellite dishes hung at precarious angles, dangling wires, lots abandoned to gravel and weeds. You notice you're the only white person left on the bus.

Finally, you reach a bus depot. Everyone gets off—end of the line. You ask the man how far it is to his place, and he points to a concrete apartment block in the distance. To get there, the two of you walk along the side of a six-lane highway; a thin metal fence separates you from the traffic. Several times, you look back. A glimpse of the sea or the city would reassure you, but you're too far out for that.

You cross the road via an underpass and cut across an empty lot. The apartment building is fifteen or twenty stories high; the concrete is streaked with white and yellow stains; some of the balconies sag. Inside, the stairwell is littered with beer cans and broken glass. The man climbs quickly, his plastic sandals flapping. By the time you reach his floor, you're winded.

His door's unlocked. It's a small, dim apartment. The only furniture is a fold-up table; five or six sleeping bags are on the floor. As your eyes adjust to the darkness, you make out some of the clutter—plastic water bottles, shopping bags, a hot plate and electric kettle, cans of food, a square TV perched on an upside-down plastic bucket, heaps of clothes, a washcloth on a hanger, suitcases and backpacks, a fraying power-strip, a tangle of phone chargers.

He tells you to sit down, gesturing at one of the sleeping bags, and asks if you want a beer. You nod; it's hot, and you're sweaty from the journey. He squats in front of a minifridge and takes out two tall cans of Heineken. This seems like a sign, though you don't know of what.

He sits next to you on the sleeping bag. It hits you now: you're alone with him. No one in the world knows you're here.

You both sip your beers.

Do you like football? he asks.

Yes, you say.

What club?

You realize he means soccer. You don't want to disappoint him, so you say the first team that comes to mind: Manchester United.

He tells you he supports Arsenal. Ah, you say. This is a team you've heard of. He reaches into a backpack, rummages around, and finds a red scarf with the word ARSENAL stitched in white. His cousin sent it to him, he explains, from London.

London's nice, you say.

He unlocks his phone and pulls up an Arsenal highlights video. Together, you watch the red team score, over and over. You relax. He wouldn't watch a highlights video with someone he's about to rob and kill, right?

Something moves—you jump. What you thought was a heap of clothes was, in fact, a person, who's just turned over in his sleep. The man next to you doesn't look up from the highlights video.

When it finishes, he plays another. You make approving noises at goals that seem particularly good. Is this your encounter—watching videos on a phone in a dirty apartment? A part of you wishes that the man really did want to put your head in the freezer.

You finish your beer and place the can on the floor beneath your feet. From his backpack, the man takes out a ziploc bag of weed and a little scale. Balancing them on his knees, he weighs out a gram and holds it up for your approval. You give him a fifty-euro note, and when he tries to give you change, you tell him to keep it; he needs it more than you, judging by the state of the apartment. He insists.

Do you like it here? you ask.

Here?

Yeah, you say. You're not sure what you mean either.

It's okay, he says. Not so bad.

Oh, you say. That's good.

Yeah.

Thanks for selling me the hashish, by the way. I really appreciate it.

Okay. Not a problem.

You take your money and your drugs and walk downstairs.

On your way back to the bus depot, you realize you should've offered to share with him. That would have been polite. Too late now. The apartment block looms behind you, casting a long shadow in the setting sun.

The depot's almost empty at this hour. You buy a ticket from a machine and wait. The only person with you at the stop is a woman in a headscarf, talking on her phone. You replay the afternoon, wondering what you could have done differently. If this were a film or a short story, you and the man would have learned something about each other. He might have told you how he came to live in this country, what he hopes for, what he has lost. You, in turn, would have been overcome with sympathy and grown as a person. A sublime experience of your shared humanity. You'd like to think that there is some sort of shared humanity, beneath it all. That's what prompted your disappointment at the archeological museum yesterday—the sense that there was something deeper about the Romans that you were missing. You assumed that there was something to them besides the gold and the marble, some inner experience beneath the power and profit of the empire. But why? There's a simpler solution: nothing's missing. All that remains of the Romans is all that there ever was.

It's dark when you get back to the city. You haven't eaten since breakfast, so you go to the promenade and buy a big kebab. A woman asks you for money; you give her a couple of coins. As you're feeling in your pocket, you touch the plastic baggie of hashish. The thought of smoking it alone depresses you. You walk down the promenade, and when no one's looking, you toss the baggie into the sea. It floats on the surface of the water.

Back at the hotel, you sit at the bar and order a Heineken. You are not disappointed.

# RYAN NAPIER

Ryan Napier is the author of FOUR STORIES ABOUT THE HUMAN FACE (Bull City Press). His stories have appeared in Queen Mob's Tea House, minor literature[s], and others. He lives in Massachusetts. More information at ryannapier.net and on Twitter: @ryanlnapier

# CHAPTER THIRTEEN

You see a watering hole. Reprieve from the old dusty path, it reads just above the toilet paper, right next to other passages scrawled and carved into the paint. Most of these have been here for years. This one is new. I don't think anything of it. Typically, in class, students recite lines like this all the time. It used to be that I found pleasure in the way these young writers had memorized and adored the novel my friend wrote, but it's been a decade, and while it's always nice to see my friend's work celebrated, I still wish they would memorize his other writing too. *The Automatic* was everywhere a decade ago and we celebrated the way in which literature had infiltrated popular culture in the era of young people locked into their screens. After ten years, a whole new generation has adapted it as their book. When it first came out, the spotlight found Lindsay and the university. Besides a handful of students transferring here, we didn't see a significant difference in the first year. But the following fall, our enrollment tripled and we had a couple "emergency hires" handed out to us. In fact, Lindsay's novel may have been single-handedly responsible for the college staying afloat during *The Cliff*[1].

---

1 The Cliff refers to the sudden drop in prospective college students starting in 2026. The theory was first introduced in the late 10s, when enrollment had stopped booming and there were fewer students enrollment in K-9 and secondary school. The Cliff's thesis is based on the idea that during the housing crisis maybe young could-be parents decided that the economy and their future was too unstable or opaque to make having a family seem responsible. Because of the sliding economy, people were having fewer kids because it wasn't financially survivable with more than one or two. And most of these people who had homes lost them or barely made it—struggled to make it—and the ones who didn't have homes (most of them) knew that since they could barely afford the tiny one bedroom they were sharing with their partner and two dogs, adding a kid to the mix just wasn't feasible. Some of these people had kids after some promotions or luck showing them that the economy is good to some people. But the majority of these people just didn't have kids. Cut to 18 or 19 years later, all these would-be kids don't exist, and all this growth the upper Administration counted on had no support. For

So many colleges tanked, and our enrollment shot through the roof, our program expanded, and at the center of it is Lindsay[2]. His goddamn novel gave kids thirst for writing that I hadn't seen in years. All of these students come here to learn writing from him, but they got stuck with me or Ian or Megan, or they have to take hybrid literatures with Naomi or poetry with Caro[3]. Lindsay's classes have a four-year waiting period[4].

I read those lines again, say them out loud.

I hear the squeak of sneakers and feel slightly embarrassed that I'm reciting this line to myself in the bathroom. I'm especially cranky today because Lindsay has a new novel coming out and it's the 10-year anniversary for *The Automatic* and I'm stuck in this star cluster of committee meetings burning my day into nothing. Every year it's been a tradition, but in this case, my untapped academic service has caught up to me. Lindsay always celebrates this book and I'm always invited. This

---

years, enrollment experts simultaneously warned about the looming Cliff, while also promising growth. These mixed message created a false sense of hope among the elite ego-driven institutions and that when the slow drop in enrollment started they blamed bad marketing or the faculty or whoever, even the students, for the drop, and kept pouring money into buildings, and flashy advertising, and new flash-in-the-pan programs. It looked so obvious and desperate to prospective students and their parents that even ones would could go, were so sick of the lie and so sick of the constant feeling of being pitched to.

2 He became this *King of Fiction* and subsequently unleashed an entirely new generation of aspiring writers that may have very be responsible for keeping the entire Creative Writing Industrial Complex alive and me and my colleagues employed.

3 All of these writers/teachers are brilliant and wonderful and a blessing to writing students, but they just weren't famous. Or not as famous. They were just the teachers you had to take while you waited to take Lindsay's workshop.

4 On the first day of orientation students are asked if they want to join the waiting list and are explained that's the only way to guarantee a class with Lindsay. Students get pretty let down that they will most likely get one class, but it is what it is.

year, I've had to back out. When I first told him I had to pull back a bit from all the celebration, he looked crushed. But I explained the service and that part of that was planning his anniversary reading and party. He seemed cool with it and even volunteered to look at possible venues for the event. It's pretty astonishing that he still finds so much joy in the way people read something he wrote a decade ago. It's still the thing he's most proud of and his last novel won the National Book Award.

I stop for coffee on my way to the next meeting[5]. I text Lindsay that I'll bother him in his office after my meeting. I weave my way through the mini-crowd gathered outside the shop and ignore the acoustic guitar strumming Death Cab songs from across the way, and the kids shouting about some professor they hate, and the public break up happening near the entrance of the Miller Hall, and I notice writing on my cup. It's a line from *The Automatic*. It's written in black sharpie where a name normally is: *This is Necessary*.

To the coffee, I say, "Happy anniversary." I one-hand-text Lindsay and tell him about the cup and write, "People are still reading that shit. Mind blowing." I smell spray paint and walk toward it—not that I want to, but it's coming from where I'm supposed to be. And on the wall, I see it. Two more lines from *The Automatic*. I stand there for a moment thinking about the book, and Lindsay, and why someone would put this here. After a moment, I text Lindsay about this new passage, but he doesn't respond.

Lindsay was a newly-hired professor here ten years ago with only a short story collection to his name[6]

---

5 I've forgotten the purpose of this meeting and hope some coffee will help me. My calendar just says *Meeting, Dean's Office,* and no other information. I'll remember once I get there and manically read through my emails.

6 Real Vampires was a collection of flash fiction written

(great, but barely recognized) when he walked into my office with a manuscript in his hand and asked me if I would be willing to look at it. I told him to send it to me and he was weird about it, said, "I'd rather hand it to you." It was nice holding actual paper in my hand. Many of us spent years between visiting gigs, adjunct scams, following partners for jobs, and traveling just to find work, that we abandoned our libraries in our parents' garages or our wealthy sibling's studio spaces, and put everything onto screens. Anyway, this book was different. I read it viciously from cover to cover and then started reading again. The next day I brought it back with a couple sticky notes on it, telling him "it was unreal" and he thought I meant it was bad, but I meant it was incredible. When I asked him what his agent thought, he told me he didn't have one and he wanted to do this differently—DIY and indie—he wanted to create a slow burn of a mythos[7]. For some reason obsessions were born. Some romanticized Lindsay's *message*— the way the kids in the book were dead-bound on making it to

---

about monsters who either lost their power, can't use it it anymore, or just simply forgot about it. But the characters are just hanging around and suffering like characters in a Raymond Carver story, or someone in early Irving. They just happen to be monsters. In interviews, people asked why he wrote sci-fi and fantasy, and he said he didn't—that these are just people whose names we recognize as monstrous, but that he writes literary fiction, that he just finds the domestic much more satisfying if the names offer the reader a pathway to an imagination that might never be accessed.

7 He wanted to self-publish, build a digital campaign and a website with hidden gems and secret pages, and social media. Mythos building. Everyone at the school thought it was a bad idea, but he insisted that this book had to be grassroots, had to be grown organically, and needed to "not be tainted, by the publishing machine." But he convinced us it was good, and so we supported it. We weren't surprised when it barely birthed a whimper of acknowledgment in the first couple months. Its first review was in some online journal I'd never heard of. [*Wolf Reader*]. Two weeks later it was on every platform and littering social media, but Lindsay seemed prepared for what was coming for him. We watched a book go viral and our friend was responsible.

digital space but were unable to ever get there: their pathway became artificial in many ways and real in others. Others obsessed with the rebellious undertones and criticism of Capitalism and wealth, without ever saying it. And others obsessed over the representation of the kids with loving parents and well-meaning adults, who simply failed to protect them. It was simple and apocalyptic and ended triumphantly sad. But everyone always talked about the writing, about the dialogue, and the characters and voice. Somehow Lindsay knew what he was writing was special and trusted that knowledge and instead of letting any editor touch it, he showed his friends and put it in the world.

The hallway is crowded with prospective students and families for Admitted Student Day or something. One of the counselors slaps my arm as I pass and shits out, "Most of them are here for *writing*."

I make my way through and into the Dean's office. His assistant's on the phone and just sort of nods their head at me to go into the conference room. No one is here, and I look out the window at the movement of the matriculated hustling between buildings or vaping. I put my hand on the curtain and there's something wet. Paint. My hand is green, dark green. I inspect the curtain and there's a ton of paint, clearly, the word *Most*. I pull the current shut partially. It's the beginning of the next sentence. I put my bag down and march out. They're off the phone and I ask, "Do you know who did that?"

They clearly don't know what I'm talking about and look horrified.

"Did you do this?" they say.

"I thought you did," I snap back. "Do you know who..."

I know the answer before they even respond.

"What does is say?" they gasp.

"If I had to guess it says, *Most of us have lost the will to find a way back to our real homes—we've learned to camp out near the best sources of energy and heat.*"

"What's that?"

"A joke." I start to pull the blinds open more. And they stop me, close the blinds and ask me not to say anything to the Dean.

I agree and start back for my spot when Mark from Social Sciences walks in and apologizes for being late, even though he's three minutes early and has arrived before anyone else. Like always he sits at the other side of the table, across from me, and asks me how things are going in the House of Myth, laughing to himself. Slowly others begin to pile in.

I spend a good hour listening to a faculty member complain about how the broken copy machine is affecting retention. The hour we blew through curriculum proposals, discussing next year's round of visiting writers, and the last 10 minutes complaining about the Administration's new job listing for a VP of Collective Governance, which turned out to be their answer to the college community pushing for a less top-down leadership strategy. I can barely pay attention. I'm thinking about the sentence painted onto the curtain. I'm thinking about the stall, the coffee cup, the wall, and what's next.

I text Lindsay[8] to ask him if his publisher has some weird guerilla marketing campaign[9]. He doesn't answer, but if he did it would be the refrain, *Haha that*

---

8 Who doesn't fucking respond and it's getting annoying. Usually he's up in my shit.

9 His last novel painted QR codes onto every bus stop sign from downtown to campus and back out. They did the same for the route that the main characters rode in the book. Before that they wallpapered pages from a controversial scene where his characters destroy a bank headquarters and decapitate the CEO. The wallpaper was everywhere, multiple cities. But Lindsay did that same shit with *The Automatic*. There was wallpaper, QR codes, social media, music, soundtracks, playlists, there were talking points and podcasts, and alternative scenes, and character profiles and teasers. In many ways, his new big publishers are learning from him. They just have the money to do more.

*book will never die*—the ongoing joke that no matter how many masterpieces he writes, the only thing he'll ever be is the author of *The Automatic*. I read his new book a few weeks ago and told him it's the best thing he's ever made. He smiled like he already knew and thanked me. I compared it to *The Automatic*, but there something about his new book that pushes him beyond that brash, innovative, and untethered author of ten years ago, and shows a level of polish and restrain against a portal of chaos. He laughs at this, but even though he writes and publishes rather prolifically, he doesn't want *The Automatic* to die. He will always be proud of it. He will always celebrate it.

Last week, Lindsay and I were out talking about our students, when he brought up what we all experienced—the worship of *The Automatic*, the cult of personality, the way in which it never seems to stop. No matter how hard Lindsay worked to humanize himself, the awe continued. We talked about the authors who eventually lost that kind of attention and love, and the kinds that never have. Lindsay kept talking about how he's coming up on his irrelevance, on his journey back into the maw of obscurity. It's like he can't accept that he might be one of these gods of writing. Though at times he seems to bask in. He looks genuinely lustful when he tells me about the rumors he's heard about the gathering of kids lighting candles and standing in a circle after poetry readings and reciting lines from that book, or about the tattoos, or about the kids who have committed their lives to the words Lindsay wrote during a depressive winter break where he didn't know the point of it all. Before his fame, students hated him, faculty hated him, and he was severely unhappy[10]. The level of

[10] He was just a softie surrounded by students sick of being told they needed a college degree to do anything with their lives, while the job markets squeezed out any prospects for their future other than basement living and service jobs at places that don't support tipping. Lindsay went home every day after class unsure why he choose this path, and why as lucky as he was to land this gig, how

fame added a layer of respectability and awe where his students always gave him the benefit of the doubt, and people gave him the room to be the teacher he was.

I walked to the other side of campus to where the gym and practice stadium sit. My next meeting happens at the Administrative Building. We are supposed to be about enrollment within our departments, but all anyone can talk about is the successes at the college for the last decade[11]. During *The Automatic* boom, the college funneled hundreds of thousands of dollars into marketing Lindsay and *The Automatic*. Kids from all over the country applied to come study with Lindsay. He carried his popularity around so much that it was hard for him to write for a good year. As we struggled to find our footing and establish our program, the college was for once putting all its force behind us and the program. The absurdity of how the Administration pivoted during the desperation with nonsense policy changes, nonsense hires, and nonsense statements about the health of the college[12].

---

useless it all was. Then he wrote. He wrote something that felt feral, but electronic, as if as he was trying to find an escape and at the edge of a wilderness beyond and a door emerged into a digital space of dissociation. He called the process *feral.*

11 Of all the colleges that folded during *The Cliff,* we grew—more specifically, our writing program grew. A school in Ohio tried to turn their liberal arts college into some STEM or Polytechnic College and attempted to decimate the Humanities, only to be embroiled in protest, community push back, accreditation scrutiny, and a financial scandal. A school in Chicago, with a four-million-dollar deficit convinced themselves they needed a new shiny Student Life Center and Initiatives expansion.

12 In this meeting it's clear that people miss the toxic days when all we did was panic about enrollment—now we're just coasting off the success of the last few years. We were all certain that our college would fail and that our doors would close, as the Administration kept bulking the cabinet level with corporate-thinking robots. According to financial documents, we were two years from closing if we didn't get the boost of enrollment that came. By that time, we had adapted to the student need and it was clear that Lind

I fumble my way over to Lindsay's office hoping to catch him before his Short Fiction Seminar, but there's a student in his office loudly talking about the unreliable narrator of *The Automatic* and starts quoting a passage of the book. It's one of my favorite sections—a young marketer rants into his telemarketing headset about socialism as the death of the gods who gave birth to the glorious age of American Capitalism. Lindsay, in his way, is super appreciative and thankful. And the kid doesn't say anything.

When the student comes out he looks at me and frowns—eyes burning into mine, locked, until he turns and carries down the hallway. He's wearing a black T-shirt that says *A LONG PREGNANT SILENCE* across the back. It's a refrain *The Automatic*.

"I can hear you breathing out there," Lindsay says from inside the office. "I know you're trying to squeeze in some shit-talk before I impart my wisdom onto these poor kids."

I wander in. "You know, quoting your own nov-

---

say had some strange power at the college. If he didn't get his way, he would threaten to leave. Then they'd give him what he wanted. The truth is, he would never leave. He demanded we dissolve the board and cabinet, and focus on a shared governance, collective cabinet and they balked and called his bluff. But here we are now many years later, still fighting that top-down machine. The truth is, these meetings ten years ago were awful. The Administration's pressure to "give students what they want," which really meant, "our data shows that this is want students want, so stop listening to the students," created silos at the college, and we all started fending for ourselves with the minor budgets we got. So, here we are now, still trying to break free of those silos, trying to create a collective, and Phil is stuck in the past, insistent that no one cares about what he's doing or what his students are doing. It's hard to admit that three students left the school because the second housing crisis took their parents' home, and when they protested the banks, they were arrested. Other kids left because their parents took out mortgages on their house to finance their education and lost their homes. Others left because there was no hope left. Ten years ago, we were fighting to keep our department funded. Ten years ago, we were all worried about being jobless. Ten years ago, Lindsay released *The Automatic* and changed our trajectory.

el is really stupid, even though it seems to be all the rage." I sit down and say, "That student OK?"

"Diagnoses can't be the only reigning principle," he says. He's probably responding to all my texts.

"Jesus, you too. Quoting your own shit is a little sad. Anyway, that student of yours basically eye-fucked me on the way out. Did you hurt his feelings? I know sometimes this little nice-teacher act goes awry and you've got students with hurt feelings because *you're just so honest* and your good intentions can't save a messy opening scene."

He just shrugs. His look is clear. He's still proud of the book. I think he's afraid of the day it stops meaning something to people[13].

"It never stopped meaning something, Lins."

He smiles.

"You should write about this." We let the moment linger a little bit and he moves past me.

He pretends to throw nothing at me. "Gotta slide on. I got minds to expand."

As he walks away, I shout, "Stop quoting your own fucking work."

I wander down to my office. I check my watch—twenty-six minutes until my next committee meeting. At my office, there's a yellow piece of paper tacked to my door. At first, I think it's a student leaving a note about missing class, but it's a lot of writing. After a minute it hits me—it's more of *The Automatic*.

My next meeting is fine. It goes by fast[14].

---

13 Every student that comes here because of this decade-old novel wants to hear more about the book's creation, its meaning, its author. The obsession turns into a respect for the craft and the human who created it. They become invested it how it was written, but not just that—what Lindsay was trying to say. These students memorize the whole book, talk about it like it's some kind of sacred text that deserves to be learned. This novel became a manual for teaching people how to craft good writing. Whether that was a reality or not, these students believe it.

14 The last meeting was the final planning session before the

◆

Lindsay doesn't show up for dinner. I wait close to thirty minutes, sipping at my beer before I actually call him, though his text messages are backed up with strings of texts about how late he is. When he doesn't answer, I scroll back through the messages and notice he hasn't texted me since last night. That's rare. Usually my phone is buzzing with numerous texts from him about anything from *SNL's* audacity, to teaching, to an idea he has, to someone he's dating. But nothing. His last text from yesterday says *Gotta chat with this student waiting for me. I'll hit you back.* Then nothing. So here I am. I haven't talked to Lindsay and he is apparently not showing. I sit at the bar for another twenty minutes and send another slew of texts before I actually call him. It goes straight to voicemail and I leave a message. I finish my beer and head back to my car. For a moment, the city is quiet and still, but slowly the volume rises: Car sounds, chatter from the bar patios, clacking of heels and boots, a few clusters of laughter, and a couple dogs barking. When I get to my car, there's someone standing there. He's got his hood pulled up, but he's leaning on the car like a dweeb waiting for the Internet Café to open.

"Can I help you?" I say.

"The alley's too dark to see," he says.

"Chapter 7," I say. This kid is in on the little game. "It's the first thing you say to the banker." I hope this commentary will shove him into reality. Maybe he will give me some insight about all this. I don't know why I care so much, but it feels like I'm getting pranked.

He just smirks at me and walks off backwards, eyes still locked on me.

---

big anniversary weekend events and we had some last-minute emergency changes with some double-booked venues on campus. We figured it out and now I've got another meeting. I thought that was last one.

"What do you want, asshole?" I yell after him and then immediately try to call Lindsey's again. I leave him a message: *Your fucking book is stalking me and these kids are running around playing characters. What fucking stunt are you pulling? I'm fucking hungry, but it feels rude to eat without you.* I pause and I climb into my car. The asshole climbs into a dark van across the street and the van pulls away. I start the car. *Look, dude. I'm coming over. I'm fucking hungry and I'm raiding your snack drawer.*

Lindsay's house is piles and spires of junk, his books scattered across the floor, as though his book cases vomited their contents. His manuscript pages scattered, his clothes, his shoes, his hats and gloves, his records and snacks. I call 911 before I take three steps. At first the scene mutes everything, but by the time I'm in the kitchen staring at a trail of Oreos and tortillas, I hear it. A voice, a loop of the lines. "The kids had nothing to say, but the line had wrapped itself out the door and into the parking lot—all these people dumping their paychecks into the safes. I could hear the sound of grackles stalking the concrete, dragonflies buzzing near the palms."

This is the next moment in *The Automatic* after the narrator meets the Banker. I know the very next line will be when the narrator gets inside the bank and witnesses the upload for the first time. Followed by the moment he uploads himself into the void, the first time he feels the digital waves pummeling through his brain. The moment he's hooked in[15].

15 When the dust settled and the spectacle of the viralness of the novel subsided, the critics descended. They talked about Gibson and *Neuromancer, Catcher in the Rye* as written by Chuck Palahniuk, Bret Easton Ellis reimagined by MT Anderson, Philip K. Dick writing Raymond Carver, Murakami writing Ted Chiang. The minimalism of the writing heightening the maximalism of the landscape, of the world, and imagination. They thirsted for his next book, wrote about his first collection, devoured his previous stories, and tried to tie the connections between the past and his future. But Lindsay had broken out of his past and the future was all that was left. He would spend the next ten years writing around the worlds he created in *The Automatic*.

By the time the cops are done I'm convinced they are uninterested in my worry. They're also completely unhelpful. I catch them rolling their eyes when I explain the lines and the premise of *The Automatic*. They're asking about his mental health and if he has enemies because of the state of the house. Because Lindsay is famous, the place is trashed, and there's the weird recording, the cops file Lindsay as missing. I wander out to the car and there's a cop standing by it. He asks me if I'm OK and I say no. And he goes, "Underneath the Dakota burn out, where the dark overtakes light."

"Not you too?"

"That doesn't happen till towards the end, but I'm just saying, I recognize the writing everywhere. Just can't figure out why anyone would be running around campus carving lines from some fucking decade-old book everywhere."

"Anniversary? Some psycho graduated from *Catcher in the Rye*."

"When you said that I thought you were one of them, that maybe you would know what happened to Lindsay."

"Graffiti? I'm a cop, not a teenager." He pats my shoulder and heads back to his car.

After he drives off, I notice the red streaks painted over the concrete. I walk into the street and there are lines spray painted down the road. It's the next scene, the same one I had predicted to the cops when the narrator gets inside the bank and witnesses the upload for the first time. Followed by the moment he uploads himself into the void, the first time he feels the digital waves pummeling his brain. The moment he's hooked in. I follow the words for blocks and around the next turn into a cul-de-sac, where a van pulls out of an alley and stops in front of me. The door slides out.

"When I came to, I knew my truth would be plugged into that space," someone says from inside the van.

"Where the fuck is Lindsay?"

"I know the way through it. I just haven't put together the plan. It's not time yet."

And the van peels out, past me and out the way the writing came. I chase it, sprinting faster than I ever have, but I don't stand a chance and by the time I'm past my car, the van has vanished into the next street.[16]

◆

Three days this carries on. My feeds are colossal pileups of news stories and what-ifs. On the eve of the Anniversary, a detective shows up to my place. This young-looking suit stands in my doorway as if he doesn't want to be there, some weird kind of smirk on his face. I'm clearly worried and half-manic, with this urge to pace around the room. I keep staring at my phone every four seconds waiting for Lindsay to respond. He must notice, because he straightens up and says something about ironing out the details surrounding the disappearance of Lindsay, and mentions, stifling a smirk, all the lines from *The Automatic* written all over the campus, in stalls, on walls, on the dirty window of my car, on the chalkboard in my classroom, on the white board in the lecture hall, handwritten pages slid under my door, spoken in a crowd, a student at the back of room saying a line. When I finally stop my list and explain that all the lines have made it to the end of the book and are now working their way back to the beginning, he looks at me and cocks his head to the side.

"How far has it gone…" he stumbles through his thought. "I mean, how close are we to the beginning of the book now?"

---

16 Nothing happens. No news. I revisit all the places I found his words and they're still there like a sick joke that lingered too long and no one thinks it's funny anymore and no one can figure out why the joke even needed to be uttered. I call the police a few times a day till they threaten me with arrest if I call again.

I walk back through it all. These lines have crept back into the first chapter[17]. And for the first time in days this detective seems interested. He asks to come in and I invite him in. He sits across from me and I offer him water and he declines and asks me to walk him through it again. He's not the smirking suit he was minutes ago. Rather, he's actually listening and taking notes. He wants to know when I first noticed, when I made the connection. He wants to know about Lindsay's mental health, and finally at the end of it, he levels with me.

"Honestly, we have no real leads, but this gives us something to think about."

"I just don't know why you guys wouldn't listen to me in the first place."

He seems actually ashamed when he says, "We thought it was a prank for the Anniversary, a student. Especially with all his lines written everywhere. I don't think we knew it was as extensive, and we didn't take all the culty stuff seriously. Rumors can be misleading."

I nod even though I don't agree.

He asks, "Is the order exact?"

"The what? What?"

"The order of the words from the book are they exactly line by line or are they kinda, like you just happened to stumble across these? Like was it lucky or was it orchestrated."

I'm not sure. "Could be either. I mean it's close to exact."

He tells me it might be good to walk through all the interactions, map it out, and see if anything shakes loose. He says he'll come back and see if he can pluck something from my little map. He's convincing.

I sit on the couch and look through my phone again, hoping I can learn something from the lack of contact, from his last couple texts or last voicemail. I

---

17 I've lost track of all the places now, but we are careening back toward that stall. Somewhere I'm gonna find those same lines carved into something, or shouted at me, or something.

think about all the rumors of the gathering of students reading *The Automatic* out loud to each in candle-lit rooms, about the students lined down the hall to talk to Lindsay. The detective made it clear that these geeked-out book clubs or late-night reading series were just the product of bored creative writing students hell-bent on creating their own importance in a city drenched in the aura of a famous writer.

I get my notebook out and start jotting down the references and where I remember them being. I rip the pages out and start building an actual timeline. I grab the book and start matching everything. Sometime hours later, I look through all the missing lines. It's all pretty exact, line by line. I'm only missing a couple things: The banker says, *I can hear you breathing out there. I know you're trying to squeeze in some shit-talk before I impart my wisdom onto these poor kids* followed by *Diagnoses can't be the only reigning principle* followed by *Gotta slide on. I got minds to expand.* Reason doesn't track, but the process I can see. I still have questions.

From behind me, I hear something shuffle across the room. I turn to look—something dark dashes across the room in my periphery. Jolted, my stomach dropping, I try to stand, but everything cuts to black.

When I wake again, I'm being dragged through my living room, a burlap sack shoved over my head, hands and ankles bound in rope. It burns a little. I hear many footsteps, my back door creaks, a van door sliding open, my body hurled onto a van floor. The van door slams shut and the noise of my neighborhood gets choked into silence. I ask what's happening. I beg for answers. No one says anything. I throw my body against the person next to me, throw my hands down, kick my feet. The walls of this van are soft—my movements, our bodies slamming together are drowned out—and suddenly something quiets me, my head sparks into splotches, and starts to fall.

◆

The throat-starch of a desert evening, mouthfuls of sand and no water. I don't know how long I've been out, but the blindfolded drive out was bumping and strangely quiet, like the van was a moving sound booth. I could taste the desert when they pulled me out of the van. Desert floor crunching under my feet, the sound of others breathing beside me, the wind pushing my clothes against my skin. I don't know how far I walk before they stop me, push me gently to my knees, and pull the bag off my head. Dusk has cranked into evening, a circle of people in dark cloth and hoods hold lanterns in front of their faces, lines from *The Automatic* burned into the ground in front of me, leading out in to the plummeting dark, where I see Lindsay, sitting, legs crossed watching me from across the circle. I hear the whispering again from everyone holding lanterns, and behind me, and out in the dark edges, rising from the darkness. A moment later, Lindsay pushes himself up, and he walks over to me. I can make them out now. Thirty, maybe fifty, of them. They're holding ropes and hammers and Lindsay crouches in front of me. From the glare of the fire-light, I can make out a small tear growing in the corner of his eye. He can't look at me for a long time. I try to talk, but he just says, "This is necessary." A fire blooms out from the darkness. I see a watering hole. Reprieve from the old dusty path.

# JOSHUA YOUNG

Joshua is the author of six collections, most recently, PSALMS FOR THE WRECKAGE (Plays Inverse Press 2017). His novella, LITTLE GALAXIES, is forthcoming from Los Galesburg and his chapbook, WEEKENDS OF SOUND: A 764-HERO MIXTAPe, is forthcoming from Madhouse Press. His writing/drama has appeared in Gulf Coast, Adroit, Puerto del Sol, Court Green, Fugue, Salt Hill, Bat City Review, cream city review, Nightblock, Vinyl, among others.

# CHAPTER FOURTEEN

You see a watering hole.

Reprieve from the old dusty path.

"I'll race you there," says Dad, already sprinting.

Everything's a competition with him.

According to Dad, "You're a soldier and it's time to go to war with your own physical limitations and it's gonna be really barbaric and really insane."

That's why he's dragging you on this 20-mile hike at peak summer suffering temperatures.

He wants to see what you're really made of.

Dad flexes, declaring, "We don't care about the heat, we're freaks!"

He's a military man.

He went through some abject shit.

Like really punishing, freakin' insane, brutal, dungeon slayer shit.

He wants to put you through the same paces so that one day you can carry on his legacy.

You're sweating buckets trying to keep up with him.

He's pushing you to the ultimate limit of physics.

Running toward the first water source you've seen for miles, you notice that it's filled with hypodermic needles, big dick pills, and gasoline canisters.

A wreath of mutated guppies circle the rim.

Three-eyed lizards and tentacled crabs splash around in the muck.

As you approach, the chemicals smell stronger.

Your nostrils burn.

Dad flexes his entire torso.

His skin is so tight around his muscle that it sounds like old leather when he flexes.

Dad points to his pecs and calls them 'devastating.'

Roid rage brigade, y'all.

He yells, "No rest for the wicked, baby! All or nothing, Semper Fi, do or die, terminator baby!"

Dad ties a camouflage bandana to keep the sweat out of his eyes.

His Punisher tanktop is on backwards.

He's on his sixth energy drink.

While Dad has all the characteristics of a human being -- bones, blood, skin, muscle -- his depersonalization is so extreme, has become so ingrained, that his ability to feel empathy, compassion, love, has been exterminated.

He's the victim of a slow but persistent erasure due to years of steroids, military brain chemicals, stress on the body, stress on the nervous system, and erectile dysfunction.

Fueled by testosterone and caffeine, he is simply imitating reality the best he can while hurtling through life as a wild, musclebound beast with only a dim corner of his mind functioning.

He grunts incoherent words that sound vaguely human while washing his face in the watering hole.

Absolutely sickening.

Thick black ooze drips down his razor-shaved skull.

He tells you to drop and give him twenty.

He says, "You will obey the Greek god, the mighty Thor, the ferocious Achilles heel, erm Achilles. Take notes. I'm like Hercules. I'm a Greek god baby, and I'm about to open a Pandora's Box of whoopass."

Thick and veiny spider webs of blood pump from his waxed chest.

His shoulders are mountain peaks rising past his ears.

His arms are pythons digesting small dogs.

His legs are the size of a mosquito's.

Centrifugal force depends on gravity acceleration, and you know that if you kick out Dad's legs, you might have a chance to escape before you die of dehydration.

It's now or never.

Time to stride up Mount Olympus and charge freakin' Stonehenge, that mountain of masculinity that is Dad.

You stare at him, so filled with rage that you can hardly speak, but somehow the words come, "The sirens are calling you home. Can't you hear them? Your day of reckoning is here. All you do is point and laugh. You bastard. You dragged me to this godforsaken place. It's judgement day. You will ask for mercy, but it will fall upon deaf ears. This ends now. I'm so damn thirsty."

Dad nearly topples over as he bursts into deranged laughter like Woody Woodpecker.

You seize the moment, and in an act of what feels like self-preservation, but in retrospect is a sort of self-assertion, you sweep Dad's legs out from under him.

He falls over, raking the air with his nubby fingers as gravity pulls down his girth.

There's a thundering smack as his back flops against the water.

Dirty ooze seeps over the rim like pus out of a lanced cyst.

You slowly release the breath you've been holding in.

A smell like sulphuric acid pollutes the air.

Dad resurfaces and immediately devolves into angry and incomprehensible gibberish.

The three hundred pound beast has a crazed look in his eyes.

He rubs his over-prominent brow.

He says, "Clouded this boy is, very, very clouded! Anger is the path to the dark side. Anger leads to hate, hate leads to suffering. I sense much anger in you."

He tries to grab you by the ankles but you're too quick.

You clench your fists and take a step backward.

You can't decide where to look, feeling vague, misdirected resentment, almost compulsively, toward everything around you.

So you stare into the watering hole, that deep, frothy abyss.

You swear it winks back at you.

Then suddenly, as if on cue, there's a rumble from beneath the earth.

There's a flash as the watering hole erupts, slime spewing upward, smiting the sky.

The ground quakes and crumbles in on itself.

You feel the heat from the watering hole intensify.

It's overwhelming.

Dad's eyes widen.

His teeth gnash through tongue as he wails.

Flesh melts from bone, liquefying as his skeleton twitches in a herky-jerky motion.

By the time the fountain of sludge ceases, Dad has all but disintegrated into the black goo.

You half expect a priest to appear out of the ether to read him a final sermon as he leaves this corporeal dimension, or at the very least a doctor to pronounce him dead on the spot.

Dead.

You didn't mean to kill him.

Fear resonates through your brain.

It permeates throughout the body.

You scream for help.

The sound of your own voice only catalyzes more fear.

You slump against the ground.

A gale rises from the trail, battering your face with sand.

You close your eyes and listen to the sludge rumbling under the earth.

There's another sound as well.

You listen closer.

You concentrate.

It sounds like a whisper at first, but soon the

voice becomes clearer.

The voice says, "Come here my child. Follow my voice."

You think you're hallucinating at first, but then the voice speaks again, "Come swim inside of me, my child."

You say that you don't want to go swimming.

The voice says to step into the watering hole.

You say no way.

The voice says that you have desecrated sacred ground and that if you don't climb into the watering hole you will be killed in a cataclysmic meteor shower from the heavens above.

You say fine, and step into the watering hole.

You're immediately mired.

The more you move, the more you sink.

You sink for what feels like days until you are consumed by nothingness.

You forget all about Dad.

You lose yourself in the black hole of time.

In the dark, you see things so pure that your heart cannot turn back.

You see how humans are genetically encoded with fears that come from billions of years of really punishing, freakin' insane, brutal, dungeon slayer survival of the fittest.

You see how people struggle every day.

They are all just trying to be happy.

Trying to be comfortable in their own skins.

Trying not to be too hot or thirsty for any long duration of time.

Trying to fully experience the moment.

Trying to love one another.

Trying to reach their potential.

Trying to leave behind a legacy.

These are natural instincts that get pressed down and forgotten until they gurgle to the surface in a simmering swamp of resentment.

They infect the main water supply, slowly melting you from the inside out until you're old and angry and hallowed out of every last hope and dream.

It's like reaching a destination and realizing nothing happened along the way.

Just devastating.

A white light consumes you.

You awake lying on the side of the trail covered in an amniotic fluid-like substance.

Upon further inspection, you realize that it's sweat.

The sun is setting in the distance.

You look up into the pinkest parts of the sky.

You look through the pink, beyond the horizon, and through to the other side.

You see the sky in cracks, and sludge exploding through the cracks and falling like rain and sludge covers the world.

Dad is standing over you.

He's no longer a skeleton, but a callous-covered man with arms the size of cement mixers.

He's struggling to maintain any kind of composure.

His nose is twitching.

His teeth are clenched.

He smiles, but no words come out.

You make eye contact.

His eyes are steady.

You notice your reflection in his pupils.

It's hard to make out, but leaning in closer you can see your half-consumed torso slowly sinking into the void.

# BENJAMIN DeVOS

Benjamin DeVos is the author of HUMAN FISH, THE BAR IS LOW, and LORD OF THE GAME. He's the head editor of Apocalypse Party and lives in Philadelphia.

# CHAPTER FIFTEEN

"You see a watering hole. Reprieve from the old dusty path. You stop."

The banjo player was nearly asleep already, the words coming in halted.

"I could stand to take. Another. Beer."

The fiddler watched the banjo player's eyes close, then turned fully back to the road. The sleet had changed over into snow but the ground was too warm for any of it to stick.

*Bridges'll be the only real concern,* he thought.

They'd left the Stoned Inn & Tavern about forty-minutes ago, long enough for the banjo player to go through two "road sodas" and half a pint of Old Grandad, and they had at least three hours til they reached Louisville, where they had a weekend residency at the Local.

"How ye holding up back there, Pots?" Michael asked.

The guitar player groaned but did not open his eyes.

"Alright then," Michael said.

The wiper blades squeaked against the warm windshield like a bow in need of rosin.

Hank Williams sang about seeing the light.

How many gigs had he played with the banjo player, that heralded outlaw prince? Ten dozen? A thousand?

*Too many,* Michael thought, shooting the sleeping banjo player a sidelong look, feeling immediately guilty for hadn't the man pulled him free and clear of Toledo? Hadn't the man got him on the road and put a little spending money in his pocket?

*Of course, of course,* the fiddle player told himself. *And I'm thankful, Lord knows I'm thankful. It's just that there's got to be something more to it than this. There has to be, doesn't there? Just getting drunk and prancing around? The same old song and dance?*

*There're worse jobs to have,* the fiddle player

reminded himself.

Hank Williams had moved on to lamenting about his holey bucket.

◆

The Louisville Local was a shotgun space. The bar lined the entire right wall, bookended with the lifted stage in the back and the entrance and a few tables at the front. It was one of the city's few listening rooms. Michael thought about the first time he got to play this stage. He hadn't been twenty shows into his time with the banjo player then. Young and wide-eyed and loving every second of everything then.

Michael could see the dinginess of the place now. The wallpaper peeling in the corners of the greenroom. The water-stains lining the ceiling. How hadn't he noticed these things until now? Why did he have to notice them at all?

*If* he *could just keep his shit together, we'd be playing the Palace, not the Local,* Michael thought.

The banjo player had played the Palace, Michael knew, but this was when he was still a young phenom, an up and coming young buck he'd been heralded by the likes of Yoakam and Earle back in the day.

*Back in the day is where he seems to live these days,* the fiddle player thought.

Michael saw it every night: the nostalgia worship. The shots lined up like votive candles at an altar. The same fourteen songs, sixteen or eighteen on Friday and Saturdays or for festivals, each and every night. The same self-deprecating stage banter, the same old same old dog and pony show.

*You're jaded,* Michael told himself. *You've got a job men would kill for and you've somehow managed to become jaded.*

Michael began setting up the stage, knowing he still had at least forty-five minutes of time to himself before the rest of the band showed up. He crossed to the center of the stage and looked out onto the empty room. He started with a few scales, working with the bow and bending his knees, trying to loosen up. It didn't used to take a trick, slipping into the song, but it sure did now. The fiddler put in at least twenty minutes before each show to get himself in the headspace he needed to inhabit to get along with the banjo player and the rest of the band, which would include a guitar player, a slide player, and, for three or four songs, a female vocalist. The banjo player had these all across the country: his women.

*I used to be able to shut my eyes and become the song. Now I have to think about what's coming next and where the fitting in is.*

Was it the years of babysitting that did it? The countless nights spent tracking down their payday because the banjo player was holed up in the van or a corner booth drunk off his ass, was it just that? Or all the nights playing the same old songs, but playing them proficiently? All those nights going to sleep knowing that he did enough for those songs but were those the songs he should be playing?

*Are these the songs for me?* he wondered for what could've been the thousandth time if it were the first. *Is this it?*

◆

There were moments where Michael wasn't sure he was fitting into the song any longer. Stark, scary blips where he felt alone and naked before a wall of billowing sound. The only way out he'd found was to grind his teeth and rake the strings with the bow, hoping against hope that he'd slip back inside the song somehow. Sometimes the song seemed so seamless that he had no place.

It made him think of the toys all children had: the blocks of shapes and their corresponding holes in the board. Did Michael's perfect circle still fit the banjo player's water-logged board? Sometimes he felt like he was crammed in there, forced into place, cramped.

*Be humble,* he reminded himself.

◆

The banjo player spent most of his time on the road, his live shows having the reputation it did, and the recordings never really doing him any sort of justice. He put them out just to stay on the road.

"Ye gotta go where the money is," was one of his favorite sayings.

All the players in the band were known to be hot, each a burning ember in the fire was how the banjo player described his band in all the interviews.

Michael wasn't sure his ember was catching anymore. He'd opened his mouth to talk to the banjo player so many times but couldn't find the words, the right ones.

*I don't feel it anymore.*

*I'm not here most of the time.*

*This is starting to feel like Work.*

Each night another bar. Two sets, three hours' worth of music. Then the breaking down and the loading up. The miles of darkened highway. The miles of a mostly quiet van.

*Is there more to life than this?*

◆

The days stacked up like a burn pile and he envisioned a song with wings. A song that lifts and dips and swells and chortles. Something ready to catch fire. It came to him many times during the day and especially along the darkened nighttime highways crisscrossing the Midwest. He found himself fretting the fretless circle of the steering wheel, shapes corresponding to chords imagined. A song with no words, just the agonized sounds of being and nothingness, minor and passing.

Michael wondered if the banjo player still heard songs such as this. He wondered if anybody had ever heard a song such as this. A song with folds; a song with creases. He knew he didn't know how to discuss what was happening in himself.

There was a rock quarry they could swim in just outside Knoxville. A roadie had showed them the spot a few years back after a college party they'd played. Michael hoped the next day would be clear and warm enough for a swim. He needed to pour himself into a larger pool, dip himself in the deep, murky water, and hopefully emerge cleansed and renewed.

He set the fiddle down, leaned it carefully against the Deluxe Reverb, and just stood under the lights of the empty stage with his eyes closed seeing the leap off the cliff into the quarry. He felt the wind whip at his cheeks, the smell of the stagnant water getting stronger, his feet filled with pinpricks as he plummeted.

◆

The faceless crowd shuddered like the flickering static of a television set. There were no individuals out there to Michael, they all melded and bristled collectively. He hit his marks. He found the heart of the song and gently squeezed it, getting it to open and pump.

The banjo player had been hard at it, before soundcheck even. Michael could smell it on him from across the stage. Three-fourths of the way through their first set and he was already missing the one and dragging out the four more than halfway through the five, cramming the last lines into the chorus, fucking it all up.

Michael stomped out the one, hoping to beat the song back into its proper rhythm imagining defibrillator pad jolts, the song arrhythmic, a live, skipping record. He yipped and cawed like a crow when he wasn't voicing anything in particular, near enough to the mic for the ghost version to slip in, high in the mix.

But there was only so far he could stretch the tearing canvas of their sodden music, the songs pulled loose like slippery threads. The songs ended with prolonged flourishes that Michael assumed the banjo player overdid to make up for undercutting all those verses, burning all those bridges, not meaning to be so hackneyed, worn out like a bad gasket, rust leaking through, corroding the innards, but being so authentically.

Michael finished the first set knowing he wouldn't say a thing to the banjo player during the break. He knew he'd feel like a skater on thinning ice for the rest of the night. He also knew this meant the van ride wouldn't be enjoyable. Whoops and hollers or curses and prayers. Another stop in the night, some roadhouse on the edge of nowhere for more, more, more drinks. Pulling into the motel at five or six in the goddamn morning.

He held the fiddle like a child, unconsciously, and wished he could just chase the balloon like he could when he was a kid, the song dangling just out of reach and with each stride knowing you'd have it, now, no now, now. Michael watched the banjo player drop his instrument onto the rack, pick up his sweating beer, finishing it in three long swallows.

Another set in the books.
*Gulp.*
Another night drinking more than I should.
*Gulp.*
Another endless highway night.
*Gulp.*

◆

One of the barmaids had a joint. They passed it around

around out back, beside the overflowing dumpster, each nodding and avoiding each other's eye contact, talking about Bob Wills and Scarlet Rivera. The conversation broke in like a tired denim jacket, they were distressed at the elbows, each aching in some shiny, apparent way.

She saw the banjo player going at his Mega Gulp, made a show of sniffing, then she snatched it out of his boiled sausage fingers. She popped the lid off the styrofoam cup, looked at the liquid inside, sniffed it again, then took a long swallow.

"Thanks for sharing, asshole," she said. "I've been givin' ye free shots at the bar all night and ye don't even offer the booze ye ain't supposed to be sneaking in and out of the premises."

The banjo player had this laugh, a booming, crackling thing. A blown speaker laugh: worn, torn, & forlorn. That was one of the things Michael could say he didn't hate or hold against the man lately, not that he'd make any real show of his displeasure with The Situation. He held his breath and waited to resurface. He took the joint carefully and inhaled until he felt filled to bursting, then he let it all go.

*Out,* he exhaled.

The chains, *a barn reading come see Chained Rock, Pineville, Kentucky,* slackened around his heart but did not come undone. He felt a brief warmth there like a sunny moment in late December; not enough to catch fire on but enough to warm and loosen the fingers.

There was a broken mirror leaned against one of the dumpsters, a large puddle around a backed-up drain in front of it. The fiddler kept stealing glances at himself through the reflection of his reflection on the pool of water amazed at the clarity of the image despite the murkiness of the water.

"Well, y'all," the bartender said. "Guess we better all get back at it."

Michael watched the door close behind her, not wanting to look at the banjo player or the rest of the guys. He took another look at his reflection while they smoked cigarettes and kicked lose chunks of asphalt across the parking lot, waiting, like always, on the banjo player to call time.

# A.S. COOMER

A.S. Coomer is a writer and musician. Books include MEMORABILIA, THE FETISHISTS, SHINING THE LIGHT, THE DEVIL'S GOSPEL, THE FLOCK UNSEEN, MISDEEDS, and others. He runs Lost, Long Gone, Forgotten Records, a "record label" for poetry. He writes songs, plays guitar, and sings in The Coomers. www.ascoomer.com

# CHAPTER SIXTEEN

You see a watering hole. Reprieve from the old dusty path.

A man walking with a walkman radio and a ball cap pulled down tight above his eyes, it's like he mapped the path in his head. The air of a local-regular, walking so precisely.

There seem to be beautiful things here.

Hot dog water left in the microwave.

In and of a life you can remember, catching it even after it's found. You remember being scolded a few times, since you kept leaving it in the microwave after it was done cooking.

The sweetest thing: a Gila woodpecker with its mouth on an aloe flower squeaking like a seagull and the feeling of wanting to relay that information.

Hard time keeping your thoughts straight but your thoughts mean well. The way you leave the light on for the dog, the delicacy of a dry heat.

But it's a dry heat here, too, so no worries. Living in a house on a street both ways—a to-and-from kind of place. Where there's a bunch of boys always gearing up to hunt rabbit and snipe. It's not much more scary than in cartoons. Though there are always implications. Who had the idea to begin with and who wanted to follow along and who did.

Natural drains list #: brook, arroyo, ditch, gully, gutter, rut, gulch.

: will have to dump out the diamond ash because something's all blocked up, it's just not good to keep around or to have on hand this time of year.

A squandered opportunity for some relief: it's Friday everyone's saying things about finally being here.

You get so lost you have to retrace your steps past the same thing a few times, between delta and dam. There was a cat hunting ducks at the end of a little concrete jetty. And who was that hack on the shore? –oh god I could cry.

Refusing to call it jealousy.

Crying to a sitcom

Crying remembering re-runs.

A man named Mulch got caught handing you a pot of water to boil.

You see a watering hole. Reprieve from the old dusty path.

And that's that.

# NATHAN DRAGON

Nathan Dragon was born in Salem, MA. Dragon co-founded Blue Arrangements and has been published in NOON Annual, Hotel, Fence, and New York Tyrant.

# CHAPTER SEVENTEEN

*You see a watering hole. Reprieve from the old dusty path.*

That's a thing I want to reiterate — you're trying to look for the full story. Moses exhausted, hungry, thirsty, and bleeding but forcing himself to continue, some say for more than a week, until he came to a watering hole. It started with a fascination with cities and how they work, and what's going on in them right now. That led me to the only thing that was tractable in discovering that, which was bicycle messengers and truck couriers roaming about, delivering packages.

The product is what you make of it. Moses threw himself under the shade of a tree.

> There is no law of right which consecrates dullness. The concept is so simple and so open-ended that people can make of it whatever they wish. They seek value and they add value. The product is what you make of it.
>
> The whole bird thing: bird chirps sound meaningless to us, but meaning is applied by other birds. Male Trumpeter Finch at Desert National Park #Rajasthan #India last month! Several small groups were dropping in to a watering hole by the main road that runs through the park. California condors! If there's a watering hole somewhere near a feeding site, they like to clean themselves very thoroughly and will sunbathe right after to dry their feathers.

This may be cliché to say, but when you speak truth to power, the ramifications can go a lot of different ways. Suddenly you have all these people on the street roaming about, and they're able to report on everything they see.

I don't really want to comment on whether I'm okay.

*You have wandered the desert for far too long when suddenly, you see a watering hole in the distance, guarded by an ambush of hungry tigers. Maybe the water is a fata morgana, maybe the predators are. What do you do?*

In the early days, I bought into the idea that the Internet would lead to a better world, that the truth was out there and that we didn't need gatekeepers. But I don't go back in time.

> I don't go back in time. You're kind of as good as your last update. That's what you're currently thinking or doing, or your current approach towards life. If that really interests me, I go to that person's profile page and read back a little bit. But in terms of my timeline, I'm just not obsessive about going all the way back in time and catching every single message that people have updated about. It's only relevant in the now, unless I'm fascinated by it. They have Moses and the prophets; let them hear them.

At that time, even in the very early stages, I had this strange feeling that I had never had before — that this was something big. I felt it from the onset. People must have thought I was a crazy person because of the way I treated it. To the right I could see a church I took a step in that direction first But to the left there was a watering hole where they were whiskey drunk And now that's where I wanna be I may not be perfect But I've always been true. Climbed up from the bottom for the last time.

That may have been detrimental.

The little eyeballs were watching. The main mischief lies in the strange devices that are used to support the long... Lol, I couldn't think of the term "hallucinating" and just said "that thing when you see a watering hole in the middle of a desert."

I don't really want to comment on whether I'm okay.

> I don't know how people do it. I personally can't do it. I don't follow people in the traditional way. There are a few people whose messages I get delivered in real time via SMS.
>
> Actively taking things out of context can be helpful for analysis precisely because it creates a cognitive disconnect. And yet you let your architects do the same thing over and over again for three centuries, and expect to be interested by their architecture. I'm more interested in their particular interruptions.

*Change can hurt. There are no secret places left. What do you remember/think about your role?*

I am very passionate about certain things and I will get passionate about certain things I believe in. He's a very shrewd businessman. When we watched Planet Earth together, i told him my fav mammal...

> That's a thing I want to reiterate—

...my fav mammal was prolly an elephant. & there were baby elephants n i rly loved those, n so did we. There was this part where a herd of elephants had to brave a sandstorm to get to a watering hole, n a baby got lost... we cuddled n rly bonded over the lost lil baby elephant.

> That's a thing I want to reiterate — You're either a tree to climb, or you're a watering hole, or a parking garage. Or a stick to swing around. In the early days, I bought into the idea that the Internet would lead to a better world. He didn't want it, though. He was trying to find ways to get out of it for a while. For a few months, six months before.

Yeah, he had the power. Looking back, it seems to be the right thing now. It worked out, right? You understand why? You understand the potential implication of what you're saying?

I don't think I want to comment on that. He's a very shrewd businessman. That's his business — to isolate and spot value where it is. There's a difference between being fanatical — and I hate to say that I was fanatical — but to be extremely passionate like I am or being very super rational and calculated like he is.

Think about it — he had the money. He had the power. They didn't really do anything. He didn't feel as though he needed that structure anymore.

> In the early days, I bought into the idea that the Internet would lead to a better world. But the internet is not what I thought it was 20 years ago. It's not a utopian world.

*You are outside of the building. In front of you is an expansive desert, peppered with dried sagebrush and Joshua trees. All you can hear is wind. A dusty path leads away from the building towards more crumbling structures in the distance. The sun is setting to your right.*

I haven't spoken with him in 5 years. He has his own ideas about how life works.

> Stop by a watering hole, have a drink. Lean down to the sink like a wary antelope at a watering hole.
>
> There are no secret places left. If you have a favorite watering hole, or restaurant that used to be off the beaten path, Google maps is currently bringing 1000 people there.

He was a nice guy. Was he doing anyone a favor? Was he really doing favors? Hard to say. Was it a calculated move? Definitely. Was there lots of thought put into it? Definitely. He definitely made a lot of money. That was a phenomenal investment. He got a great deal.

I don't really want to comment on whether I'm okay.

> There is no law of right which consecrates dullness. That allowed me to create this visualization: the little eyeballs were "watching." The concept was watching before we kind of switched it and developed it into "following." So you could watch or unwatch someone -- but we found a better word -- follow or unfollow.

It kind of turned me off from collaboration for a while which is something I really enjoyed.

*Now we have another entity roaming about the metropolis, reporting where it is and what work it has, going over GPS and CB radio or cellphone. And then you get to the emergency services: ambulances, firetrucks and police—*

The working name was just "Status" for a while. It actually didn't have a name. I pitched it at a board meeting.

> Let us think for a few moments —

One of the very last board meetings, I think.

> Let us think for a few moments what romance and utopianism mean.
>
> First, romance. It needs someone who's not just mesmerized by its sparkliness, but can see it as a product. Who can look at how people are actually using it and how people want to use it. The problem, of course, is that it can show who you really are.

He started talking to me about this idea of status and how he was really interested in status. That allowed me to create this visualization -- I was looking at stuff like how people were communicating on MySpace and other social networking things and seeing how people were trying to communicate and seeing how systems weren't really designed to do what people were doing with them. But people were trying to communicate in a certain kind of way. Non-synchronous. Non-realtime communication. I was looking at stuff like how people were communicating on MySpace and other social networking and I don't know if they fully got it. A Follow is a connection. A Like is a connection. It just *postpones* the economy. It need not hurt it. We were sitting on Mission St. in the car in the rain. Bicycle messengers and truck couriers were roaming about, delivering packages. We were going out and I was dropping him off and having this conversation. There was a moment where it all fit together for me.

> And now utopianism. That is another of the devil's pet words. The working name was just "Status" for a while. It actually didn't have a name. I pitched it at a board meeting. One of the very last board meetings, I think. It's really hard to define because we're still coming up with the vocabulary -- but I think it's defined a new behavior that's very different than what we've seen before.

> I don't know if the other guys got it. They kind of got it. But I don't know if they fully got it. They saw it as a distraction.

If you look at any big internet thing, you see it's basically a big hive of connections. A Follow is a connection. A Like is a connection. If you study what the really big things on the internet are, you realize they are masters at making things fast and making people not think.

> There is no law of right which consecrates dullness. The proof of a thing's being right is, that it has power over the heart; that it excites us, wins us, or helps us.

> I have delayed you by the consideration of these two words, only in the fear that they might be inaccurately applied to the plans I am going to lay before you; for, though they were utopian, and though they were romantic, they might be none

> the worse for that. But in fact they are neither. We often think the internet enables you to do new things. But people just want to do the same things they've always done.

What we've been trying to do is really reimagine the way we display a conversation to make them easier to read, the participants and actors in that conversation more discernible, so that the authoritative voices, the people who started the conversation, the people you follow in that conversation, will be more recognizable. That allowed me to create this visualization. The little eyeballs were "watching." So you could watch or unwatch someone. Afterwards, I was a little shell-shocked. I was like, "Wait ... what's the value in building these relationships if this is the result?"

> Now, therefore, if you feel that the present world is unattractive to you, I say there is something wrong, either in the world or in you. "Well, but what are we to do?" you will say to me; "we cannot make architects of ourselves." Pardon me, you can—and you ought. We have certainly not reached the final evolution of social communications architecture.
>
> Well, but, you will answer, you cannot feel interested in informational architecture: you do not care about it, and cannot care about it. I know you *cannot*. People do not know that you cannot successfully innovate in an existing organization unless you systematically abandon. About such architecture as is built nowadays, no mortal ever did or could care. You do not feel interested in *hearing* the same

thing over and over again;—why do you suppose you can feel interested in *seeing* the same thing over and over again, were that thing even the best and most beautiful in the world?

We have a dedicated team who does that.

Whatever the case, no one would argue that this particular aspect of this system is a force for good. I had dinner the other night with a famous person who does (or did) read their replies and who was quite upset at the abuse he'd seen. I felt for him. We've enabled people to be nasty in a new and visible way that didn't exist before. Frankly, I rarely post anything other than a link, because I don't enjoy debating with strangers in a public setting. And yet you let your architects do the same thing over and over again for three centuries, and expect to be interested by their architecture; but there is no law of right which consecrates dullness. People just want to do the same things they've always done.

Moses threw himself under the shade of a tree.

We were sitting on Mission St. in the car in the rain. We were going out and I was dropping him off and having this conversation. He was a nice guy. Yeah, he had the power. He got a great deal. I don't think I want to comment on that.

They have Moses (Laws) and the Prophets(ELIJAH) let them hear them..... If they do not hear THEM neither will they be convinced if someone shld rise from the Dead!

I worked on a game for a while. It didn't really come out the way I wanted it to.

# JAMES TADD ADCOX

James Tadd Adcox is the author of a novel, DOES NOT LOVE, and a novella, REPETITION, and is an editor at the literary magazine Always Crashing. His work has appeared in Granta, n+1, and The Collagist, among other places. He lives in Pittsburgh.

# CHAPTER EIGHTEEN

You see a watering hole. Reprieve from the old dusty path. Another obstacle for my vitamins. I cut out her rhyme. Only a part in the hair visible, pale round the well's rim. Snipped out her capsules to double mine, slash pattern smile, dots on brick. How to baptize an aphorism into evidence.

I do my multiplication tables in blood. An unpopped kernel of popcorn swells behind my left eye. If the weather seesaws, I will be forced to prep a muscle for extirpation. Looks like someone tossed a stick of dynamite in her bedpan. Sticky bindings pollute the slab. She needed to stay about the periphery of anyone's approval to feel safe. Raking in the life sentences.

The only thing I mean to convey will be the charges brought against me. I am addicted to chewing mothballs and running lace between my two front teeth. A bouquet ground into her morral accentuated specks of maidenhead inexorably burst, crux to nostril. Enough to decongest a prostate.

Come reincarnate, gormandized target, indentation of every rape girdled on air. I like my totems chunky. She could contour the sincerest affection until it came out more subliminal than meant. Had to staple a staple in my scalp to anchor thoughts. Picking through the florescent muss our race made, the regime of me. The last government detonated from faith, consent gone the way of the dodo. The malice of a law is in parentheses.

Phonetic bass beat coital stultification, caravans scratching intricacies on the horizon. Any skyline can be used as a leash. Shoving still-wrapped candies down her throat, mites preserved in cream, shit fanning under like the tabernacle sneezed. The full ordeal of courtship: someone tried to draw a girl around ten tons of pork chops and mashed potatoes, a life abandoned to appeetite. When the cock dried up into a family, dinner took its place. Weddings reboot twice in hell.

That birth chute crowded with dairy snacks, factory farm for stretchmarks, still wanting to split the carbs while she trifled to bend over, pinup pictures of her youth sagging down the wall.

Help us prune in the pool as a species.

# SEAN KILPATRICK

Sean Kilpatrick studied forensic photography, holds a Master's in writing, is published or forthcoming in: Boston Review, Columbia Poetry Review, evergreen review, NERVE, FENCE, LIT, VICE, BOMB, DIAGRAM, New York Tyrant, Sleepingfish, Obsidian, Vol. 1 Brooklyn, The Quietus, Hobart, gay death trance, La Petite Zine, Pindeldyboz, Expat Press, tragickal, fluland, Terror House, NOÖ Journal, Jacket2, Exquisite Corpse, MiPoesias, Forklift Ohio, Arsenic Lobster, Melancholia's Tremulous Dreadlocks, Sixth Finch, Epicenter, Skidrow Penthouse, The Lifted Brow, Black Sun Lit, elimae, Alpha Beat Soup, and completed several small books with various presses, including ANATOMY COURSES with Blake Butler.

# CHAPTER NINETEEN

YOU see a watering hole. Reprieve from the old dusty path. YOU start across the one hundred yards of yellow land separating YOU from your first drink of water in three days.

YOU stifle your excitement and barely allow a grin. YOU know if YOU smile any wider it'll crack those sunburnt lips. YOU instead let your legs express the emotion. Each step toward that water is made with more urgency than the last. The remaining coins in your pocket clang against one another.

YOU continue at this pace for seconds before YOU suddenly slow. The reason for the slowing of your pace: YOU see THEM at the watering hole.

THEM is a brown woman in her 20s with her black hair down, over the shoulders of a dark blue pioneer dress. THEM is crouched at the watering hole.

YOU continue walking, slowly. Without your glasses, YOU squint. YOU blink. YOU squint some more. YOU blink some more. It's no mirage, no trick: THEM is still there, at the watering hole, a hand cupping water to her face and neck. YOU see that her dress and hair and skin are caked with dust, as if she too has been on foot for days.

As YOU draw nearer to the watering hole, THEM becomes alert. THEM stands and turns to you. She is pregnant. Far along. THEM keeps her eyes down and her mouth taut. She is submitting to YOU and, satisfied, YOU allow your tense shoulders and neck to relax.

YOU move your eyes from THEM to the watering hole: the water is dirty, rancid, tinged brown. Dead flies float on the surface.

YOU:
Mind if I—?

THEM shakes her head.

YOU crouch to the watering hole. THEM stands a few feet away, watching as YOU cup your hand and bring water to your mouth. YOU do it again and again and again. Eventually, you can't resist. YOU submerge your face in the water.

Down here, beneath the surface, YOU feel relieved. YOU feel safe. YOU are protected from the cruel sun, from the cruel earth. YOU hear so little. YOU see so little.

When your throat and lungs can take no more, YOU come up gasping for air. THEM has moved to the other side of the watering hole.

THEM:
I knew you'd come.

YOU:
Did you now?

THEM:
You're here to hunt.

YOU:
I am. I'd be doing that right now if your kin hadn't taken my things in the night.

THEM:
You're here to hunt me.

YOU:
What else is left to hunt?

THEM paces on the opposite side of the watering hole, growing comfortable with the act of looking at YOU.

YOU:
Unforgiving land for a pregnant lady to wander, wouldn't you say?

THEM:
I'm not wandering.

YOU:
I don't see any water buckets. Don't see any arrows. You're not even wearing your own clothes.

THEM:
One doesn't wander their home.

YOU:
Sure they do. I did until I was 25. Headed this way once I got sick of beating my head against my father's walls.

YOU sit on the bank of the watering hole. YOU lean back and look up at the sun. When YOU return your eyes to center, THEM is staring at you.

YOU (cont'd):
You know, I've never been any good at hunting. Most of us aren't. I knew it the first time my sister took me out into the woods. I was six or seven years old and we were after whitetail deer. That's what my sister was always after. Good meat, real good meat. Lean, but tender, not like the game out here, not as wired for survival. You can taste that in the blood, you know, that relentless fear they live

with. It's different—different than being spooked now and again. Anyway, I was too impatient for it, waiting for those whitetail to appear, the sitting still, the quiet. Even now the only time I can sit in silence longer than a few minutes is when I sleep.

THEM:
And when you sleep, you let your horse get stolen.

YOU:
Any other day, I wouldn't think that was very funny.

YOU shrug your shoulders.

THEM (cont'd):
If you're bad at it, then why do you hunt?

YOU:
Simple. I love killing. That's one thing the whitetail did confirm, the day I finally played the game it wanted me to play and I put an bullet right through its heart.

YOU stare at the rancid water.

YOU (cont'd):
If there's one thing I appreciate about your people, it's that: I can sit here and tell you that I like to kill and you don't fall into a panic, like some dainty white woman back east would. You're not afraid to admit that you like killing.

THEM:
I don't like killing.

YOU:
Then you're in the wrong place, sweetheart.

THEM:
No, I'm not. I told you: this is my home.

YOU:
What is?

YOU motion to the north and south and east and west, at the oceans of plains stretching far beyond what the eye can see.

YOU (cont'd):
This watering hole is your home? The tree
I passed ten miles back?

THEM:
All of this.

YOU:
You can't have all of it. Not anymore.
That's what the hunting is about, and you
know it. It's about the shifting of
perspective.

THEM:
—the shifting of my perspective. Not
yours. You want me to see my homeland
in a way that I'll never see it, and you ask
nothing of yourself. No shifting of you,
no shifting of them, whoever it is you
speak of. Where is your homeland?
Where do your people come from?

Where do your people come from?

YOU:
Born in North Carolina, raised in North Carolina. Before that, before me at all, was Scotland.

THEM:
Scotland?

YOU (cont'd):
Mmhmm. My family was one of thousands run out of their homes. They escaped here, to America, and settled in North Carolina. But they were never really settled, were they? Can the systematically oppressed ever truly feel settled? Can they? Huh? But they settled nonetheless. God, I hate that word, settled. Settled. Settled. I don't think any of us were meant to be settled. I really don't. But thousands of years in the making, here we are. And there you are: wild, free, bred to roam. Relics.

THEM puts her hand on her belly and walks into the water, stopping when the water is up to her shins.

YOU (cont'd):
Don't you see what's happening here? What's been happening? Oppressive systems are built by jealous men. They always have been. And this system is swooping you and your people up.

THEM:
Where will it drop us?

YOU:
Wherever it wants to.

THEM:
And your life is unaffected by this?

YOU:
My life is supplied by this. I'm an agent of the system and I'm handsomely rewarded for the work I do. Does that mean that in my soul I support the system? No. But I don't think my soul factors all that much into this life.

Without so much as a shift in posture, THEM's water breaks. As THEM's water reaches the watering hole, there are small splashes, and there are ripples that follow and make their way to the watering hole's edge.

YOU stand.

YOU (cont'd):
Hey there, whoa—are you okay? Maybe you should sit back down.

THEM:
I'd rather stand.

YOU remain standing, caught between helping THEM and staying put.

THEM (cont'd):
Sit. I don't want your help.

YOU raise your hands as if to say, "Fine then." YOU sit.

THEM (cont'd):
Tell me: if not for the soul, what do you

believe this life is for?

YOU remain silent, in thought.

THEM (cont'd):
You do believe that you have a soul?

YOU:
I'm not sure if I do.

THEM:
Then why do you kill? If it does not
please your soul, what is it pleasing?

YOU:
My brain, maybe. My hands and mouth.

THEM:
That tingling you get—

YOU:
—the buzz, yes. That tingling, that hum.
So you have killed?

Again, without grimacing, without changing her posture, THEM gives birth—into the watering hole her offspring drops,

YOU stand and hurry to the watering hole.

THEM remains still.

THEM:
I believe my soul is in my brain, that it's
in my hands and in my mouth. I believe
my soul is in my skin, and that the hum
after a kill is just one way my soul chooses
to talk to me.

YOU stand feet from THEM, crouched, your hands plugged into the watering hole, frantically searching for THEM's offspring. It takes seconds for YOU to realize that there is no umbilical cord hanging from THEM.

THEM (cont'd):
Maybe the only way you could understand
this is if the system had passed over you
and your family, if it had left you in
Scotland, but my soul is in that tree ten
miles back. My soul is in this watering
hole, and my soul is not happy.

A SNAKE leaps out from the watering hole and bites YOU in the throat. YOU gasp for air. YOU swipe at the SNAKE with your hands and miss. YOU miss again and again and again.

THEM remains standing. She watches as the SNAKE bits you on the cheek and forehead.

YOU slip on the mud beneath the water and fall beneath the surface. Water goes over your chest, over your face. YOU come up gasping for air.

The SNAKE keeps biting you. On your hand, on your ear. Again, your throat.

THEM walks to you through the water. Her belly is now flat. She leans down and quiets her voice to a whisper.

THEM (cont'd):
I know that the current of your people is
too strong, and that a choice by you to
swim upstream would mean death. I
know how this ends. I know we all have
our parts to play. And I know that the

only thing you and your people will do to dull the tragedy you bring is talk. Talk and talk and talk.

# GARRETT DENNERT

Garrett Dennert is an American author who was raised in Hart, Michigan. He currently resides in Seattle, Washington and is the founding editor of Orson's Review.

Garrett's stories and essays have appeared in Barely South Review, Midwestern Gothic, Monkeybicycle and Whiskeypaper. He authored WOUNDED TONGUE, an ambitious dystopian novel, and is at work on his next novel, as well as a story collection and a children's book.

# CHAPTER TWENTY

*for Elizabeth Aldrich*

You see a watering hole. Reprieve from the old dusty path. I love him in a way I can't explain. I first saw him through the glass, at ten in the morning, standing with the others, separate but equal among the crowd, his right knee at an angle, not in supplication, more contrapposto, a word I know the meaning of without having to look up. Mostly used among artistic types, of which I am not. The group he was standing with was all white, the blacks had their separate corner, their heads severed by the manufacturer. How did they feel, not having a mouth, a voice, for all eternity, to be clothed, fondled, and stripped of personhood before the next white sale over Labor Day weekend? I knew I had to have him. I opened the door – LAST DAYS! – and walked to the area where he was standing, naked as the day he was extruded from the machine. A few scarecrows milled about, fondling sales tags, considering candelabras and floor length faux furs. Every overpriced item knocked down, eighty percent off, buy two get one free, won't last long!

◆

Perhaps you think me a bit strange. It has taken a lifetime to become this strange, this unsettled. Third grade, Mrs. Jacobsen's class. The girl wore pants I thought a boy would wear, ugly brown fabric not meant for a girl's body. When I thought of girls my eight year old brain thought cotton, white, puffy, strange brown pods filled with the future, and when I thought of a boy's body I thought corduroy, clean sharp lines funneling into the center of everything I knew. Girls' bodies were foreign, my Dremeled thumbnails prying into a slit and still nothing, ungiving, and I could spend an hour with a girl's body and still not understand. She wore a watch, an adult watch, a thick wedge of silver on her left wrist, its heaviness masculine, and I laughed at the foreignness of it – SEIKO – where did you get it? It's my father's, she said, why does he let you wear a boy's watch, Because he's dead, and I didn't say another word, and in class, sitting next to each other, next to my first love, because geography said so, as it always does, I met her in class and now I love her, I met him at work and now I love him, my father met my mother in a bar they both decided on that night, and now here I am, all our lives, our loves, determined by accidental geography, the room smashing two strangers together until one utters the other's name, for the first time, and before long they are off to lunch, off to city hall for the license, for a piece of paper that declares yes, this is real. But this was before all that, when life was simple, when it was clocks, and recess, and an American flag draped over green alphabet placards hung in place before I was born. Her hair was long, and blondish brown, and parted in the center, like all the other girls I knew. Her name was the only name I spoke aloud, and each time I did it was as if I were giving her even more power over me. We pulled our chairs together, Mrs. Jacobsen shouting CHECK EACH OTHERS WORK, TEST EACH OTHER! I thought how lazy, shouldn't you be doing this, with her sharpened nails that had dug into my biceps more than once, shaking me, as my mother did on occasion, and I could only laugh, that was my reaction, I laughed and she shook me harder, as if she would knock the worldliness from my eyes, He's stubborn, you know, I heard my mother tell my father, he's stubborn, he'll sit there at his plate and he'll stare at it until finally I tell him get up and take a bath, get ready for bed, but of course you'd know that if you were here, and I have been a slow eater ever since, my beautiful other half, chosen by electronic geography, the internet, finished ten minutes before I stomach the final bite, a slave to food yet somehow hating it, and her name was Tracy, Tracy Green, which sounded very simple, but wasn't. It's my dad's watch, he gave it to my mother and my mother gave it to me, and now I remembered that movie, but this was before that movie, this was 1978, and the only movie playing in my head at that time was filtered sunlight through carob leaves, and I had not yet met death, and as we sat in the classroom, Tracy and I, she tested me, tested my excellent spelling skills, and as we sat next to each other our knees touched, and it was at that moment I fell in love. I followed the lines of her ugly brown pants to the center of everything, a bald, strange fruit, and I had seen other fruit of the same kind on one occasion, Stephanie Jones, but this was different, less animalistic, perhaps due to the classroom setting, and the clock, and the paint on the wall, which had slowly yellowed through a million recesses, YOU KIDS PIPE DOWN! which reminded me of my mother, of something my mother would say, and I hated Mrs. Jacobsen, hated her nails in my flesh, her old, cracked face, her onionskin lips in a permanent rictus, the rattle of the whistle at the end of her ruined neck, a wooden ball in a metal case, and my friend Mark gave me a whistle just like Mrs. Jacobsen's, and once, when we were on the field, far from the adults, I drew the whistle from my pocket, put it to my lips and blew myself into the principal's office, what do you think you're doing? Mr. Butler sighing at the overly-familiar sight of me, my slanted eyes, touch your toes, the slap of wood against my ass, a paddle of some kind, tennis? I am terrible with sports, don't care, and at the end of the state-sanctioned punishment, more laughing. Do you want another? No I answer as I walk out the door laughing.

◆

Do you want to see something, Tracy asked. We were on the playground, my whistle tucked safely in the top of Mr. Butler's desk drawer, near the teeth-worn Ticonderogas, weapons seized from future rapists, murderers, and the all too common drug dealer. We sat hidden in the concrete tunnel, away from the other children and the nosy, ineffectual adults. Yes, I said, expecting candy, or jacks, a game I didn't understand, being a boy, and suddenly her finger was in my nose, the acrid pungency immediately recognizable, the sulphur under her fingernail, and the shock of it knocked me against the sharp-pebbled surface of the tunnel. Her cheap plastic eyeglasses became darker, more masculine, almost military, and I wondered if they too belonged to her dead father. I must have made a face that stunned her to embarrassment, the joke quickly souring. I had never smelled the animalism of a girl before, all the mystery of the world exposed in direct sunlight, the grass already dead as if summer was just a final bell away, the 2:30 chime signaling the kids, who moved like starving dogs, towards the water fountains, the expectant teachers, the lucky few with parents already waiting for them in queues at the front of the school. I was a bus rider, as was Tracy. We were poor, working-class, white. She was deposited every afternoon at the entrance of the Lazy Daze Trailer Court, whereas I was three or four stops later, a small brick home that felt more real than a tin box, and before she left her seat for the door, I looked down my small pointed nose at her and saw her for what she was, garbage, and I wondered how a girl who was born a girl knew enough to do what she did and present it to a boy she loved. That may have been the moment when I was off girls for good, because next year was fourth grade, and fourth grade was very different, transitory, a nothing year, and then came fifth grade, and a boy who sat three seats in front of me, and as the bus pulled away from the entrance to the mobile court, the trailers poking above the ratty wooden fence like empty beer cans lined up on a drunkard's windowsill, I looked down at her through the handprint glass, my classmates' lifelines grimy and impermanent, and she stood still, a small dirty negative of what should have been a normal life, looking up at me as the bus headed towards forty-third avenue before turning right, and I knew I would never speak to her again, and years later,

the hall, I remembered our playground encounter, and how, once something wicked is revealed, it can never be made right again.

◆

Holding someone's hand in your hand until their hand disappears, until you become one, their body and your body indeterminate. This is the definition of love, is it not? When we forget someone is there, when they become us? Moving from the other to the us. Her father was a soldier in Vietnam, a man who didn't come back. I was five years old when we pulled out of Saigon like a cheap date, and none of it meant anything to me, other than people saying Vietnam, Vietnam, Vietnam, as if conjuring someone's hand they remembered to forget. She lived with her grandmother, Mrs. Thrasher, who had a different surname than she did. Years later, when I was a skater in high school, when I bought the newest copy of *Thrasher*, I'd think of her for a moment, of her grandmother, then her, I would recall us horizontal on the cement slab in her backyard, exploring each other's bodies using only our hands, our fingers. She was a year older than me, had already been institutionalized. I would be institutionalized a year later. And now we are six. There was no grass in the backyard, only powder thick and heavy as cinnamon, silt on an ocean floor that had died a million years ago, and when she took my hand and led me to a powder blue toolshed, the door hesitant, unwilling to show us its secrets, she pushed through violently, as her father must have pushed through the sweltering foliage of Vietnam. Her grandmother sat in a recliner most of the time, watching a dead television, waiting for her son to walk through the front door. I remember all the green on a spotty Trinitron, and now and again she would bang the side of it with a very unfeminine hand the size of a pork chop. Stephanie, get your mama a glass of water, would you honey. But Mrs.

Thrasher mostly wasn't there, and didn't notice when her granddaughter and I disappeared into her father's toolshed, the blue fiberboard swallowing us, blasted by the sun, chips of paint dropping to the powder, disappearing into forever. She was a boyish girl, her hair blonde and much shorter than mine, my hair over my eyes like a visor, the tip of it slicing through a lazy eye until I looked only half-Asian. There was a mirror duct taped to the wall, adult height, the tape retracting from the glass, due to age or the incredible heat, or both, until only grey threads remained, and if I wanted to peer into it (I didn't), I'd have to stand on one of the empty metal milk crates that littered the dirt floor. Stephanie partially closed the door until only a slice of sunlight highlighted the dust motes falling through the air, each dust mote an individual planet landing on two black suns. She took a plastic water bowl partially destroyed by a missing dog, turned it right-side up, and dropped it on the ground, then turned an empty metal milk crate over the bowl, unhooked the button of her jeans and thumbed her jeans and panties to the floor. Watch me, she said. I got down on my knees, the kneecaps of my jeans powdered red. I looked at her essence, through the metal grating, everything that made her a girl bald and open to the world. I was far too young to realize this was a wound men would travel for, would kill for, for all eternity. The water came, flitting around the bowl, hitting it, peppering the dirt around us, the sides of the bowl now reddened by water and dust. Stephanie was laughing. Can you see it? Yes, I said. The water continued until she was done. She pulled up her panties and jeans simultaneously, like a boy. Now your turn. I moved the milk crate aside and unzipped, the thumb of my childhood no larger than an inch. It looks funny, she said. I aimed and pissed into the bowl, a much better shot than Stephanie. She marveled at the mechanics of it, or I imagined she did, her face open, in awe. Boys have it easier. She didn't say this, we were only six, but I heard it in my mind, as if she whispered it directly into my auditory cortex, and a warmth traveled up my spine and terminated at the crown of my head, as a halo, a warmth as beautiful as it was rare. I've only experienced it a few other times, once while working with my bees, the veil vacuum-sealed as a few angry bees pelted the mesh, and me dumb, loving, a stupid animal. Many years later, in my very early thirties, as I sat at my baby brother's kitchen table while he dealt high-grade cannabis to a boy who worked in a fast food restaurant, a boy whose name I don't recall, I'm not even sure I ever heard it, he was maybe eighteen or nineteen at most, and when he left my brother's house I told my brother, with my sister-in-law standing at the stove, making dinner for us, I said I'd _______, because I was stoned, and talking to myself, not knowing I was speaking aloud. My brother laughed and Lilly laughed, a huge great laugh that threatened to split the ceiling of the mobile in two. The following weekend, as I again sat at my brother's kitchen table, stoned, drunk, deliciously warm, feeling an unbelievable love for everyone in the room, and the boy knocked on the door and my brother yelled WHO IS IT, to which he replied _______, and Lilly laughed and shook and her breasts heaved when she did so and she said Oh god it's lemon meringue, and when the kid came through the door he said hello and was very skittish around me, the dark-haired devil sitting at a second-hand Formica table. My eyes lingered on his body, coaxing the shadows, the knobs of bone, where his kneecaps should be. He didn't stay as long, the chat perfunctory, as if someone was waiting in the car for him outside. What's wrong with him? My brother, who is named after my father, said I told him what you said, about the lemon meringue pie, and I laughed and Lilly snorted so hard it was as if her brain had suffered a sudden air leak. Well what did he say? He says you're crazy, and after that he was lemon meringue until he stopped coming around.

◆

In sixth grade, now twelve, with a body doing things I didn't understand and couldn't control, I walked with my girlfriend Nikki Real (pronounced Ray AL) from school to home, as we did every day, her parents living three doors down from my parents, and her father liked me, though he always called me Jeremiah, rather than my name. Whenever I stepped through the door, if Mr. Real was watching television on the sofa, or lying on the carpet watching television, a great big mass of a man, he'd say Jeremiah was a bullfrog, was a good friend of mine, and I would laugh and nod and become egocentrically shy, unable to speak, as Nikki and I moved toward the kitchen, toward her mother. The days fell and set, and it was always Nikki and only Nikki, so when we walked to school one morning and a girl joined us, halfway up the block, the two girls speaking as if I weren't there, as if I were only a boy, I was surprised. The girls continued on, speaking in hymenoptera rhythms I didn't understand. I looked at our guest for the very first time, really looked at her, and all the years came rushing back, the overturned crate, the dog bowl. What's your name, I asked, expecting Thrasher, but then remembering that was her grandmother's name – what had happened after the secrets of the world had been shown to me that day, so long ago? My name is Stephanie Jones, the girl said, and her hair was still shorter than mine, and coarser, and she reminded me of a lesbian, though I didn't yet know what that word meant, I only knew it was a word whispered in hatred, in laughter, by my older sister when she was amongst her friends. Do you know Jamie, Nikki asked Stephanie, and Stephanie looked at me, looked at me as if for the very first time, and said Yes I know him, and we said nothing more, our secret between us, and I never bothered telling Nikki, not even years later, when none of it mattered anyway, that I had seen the meaning of the world in the backyard of a my house, in a powder blue toolshed, sitting on a crate, while I knelt, as a boy, before the woman she would someday become.

◆

Some nights Nico appears in our bedroom, loitering near my nightstand, on my side of the bed, and the unexpected shadow in the room temporarily frightens me. I pick him up and move him back to the living room, and he asks why am I moving him, he doesn't like being alone. I don't answer him because I don't know the answer, instead saying *Shhhhhhh* it's alright. I don't want him frightening my lover. We all have our secrets. It's how couples stay together so long.

◆

I miss him when I am away from him. This is the definition of love, is it not? When he is not in his chair, at his desk, his absence made greater by the empty chair, if I sit in his chair, will I be closer to him, or is a chair only a piece of fabric stretched over a foam suggestion? What does it mean to be human, with two arms, four legs, a star on the floor, an empty room, a broken heart? If I sit where he sat, I am no different than a third grade Tracy Green, and I love him, and care for him, and so I defer, because I am not that kind of man. I don't like getting in people's way, I prefer to be unnoticed, unseen. And yet something compelled me as I walked through the front door, past the orange sales signs, everything must go placards, the battered displays strewn across the floor like an indolent bomb had gone off near the registers. I looked at him, naked and white, the space where his eyes should have been blanks, as if he were peering into the eternal, while I was trapped in the temporal, the ever-present now, moving from birth, to school, to work, to here. I looked around, slightly embarrassed, though too old to feel embarrassed, too old to care. The other shoppers looked at me as I did them, bemused, wondering if I would pick him up, move him, try an arm, see if his hands fell properly at his sides. I had no idea how much he weighed, what to expect. I placed a hand on either side of his waist and lifted him as I would a potential lover, I am old but strong, my mostly-dormant musculature buried somewhere beneath all the flab, and was horrified when his torso separated from his waist, his chest and head in my hands, lighter than I expected. I laughed involuntarily, as I do at all tragedy, and a young woman fingering a faux mink coat looked up in time to catch me laughing as I placed his torso back on the knob of silver metal that held him together, brought him closer to the human species. She smiled before turning back to her coat. I thought of it as hers already because I knew she would buy it. I placed a hand between his ass cheeks and the blank white space where his genitalia should be, asked his forgiveness, picked him up, and moved him off to the side, near the blacks, near an abandoned fitting room. He stood five foot four, maybe taller, only a few inches shorter than me. The floor of the department store was chaos. I approached registers with the least amount of people near them, ascertained the small crowd gathered was far too polite for the darkness in my heart, walked back toward him, expectant, the silvery blacks reflecting the emptiness of my face, the old barber shop mirror trick played out on twenty black faces, and Nico turned slightly, almost imperceptibly, his hand reaching for mine. I looked in the direction of men's shoes, saw an old shoe queen attending to an old woman, and walked in his direction, patiently waiting for the old woman to complete her purchase. The old shoe queen looked as if he'd worked at the department store since the day it opened. He wore a rumpled black t-shirt with a dingy wool houndstooth sport coat over it, a band name or bar I didn't recognize, his untidiness somehow forgivable due to the store's eventual closure. I asked him for help. There's a display I'd like to purchase. Which one? He's in the corner, near a fitting room. Show me, the clerk said.

◆

Do I just walk out with him? That's what everyone else is doing. I hope he doesn't mind me picking him up by the ass, I said, trying to make light of it. I've seen stranger things, dear. We both laughed. I asked him if he was transferring to another department store. This is it, he said, more for himself than for me, as if he still couldn't believe it, as if saying it would somehow make it untrue. Nico was marked $75, an orange sticker just above his ass, in the dip of his back, total with sales tax $82.58. Do you have a box I can carry him in? I asked the shoe queen. No, you'll have to walk out with him just like that. I removed my backpack, placed it on the floor near Nico, and unzipped it. I looked around. I didn't care how insane I looked, love does that to you. I twisted his left hand until it came off in mine, bagged it, and then removed his right hand. I twisted his left arm until it came away in my hand, then repeated the process with his right arm. Soon his arms and hands were stowed in my backpack. I draped my grey wool overcoat over his nakedness. I picked him up by firmly holding two hands under his ass, the only way I could carry him, asked his forgiveness again, and walked out the door, into the wet darkness. A girl, maybe ten, walked with her mother near the open door. Why are you carrying a person, the girl asked. I didn't answer, only smiled, pleased the girl recognized Nico as a person and not as a plastic entity. Children live closer to the ground and see truths adults cannot. I walked from the department store to my bus stop, eight blocks, with Nico in my arms, his partially exposed ass white under the moonlight as people giggled at my weirdness. A few were horrified. When I arrived at my bus stop I felt weak from carrying him. He weighed maybe twenty pounds, but at my age twenty may as well have been one hundred. I let his foot rest on my foot. I didn't want the piss, shit, and vomit of the city to dirty an already marred existence, losing one's home, one's friends. I thought of the blacks huddled together in a forgotten corner of the department store. The white world wanted nothing to do with blacks, not even black plastic. I miss my friends, Nico said. I cautioned him not to speak on the bus. When the door opened the driver looked at me as if I were the world's biggest asshole. I swiped my bus card and stepped aboard, only paying for a single fare. An old Asian woman sitting at the front of the bus looked at me, then looked away, unfazed. I too would be her age someday, if lucky. I too will have seen the entire world, will have seen all the love and the horror it contained, and not care, but not tonight.

◆

In front of my apartment building, a ten mile bus ride from downtown, I removed my car keys from my pocket, walked to the driver side door, turned the key and unlocked all four doors, then opened the passenger side back door and placed Nico as gently as possible in the back seat. I bumped his head on the headliner. Sorry, I said, involuntarily. I removed Nico's arms and hands from my backpack and placed them on the floorboard behind the front seats. I wondered if anyone was looking out their window at this moment, watching a strange dance unfold between a man and a five foot four piece of plastic. I zippered my backpack and put it on, opened the apartment door and went inside, as if everything were normal. How was your day? Ok, I said. How was yours?

◆

Dinner was followed by small talk and the promise of alcohol. These were my nights, every night, and I was thankful my life was usually predictable. Once my lover was in the shower, I went back outside, car keys in hand, and slowly brought Nico into the apartment, piece by piece. What the hell is that? He was standing in the living room, freshly toweled from the shower. It's our son, it's Nico! I don't like it, my lover said. You need to get rid of it, right now. Why did you buy that thing? I stared at my lover, my scalp hot. I felt the anger coming on. Because they were going to throw him away, like my parents threw me away. Some things are worth saving. Sometimes they're not, my lover said. Whatever, I said. I'm keeping him. You're not keeping him, my lover said.

◆

We ordered his clothes online. Dickies, black, US waist size 27, a t-shirt, size small, PORTUGAL emblazoned in gold on a red background, and a used pair of Vans Old Skool, size 9, off eBay. Nico stood naked, contrapposto, in the living room. He stood in the darkness, an undefined white shadow. It took a while to get used to him, just slightly behind us as we sat watching movies on the sofa. His pants and boxers were the first items to arrive. My lover was standing in the living room as I struggled to pull a pair of newly-washed boxers over Nico's plastic hips. Can you help me? I pulled the pants over his boxers, over his hips with help from my lover. I named him Nico after my partner, my partner's middle name, Latin, slightly foreign, a blade of mint among the grass. My partner laughed, sounding a bit afraid, perhaps wondering if I had finally lost my mind. This is too weird, he said. I stood firm, unmoving, I don't care what you say, something I've said before, I'm keeping him, and I felt as my father must have felt, seeing me for the first time, abandoned by my mother, on the side of the road, a few miles from the hospital. Why do you love him? Because no one else does.

◆

Nico often appears in our bedroom at night, bent slightly toward my side of the bed, the corona of his white plastic hair covered by a beanie. I don't understand how I got here, hands on stove, burning plastic, burning the man I love, a dismissive remark, a deleted text, or is it illness, my mental illness, as surely I am ill, willing to throw away five years, or twelve years, throw it all away over nothing, over something unsaid, because few things are worth saying, worth hearing? Why am I like this? Men are mostly dumb animals, and do not recognize the dog bowl before them, filled with water, with sustenance, my love like tendrils down the buttons of their spine, is it too much, am I too much, why can't I leave well enough alone?

◆

I heave into a toilet bowl, drug sick, alcohol sick, and the world feels very cold against my scalp, and I could die here, and at the moment, with so much pain in my head, for just a moment, I'd be alright with it, alright with death, my death, but then what if he texted the next day and I were dead? A message sent in the middle of the night, across invisible dark miles, HOW ARE YOU, and I have been asleep for thirty years, I can't feel a thing, my heart sealed in Quikrete, and it is very difficult to breathe, here in this kitchen, the glass burners glowing orange. My hands are always sweaty, a barrier between me and the pain, I am hot-hearted, I tell him, which scares him, and I drop his hands on the circles glowing orange-red with my hatred, the white plastic immediately bubbling, the electric scent cloying, my love too much, and all I ever wanted from you was the time of day, to be close to you, without touching, because sometimes being close is enough. I place both my hands firmly over Nico's ruined hands, white over black, and the pain is intense, it's enough to wake all the dead hibernating below my feet.

◆

My heart is a Fender Rhodes. Keys and hammers meant for him alone, yet I play to an empty house each night. No calls, no texts. It doesn't matter, I hate talking on the phone anyway. Somewhere in the kernel of this lie is the truth.

Doyle

My first love was a crumpled DeLorean, 1981. I'm sure someone had died in it. Doyle drove the golf cart down the aisles, five acres of ruined cars surrounded by an eight foot high cinder block fence, the top of the fence decorated with razor wire and broken Coca-Cola bottles cemented in place. Doyle was the last of his kind, a live-in security guard. He was my father's friend. My father attended automobile auctions with him. It was nighttime, the ruined automobiles mysteriously silent after a short life filled with noise. The lot was illuminated by sickly-green floodlights that cast a pale shadow over dusty windshields, scissored doors, radiators naked and broken, accordioned cars with black collarbones reaching for me. The golf cart's soft headlights fell on the DeLorean, a spaceship that had failed to take off, its rocket boosters devoid of inspiration. Can I sit in it? I asked Doyle, the DeLorean's ruined doors exploding Jiffy Pop on a Saturday night, stay away from the stove! Sure, Doyle said, laughing, and he took my hand, which I thought strange, because I was ten years old, and didn't want anyone holding my hand. I shook him off. I sat where the dead man had sat, scooped out, his dreams scattered across the floor, the dash, coming to rest on the windshield. My jeans thin as linen, my favorite rugby shirt yellowed, you look like a ragamuffin, my mother said, and I asked Doyle to close the door, but it was forever stuck at high noon. What do you think, Doyle asked, his face a few inches from mine, as if what I said mattered. It looks like a spaceship, I said. Yes, Doyle said, it does, his hand on my kneecap. Maybe you'll have one someday.

◆

Doyle and his brother, whose name was never mentioned, ran a chinchilla farm many years ago, long before solar winds had gathered me together in my present form, and the years of working with small animals in tight cages were tallied on his fingers, his hands. Doyle came from money, and though he never said it, it was apparent in the way he moved. Someday I'll retire in California, he said, I'm just doing this to pass the time, and he said it as if time were a commodity that could be held in small silver cages. I can leave anytime I want, I don't need this, I don't need anything, and I wondered, briefly, why a grown man would need anything. Did he not have everything already? Time, space, a car, a golf cart that moved easily among ruined bodies, ruined lives. What else could he possibly need?

◆

Violence is death in a public sphere, as opposed to a private one. He laser-focused his crosshairs on me because I was more girl than boy, because I moved in my body like a girl would move in her body. I was ten years old, an unblemished canvas. I hadn't yet learned how to walk like a boy. I hadn't yet realized I was anything but me. But Doyle saw it, saw the smooth engine humming between my shoulder blades, a machine warm to the touch, bristles whirring like the grinder at the end of my father's work bench, don't ever touch that when it's on. My father loved me, his son, loved me without question, even when I set fire to the tool shed in our backyard, even when I splintered the glass door in his office with one solid foot placed firmly in the center, removing his belt yet barely using it, not into it, more for show than anything. I was his son, the last thing he wanted to do was hurt me. Isn't this what parents did, protect their children? Damn it, boy, don't make me do this again.

◆

Doyle removed a chocolate cake from the refrigerator and sat it on the Formica table with a flourish intended to bedazzle me. It worked. He opened a cabinet door and brought out two Chinet plates, which I thought fancy. The cabinet doors, made of MDF, were bubbled in the middle where the laminate was raised from the surface of the MDF, either from the heat of the stove or adhesive breakdown. He cut a large slice for me, placed it on a Chinet, and placed the plate on the table. I sat down, not waiting, spading a dirty index into the frosting, sucking on my digit involuntarily as one would expect of a child. Doyle said buy you books and buy you books and all you do is eat the covers off them. I shrank to the size of my former self, knocked down, as always, by adults. Wait a minute, dammit, his hand on my neck as he moved across the floor in a big stride to another cabinet by the yellow refrigerator. I didn't like his hands on me, and rolled my shoulders toward my neck until his hand disappeared. In a moment he was back at my side with a restaurant-style sugar dispenser, the kind with a silver metal top that screws onto a glass base. He shook the base over my cake until the lid opened and white crystals baptized the frosting. You put sugar on it? Yes, he said, and I decided I'd never met another adult like him, everyone always saying No while he said Yes. *The Rockford Files* played on a small television on the kitchen countertop, both ends of the rabbit ears balled in aluminum foil, but neither of us watched it. Time for bed, and he prepared the bed for me in the back bedroom, the singular bedroom window ablaze under the security lamp outside, pulling the comforter back and massaging the pillow like a squeezebox, and as I slipped into bed wearing my rugby shirt and jeans Doyle said you can't sleep like that, as he had said all the other times I had stayed over with him, and like a good unthinking robot I raised my rugby over my flat white chest, my hair now an electric box, unhooked my jeans and dropped them to the floor, standing in a white t-shirt and briefs. Aren't you going to take your shirt off, a question I'd heard before, from his mouth, and I replied, as I had before, my mother doesn't allow me to go to sleep without a t-shirt on. Suit yourself, Doyle said, and I crawled into bed, ass up, on my stomach, hoping he would leave sooner than later, my hands folding the comforter over me until I nearly disappeared, and it was a strange room, though I'd slept in it before. I had trouble finding myself on a floating bed in the middle of nowhere. Doyle's shadow left the open door until only a greyer darkness remained. I heard him move toward his bedroom at the opposite end of the mobile, the trailer sighing under his weight. I sat up and pulled my t-shirt off and threw it on the floor, against my mother's wishes, now clothed in Fruit of the Looms and nothing else. I touched myself briefly, as I often did while lying in the bottom bunk as my older sister snored unknowingly in the top, as I often would for hours, the milk not coming for another year, but tonight I felt nauseous, my head stuffed with pieces of cotton from the fields that surrounded us, the metal of damaged cars buffeted with cotton fluff, smoothing out lives taken so suddenly, the spider web of a broken windshield frozen on a driver's final thought, can't he see me? Did I unplug the toaster?

◆

Around midnight, much too late for me to be awake, the sweep of a minute hand on an old clock emblazoned with the words LAS VEGAS in silvery rhinestone, I grabbed my stomach and rose from the foam mattress, everything looking cheap, old, sinister. I made my way in my briefs through the hall to the bathroom with the funny toilet, one donut stacked on another, a child's recollection, opened the lid and stared into the water, cleaved in two, when desired, with a simple foot depression, and heaved into the bowl, the black filth from my stomach emptied into what seemed like forever, my ribs sore from the sugar, the maple syrup, the cake, the Neapolitan. My forehead slick, barbed-wire hair, the bathtub and toilet bowl the dirty orange of Dial soap, and still the emptiness came, up though my esophagus, scorching my mouth, my nostrils, the back of my throat tasting of the chlorinated public pool at the end of summer, the only time I walked in public wearing nothing more than briefs, because I was a Catholic boy and my mother never allowed me to wear anything less than pants, because ten-year-olds are allowed to wear swimming briefs in public, and I didn't know the word Speedo, I was from a working-class family, the lemon-yellow fabric cupping my balls surely from a fire sale at K-mart. Lean into it, Doyle said. I jumped when he placed his hand on my shoulder, emptying everything I was into the bowl, the black chunks of chocolate cake dizzying, and his hands on me, on my naked back, and I could feel his hardness pressing against my buttocks, a hand the size of a dinner plate reassuring me, resting on my right shoulder blade, and I thought how ugly everything was, and how old, and how I never wanted to be surrounded by old things ever again, and he touched me in places my mother had never ventured. I just want to lie down. Brush your teeth first, and so I did. In bed again, his fingers lighting on me like strange insects, an incredible gilled warmth closing over me, I asked if I could please go to sleep, turning on my side, away from him, the buzzing green of the security lamps slicing through the sliver of curtains. In the morning he called a cab for me. I felt important, special, all this unnecessary fuss over me, yet I also felt dismissed, as if I were a piece of furniture forgotten on a curb. As I slid into the cab, Doyle peered into the back seat, his eyes betraying his desire, my face mirrored in the pitted orbs of his heavy prescription eyeglasses. I wouldn't tell your father you overate. I won't, I said, closing the door violently, like an oversensitive girl. I knew I would never sleep at his house again.

Nico

You hold someone's hand in your hand until you both fade. If that's not love, I have wasted my life, and now I have become Doyle, except I haven't. I would never touch Nico in a sexual way. I am not a sexual vampire, I prefer spending my days with my iPhone, or reading, when I have time, on the bus, my beloved waiting for me at home in our small apartment. I have touched Nico, of course, but not like that.

◆

Sometimes, at night, after I use the bathroom, my lover asleep in bed, gifted with the capacity to sleep through a nuclear blast, I'll walk into the living room, in the dark, walk into the kitchen and turn on the soft light of the microwave, the kitchen now golden orange, and Nico is there, near the bookcases, standing as young as he was the evening prior. How old do you think he is? I ask my lover, and my lover says I don't know, fourteen? He is there, waiting for me, and I hug him, not in a sexual way, because love and sex have nothing to do with each other, no, I hold him as a father would hold his son, his son who will soon leave him, move out, find his way, place new oars in the dirty water that is the world, and

I whisper I love you, I love you, and Nico stands there, his eyes empty as ever, and it feels good to hold him, a plastic heart thumping against a human heart, and I tell him as long as I am here, nothing will hurt you, and his hands move slightly, I feel them move, he's smiling a bit more than he was before, and I know he will never age, his forehead unfurrowed by time, his hands as delicate now as ever, unbroken by the world, whereas I have a broken finger from fighting. I think of my favorite watering hole, within stumbling distance, just a few blocks from home, how in the old days I would sit at the bar with a friend, someone whose hand I've never held but whose heart is in my hand, a diversion, a comfort, a reprieve from the old dusty path. I don't kiss Nico, that wouldn't be right. He is strong, and white, his hair always perfect, and he stands on his own two feet, his eyes blind to the lies of the world because he chooses not to look, knows the world is too ugly. I hold his hand in the dark. I speak to him, tell him I want to die, and he only smiles, knowing I won't, not tonight, anyway. I have never touched him inappropriately. I have never kissed him on the lips. I only hold him because I'm dead, I'm empty, and I need to hold something, something human, in my arms. But I've never kissed him. I won't. I'm not that kind of man.

# JAMES NULICK

James Nulick is an avatar based in Seattle, Washington. His physical body was born in 1970. His new novel THE MOON DOWN TO EARTH will be published by Expat Press in Fall 2020.

# CHAPTER TWENTY-ONE

*You see a watering hole. Reprieve from the old dusty path. There is evil in the world.*

I turn my eyes away from the light and gaze at a dark spot in the distance. Having changed what needed to be changed, I kneel to wash my face and rinse the dirt from my mouth. There are bones and tree roots everywhere. Look at the state your hands are in. Look how feeble your body is. You are alone on this path. There are no people around, no precious artifacts to be dug up. There is nothing but a temporary respite from the deafening silence of past years, absolution captured in this moment as fleeting as the thirst you are feeling. Look how your blood tints the newspaper-wrapped flowers you were carrying. I am talking to myself in words that come out as images before my eyes, as finger strokes on my body, as gulps of air crushing the ribcage of the night. Fragments of you are alive inside me, traveling my veins, assembling my flesh. I find darkness in everything. In the very first manifestations of human language, in the traditional and material needs of the world, in the mechanisms of aesthetic insinuation, in the philosophical vocation of artless terrains, even in the spirits risen from my insides. I find darkness in everything and it eats away at me. And thus, the lizard crawls with the gratification of being a lizard. I take out a notebook from my pocket to write something down but the words escape me before I can find my pen.

*There are two main types of anamorphosis. In each of us, the ache for walking towards an ideal.*

I am talking to myself in words that come out as fading reenactments of Plautus' plays, memories of the character who hears the voice of Apollo advising him to kill and how the others think he is insane. Not insane, in need of a doctor. I look at my hands and see starving words from psychology books gnawing at my skin—lines, phrases, entire paragraphs describing hallucinations and carnal presences, justifications for the sentience of 4AMs: peaks of melatonin in the body. It is night. That time of night associated with enchantresses, ghouls, transhistorical rootage spilling its sap over the world's demythologized state, devils, the souls of the dead, and the absence of prayer—the witching hour. There is rust on everything, even the ground seems to have rusted away. On my skin, ambivalent words and grazes speak of ancient treatments and myths, of repressed ontological frustration and ceremonial dances from another time. I proceed to performing a post-modern examination of this night, of this hour, of this moment. I think of the thirst for knowledge and how, even when blood gushes from your veins and you are sullying the bones upon which you rest, that thirst goes hand in hand with exploring your surroundings. I get up and try to open my eyes. New theories on the structure of light are being developed this very minute. There was a time when people did not relate daylight with the presence of the sun and sight was a mere subjective phenomenon. I cannot see where my steps are going. New theories on sight are being developed this very minute. Are these bodies visible because of the eye or are they visible due to their own emissions? Someone once told me the history of colors born from a white light traversing a body of water. Regardless, it is not the outside world that I seek to cut open and examine, but the ideas and recollections that somehow became more vivid than reality itself. I have no interest in the pain my body exposes on its exterior. I believe I see and hear what no other person sees and hears. Ideal inanity—I am tracing in the stillness of open arms tendencies revealed by my discontent with metaphysics and turning life into a symbol. That does not stop me from once again opening the gates and letting all hallucinations flood me at once. The obsession with the labyrinth, the romantic soul of objects and movement, I see my body swimming. I see it becoming a dot on the horizon, impersonating yet another fictional character. Dostoevskian, perhaps—reduced to nothingness, with chains on hands and legs, swimming freely. I feel the thrusts of time passing through me like ghosts in a teeming aquatic graveyard. I see my body breathing in the virtues of water. It is not by strolling in the vicinity of a sea that one becomes a storyteller. My mouth tastes the eternal inbetweenness of the wet shore.

*I close my eyes. Enriched by the wounding search for the old cradle, a tumult breaks in my head.*

Visceral apparitions rise from my internal organs—some formless, some taking the shape of antechambers full of debris, depressed below the level of the horizon. I lie on the ground again and think of the return to the womb of time like falling fruit returns to the womb of the earth. Separating sense from being, I reach for the end of this and any other thought, unable to break away from hallucinations of unlived times. Angels, saints, devils, mythological creatures, pans, naiads. In delirium tremens, in nightmares—delusions of mind where fantasies take the place of reality and objects I would normally think of as real end up being falsely represented. Delusions of mind not affecting my intellectual capabilities. A cerebral phenomenon acting independently of the senses—can you envision such horror? An alchemy—perhaps a revolt against concrete time—tells me that I will wake up feeling different; that I will learn to live with who I am now, besotted with the imbalance of vital signs. I have been talking to myself for what feels like an eternity. Oddly, I cannot hear the sound of my own voice. "Mary Magdalen hallucinated the resurrection of Christ," reads a creased newspaper headline.

*Third day of continuous fever. Mouth full of blood. I have lost faith in the narrator.*

I've made it inside the apartment somehow. Clutching to an old Robbe-Grillet translation of Dans le Labyrinthe, I stretch out my left arm and reach for the glass of wine I left on the counter last night. I take a sip but a tremor makes me spill it. It reminds me of the Russian fairy tale motif of carrying water with a sieve—

or with a rope, like in Ukrainian folklore. I think of unfit instruments: trembling hands, serpentine mouths, chipped glasses, decanting sieves. Of fragmentary storytelling methods, of Cioranian sadness and how it rises from the ability to access universal pain with a mere tremor. Regression is nothing but a temporary solution. People rebound all the time. Outside my window, poppy fields bleed into traffic. I walk around, listening to my steps, to the sound my clothes make as they touch the floor, to the malign tension of this treacherous plot. The threat of guilt overweighs the fear of violence, providing my body with heat. I open a notebook and write something about objects without voice, objects that cannot protest, cannot engage in pleading conversations with their torturers. I write down everything that comes to mind, compartmentalizing disintegration processes I no longer wish to remember, such as hallucinations of gaze and my ability to bring deceitful light into darkness. I write about serpents of mythical proportions, sea waves, falling out of time. I write and turn my pages into graveyards full of bones I exhume in a manner similar to how I extract thoughts from inside my head. As it resurfaces, like bones eaten by the passage of time and the benevolence of nature, the past too crumbles in my hands.

*Fingers, latent on my throat. I think of raspberries and the knife I stole from a hunter years ago. What time is it in Chernobyl?*

A medical ward. All narrative needs in order to reveal itself from the other side of the mirrored glass like a mnemonic exchange between two selves leaving traces on the urgency that connects glass and skin are a couple of recurrent words. The characters have doubles. Perspectives shift imperceptibly. Labyrinthine spaces engulf the eternal hostility of memories devouring each other. I escape reality by writing about my recurring nightmare. It starts with a fall, followed by the sensation of freezing ground underneath my feet. It takes a ment, but I eventually understand that this is not where I've fallen, and that although my eyes are open, I cannot see anything. I hear voices I never heard before, I smell perfumes unfamiliar to my senses. As time passes, my eyes get accustomed with the dream and I see it—a graveyard. Statutes, flowers, holes in the ground, rotting roses, corpses everywhere. I am inside a glass box. In the distance, someone writes my name in the dirt then crosses it with a straight line. The wind awakens the leaves from their inertia. The here and now is illusory—the writer remains in the past. I lower my eyes and look at my hands and legs. I feel my face—there is no flesh, there are no lips. I seem to be existing without coherence, fragile and longing for newness. I do not have a mouth—the connection between sentences has been destroyed. I wake up and hide between words diving on the page. I hide in rivers, and forests, and the luscious rawness of a broken sky. An homage to animals living in the wild. Bewildered by an unfulfilled erotic drive, I go through hours and hours of lectures on mental illness.

*Drained by a weariness abnormal to the resting body, I reach for my notebook and write: schism-blue.*

I fall asleep again. A dream takes me into the arms of a familiar presence. I listen to his voice while I struggle to discipline my hands. It must be cold, but I don't feel it. His eyes are savage and caring. Mine follow the shapes and dots that light creates under my eyelids. His fingers caress my face and brush away my hair. Another apparition—one limited exclusively to the interior obsessions of yet another character. I am wearing a white dress with seaweed stuck to its seams. My hands move and I feel as if he and I are part of the imaginary construction of a world that chose to represent its realities through monstrous clusters of people trapped under the supervision of plural solitudes and wayward cobwebs. A space enclosed on itself. He talks about human suffering. Real and fictional individuals from history, literature, poetry. Characters thrown in perilous situations by their makers to see if and by what means they thrive. Sometimes they are bestowed with unusual powers, other times they strip them of everything, even of thoughts and healing illusions. With intimate gestures of mathematical beauty and in a whispering voice, he tells me how history uses accidents, betrayals, and agonies to build its foundation. He gazes into the distance and I remember that as a child I used to do the same. I used to gaze into the distance and imagine how prehistoric people lived, overlapping their time with mine. It calmed me. Snow falls upon my cheeks like in a Trakl poem. The dream fades but the wrath in his eyes lingers on, disturbing the waters of dreams to come. It feels like the loss of something I will never get back. Longing for lashing rain, I dream within this dream of time dripping down the skin of spring days. The chronotope of open wounds and pulling flesh reveals itself to me as an act of temporal happening etched upon the color of absence. Rain-to-come has become my muse. I kneel to wash my face and rinse the dirt from my mouth. There are bones and tree roots everywhere. The graveyard is suffocated by images of dead people projected from above. They have no mouths, no eyes, no flesh on their bones. Corpses trapped inside glass cases—fairy tale coffins tainted by amnesia and the damp rubble of pretend floods. I can still feel the freezing ground under my feet. A compulsive sense of carnal despair takes over my body. Whatever is left of my blood has separated from yours—the double, no longer confused. I reach for my notebook and write about antinomies frozen in time.

*It has only been an hour. Despair takes us again. Bury me standing.*

## CHRISTINA TUDOR-SIDERI

Christina Tudor-Sideri is an ex philosopher preoccupied with the phenomenological understanding of the world as flesh, the complimentary chronotope, existence buried within the depths of linguistic consciousness, the fall out of time, as well as conceptualizing the (absent) body and its anonymous rhythms. Her work deals with myth, memory, narrative deferral, and the imprisonment of the mind within the time and space of its corporeal vessel. She has an interest in translating Romanian poems, philosophy, folklore, and mythology. Her book-length debut, UNDER THE SIGN OF THE LABYRINTH, will be published September 2020 by Sublunary Editions.

# CHAPTER TWENTY-TWO

You see a watering hole. Reprieve from the old dusty path. Michael Snow made his film *Wavelength* in 1967, "preceded by a year of notes, shots, mutterings." It is a very simple film, among the simplest films ever made. In it, a camera fixed at one end of a loft looks across at the other end where a row of windows opens onto the street. Over the space of the film's 45-minute runtime the camera progressively zooms in, reducing the spectator's field of vision by steady decrements. This zoom, along with some slight refocusing, is the film's only camera movement. Everything else is still. Over the course of 45 still minutes, a room is offered up for our view.

The room, which is a woman's apartment, is a space for living and it is a space that is living. A hard-backed yellow chair sits against the wall. Its yellowness is voluptuous. Time collects in this simple, hard chair; pools inside it like water in a cell, keeping it turgid. The white of the walls, the shape of a radiator, and a thousand other details poke at the eye, calling attention to themselves, wanting you to look at them. The woman is an incidental resident. When she enters the apartment with a friend – and, later, to call the cops after Hollis Frampton drops dead – she does not properly belong to the space of the film. She doesn't belong to her own apartment in the sense that the apartment, the room, exceeds her. It exceeds her the way a single frame will exceed a film.

Speaking of his intentions for *Wavelength,* Snow was direct. "I wanted to make a summation of my nervous system, religious inklings and esthetic ideas. I was thinking of, planning for, a time monument in which the beauty and sadness of equivalence would be celebrated." The words *time monument* are obviously correct but to these may be added, in a clarificatory sense, the film's monumentalizing function of space. After all, the film has a single purpose – it's uniquely single-minded – and from its very first moments it is bent upon it: the achievement of a perfect mental zoom, a picking out or focusing in on the object on the wall on which the camera is trained. It isn't obvious at first what this thing is. Gradually, as time climbs up the leg of the chair and space concentrates, the mysterious object becomes progressively clearer. It's a photograph.

It's a photograph of waves.

It's not the only photo on the wall. There are others: a pair of images of two figures, one larger than the other, resembling an x-ray. The forms seem almost unhuman. The weird oblong of the head (like a giant pin) and disproportion of the limbs give them an alien aspect, as if these were photos of beings who had just stepped off a UFO. *Wavelength* ignores them. It continues its inexorable zoom until everything is annihilated, clipped out of frame. The aliens drop away. So does the room. With a breathless motion the camera passes through the photo and drops onto the waves. It continues its investigative forward motion over the flowing waves. The image is no longer still. The film is no longer a film.

All of the above is the same as to say:

The photographer in *The Omen* has his head chopped off. A sheet of glass falls off the back of a truck and slices his head clean off the neck. It does this because the photographer had perfected his art to the point that he could, while remaining quite calm, photograph the things behind other things. Call it supernatural photography, the genre of 'trick' images. A priest appears in the developing tray with a line bisecting his neck. It's a prophecy, a statement that comes true in time. A puncture had formed in the barrier between grain and reality, between the optical qualities of silver halide and the secrets transmitted to it by light. A contract was breached. The camera can see things it's not meant to see; but you won't survive the encounter. You're not meant to. A detective urge rises in you. It must be suppressed. Shutter the darkroom. Smash the lens. Something now in motion prepares itself in the wings.

# ALI RAZ

Ali Raz is the co-author, alongside Vi Khi Nao, of the collection of sex ads known as HUMAN TETRIS (11:11 Press, 2019). She received an MFA in Fiction from the University of Notre Dame, has had pieces in 3:am Magazine, Queen Mob's Teahouse, and elsewhere. She lives in LA.

# CHAPTER TWENTY-THREE

YOU see a watering hole. Reprieve from the old dusty path. The hole is no more than a few feet in diameter and surrounding it, scattered black stones. They are striking against the soot and rubble of the landscape. You are briskly gathering the stones, humming some unrecognizable melody. It is much like prayer. You begin to stack the stones and I take notice. It seems you are trying to build a sort of wall straight through the middle of the watering hole. An extended line across the diameter, stretching only a yard or two, essentially the length of the road on which I have found myself. I walk by admiring your work for a moment in polite speculation. The stones are so smooth, they slip and collide, making a pleasant clacking sound. I imagine it is the sound a marble statue would make if it were to blink. YOU continue, either unaware of my surveillance, or unmoved by it, piling the stones on top of each other, ever so gently. I can see plainly that it is all in futility. A feeling of great discomfort begins to stir within me and I begin to walk past you. Your eyes meet mine.

YOU
Do not cross.

I
You mean the stones?

YOU
Yes. Obviously. The division.

I

They're just rocks. Just a pile of rocks.

YOU

You could say that about anything. Just a this. Just a that.

I

Well, that's what they are.

YOU

The stones are a line in the sand. They are a demarcation. They're a composition.

I

I'm just passing by.

YOU

That's not an option here.

I

So I can't pass?

YOU

Well.

It is as though you haven't contemplated this line of thought.

YOU (CONT'D)

I suppose you can.

I

But you'd prefer I'd not

YOU

You're either passing through deliberately, antagonistically; or you're going another way.

I

Will you stop me if I try to pass?

YOU

I'd like to but I won't. I can't.

I

What's stopping you?

YOU

Look, I'm asking you kindly to avoid crossing it. I can't stop you, but if you cross it will lead to demoralization.

I

Demoralize who?

YOU

Me. You. Our ancestors. The chorus of angels.

I look around for something that could be described as a chorus of angels but see a blurred horizon and the silhouettes of telephone wires. The landscape is corporeal. Skeletal.

I

I don't see any chorus of angels. Just you and your stones.

YOU

I don't see them either. I was hoping they'd arrive.

I

It's demoralizing to watch you, honestly. Real Sisyphean. You're not making progress.

YOU

It's slow work. I'm not sure if it's going anywhere.

You place a hand to your forehead to wipe away sweat that may or may not be there. You're weary and the high-noon sun has been beating on your back irrevocably. I, feeling a sense of great pity that I would prefer to be empathy, look toward you.

I

That's what I'm saying. It's hard to watch.

YOU

What would you find inspiring?

I

Those stones won't stack. Look at them. They're those perfect kind of rocks you buy from a store. I have the distinct memory of stones just like these decorating the indoor garden of someone's house, when I was younger. I recall some kind of palm tree sticking up from the stones. Maybe it was a fake.

YOU

That wasn't my question.

I

I'm not looking for inspiration.

There is a long pause. Some birds are singing out of view and the low rumble of a highway echoes in the not-so-far distance. It seems as though time is passing by immeasurably fast. That the bountiful afternoon is slowly eroding into night and all houses of the world are turning on their porch lights and calling their children home. Yet somehow, you and I are separated from all of that and our moment is distilled into an impossibly pure and singular event.

YOU

Perhaps if I had some glue. Some kind of binder to keep them together.

I

I'm not sure you can glue rocks.

YOU

Mortar. Something to strengthen the structure.

I

I don't know much about structures. But I can see pretty plainly that your methods aren't working.

YOU

I'm aware. I see that. Perhaps the difficulty though...

I

Hmm?

YOU

I often believe that things requiring great difficulty are more meaningful.

I

I wouldn't agree with that. The harder something is the less likely I am to complete it.

YOU

Would you consider helping me?

I

I'm not sure.

YOU

Two people. Two sets of hands. That could be the solution.

I

I'm not sure I want a solution. This whole thing.

(I point at YOU.)

What's it for?

You ignore my question and look down at the stones. I kneel next to you. Every stone is exactly the same. Flawless replicas. I take one in my hand, rubbing my thumb along its surface.

I (CONT'D)
This is some real ingenuity. Perfect rocks.

YOU
Perfect for what?

I
For laying in dirt I suppose. For surrounding a watering hole. Or a fountain. Or outlining a garden. I suppose they have many uses. They're too heavy to be skipping stones. They'd look nice in an aquarium. They're decorative but inoffensive. I recall seeing stones like these in a museum once, a very nice museum. The artist had arranged a contraption to drop the stones on a large LED screen that displayed a series of images. Flowing water. And with each stone that dropped, one expected the screen to shatter, but instead the rock created a kind of pixilated rippling effect. I sat and watched for a while before leaving. It left a very curious impression on me, I guess. I haven't thought of it since.

YOU
Well, they don't stack well.

I
They do not

YOU
If I can't at least make a small dent in this, I'll just give up for the day. I still have other work to do.

I

Is this somehow your job?

YOU

No, this is voluntary. No one’s tasked me to do this. At least not directly.

I

Yet you do it anyway.

YOU

This is a project. In tandem with my other work.

I

What do you do?

YOU

I’m working on a piece. A musical piece.

I

So you’re a musician?

YOU

I’m a music journalist, that’s my title at least. I suppose I’m actually a music ethnographer.

I

What do you write about?

YOU

My work is mainly in tonal response psychology, musical propaganda, and political allegory in pop music.

I

Sounds very academic.

YOU

It's not, though I do suppose it sounds that way. My last publication was on a small website that was run by the inmates of a federal prison. But now, the piece I'm working on... It's much different. Maybe the most important thing I've ever done.

I

I would guess it's very important.

YOU

Important is the wrong word. Maybe meaningful.

I

Work with meaning.

You give a look of mild disdain. Rising, you pace round the watering hole.

YOU

Are you familiar with Juno Baski?

I

(Feigning a cursory knowledge.)

The name is familiar.

YOU

You may have heard a reference or

**(MORE)**

YOU (CONT'D)

seen their name in some liner notes. They've been a prolific producer for two decades. Finding their way into hundreds of charting hits, and far more that remain in obscurity, with little more than a cult following. There is, essentially, nothing known about their personal life. It has been assumed by many that Juno Baski is a pseudonym for a different producer, or perhaps a collective of many. I've had my own theories on Baski. Some I've even written about. For many years I've tracked their work. Once, I even came across a forum where someone claiming to be Juno Baski answered a series of questions about their work. They wrote, "The use of the timpani is a reference to Mahler." And "I am most inspired by the death of my childhood dog, Rilke." Things of that nature. But that was almost certainly a farce. Some audacious student's affair with experimentation and anonymity. Still it is necessary canon to the history of Baski. The imitators I mean. Baski's own work has been imitated by nearly everyone. They are perhaps the most influential working musical artist or artists.

I

To be honest, I'm not really familiar.

YOU

I know.

I

I'm not really an active music listener. I hear stuff on the radio, or in a store and I might like it but I don't really feel the need to dwell on it. To look into it.

YOU

That puts you in line with just about everyone else on this earth.

I

It's not that I don't like music. If someone were to ask me if I like music I'd tell them "of course."

YOU

I think that would be a very stupid question.

I

People ask that question all the time. Or, what kind of music do you like? To which I'd say I like it all.

YOU

But have you ever heard something that sounds like a chorus of angels?

I

Like a Christmas carol?

YOU

No.

You are standing, while I still sit near the pile of stones. You are playing with the buttons on your shirt. You are attempting to portray being lost in thought but you are not lost whatsoever, instead you are focused on what you have already planned to say and deciding on exactly what tone to say it with.

YOU (CONT'D)

(In a tone in which many would describe as patronizing but you might call illustrative.)

You know, this line, this thing that I'm building here. It's not symbolic. I'd like it to truly be a Structure. Like a picket line. A defense. A threshold.

I

Against what?

YOU

Against those who would try to pass it.

I

Anyone just walking?

YOU

I would like that, yes.

I

So you're trying to block the way.

YOU

No, I mean. This is a very small perimeter. There are many ways to pass.

I

But this spot.

YOU

I don't want people passing through this spot.

I

This is the logical spot to pass. It's the road. It's how people travel.

YOU

This spot is not for traveling.

I

To what end? I don't think you grasp that people need to get by. There is a city on the other side. And past that another. A border like this is just an arbitrary inconvenience. What are you trying to stop?

In the past I have come across many borders and found them quite laughable. Their sheer impossibility. Their incessant need to sever. When I was a child around seven or eight I learned I lived in a house on the border of two towns and I would find endless amusement in crossing between the border saying, "Now I'm here. Now I'm there."

Dancing on the imaginary line in the street. I could not discern any difference between the two towns. Both had houses that were relatively the same and children, like me, playing.

There was only a small wooden sign to signify the two separate places. The imaginary boundary was so absurd. Like my imaginary friends or my imaginary histories. I imagine telling you this story, but instead it unfolds in my head in a brief retelling, accompanied by images of my family and old cars that would drive too fast down the street.

YOU

The piece I'm working on. About Baski. Well, you see, they've released music. Their own music. Not as producer, or co-writer. As artist.

I

The long awaited solo record.

YOU

Essentially. Though, it wasn't really "released" it was placed on a private FTP server. The address sent out to a select few, with an accompanying password. There was no statement from Baski, who of course, has never made a public statement, or any private ones.

I

I don't know anything about—

YOU

But while the legitimacy of the release might be in question. I'm quite certain it's the work of Baski. Just tonally it's either them or the perfect imitator.

I

That's all interesting I suppose.

YOU

You don't find it intriguing?

I

I said so.

YOU

You said.

I

I said it's interesting. It's just I'm not particularly invested.

YOU

In the work?

I

In the biography. Or...

YOU

The music. Are you interested in the music?

I

No more than any other.

YOU

You should be.

I

I’m more interested in this border. In what you’re doing now.

YOU

This isn’t a border. Border is the wrong word. It’s a separator. Like the space between songs. The blank grooves of a record. The static sounds of a tape reel. The negative space. You know...

I

A pause?

YOU

The Baski record. It’s called “Sidereal.” You understand the difference between solar and sidereal. The way we measure time. Well, it got me thinking. Three minutes and fifty-six seconds. That’s the length of every song. The song files seem to be arranged arbitrarily. There are no track numbers. The consensus on the order of them varies but—

I

This is all interesting but I must say I don’t know who Baski is.

YOU

No one does!

I

Maybe if I heard the music.

YOU

You want to hear?

You are indigent. The birds have stopped singing and white noise of traffic has silenced. The sun is hidden behind a series of cumulus clouds, each resembling the shape of a country. One the boot of Italy. One the dual animal heads of Australia. I am reminded of gazing at the clouds as a child in yard of my house on the border. How it seemed that every cloud I saw resembled something and how quickly the associations came.

I

I think it's best I left.

YOU

Just listen.

I

I don't hear anything.

YOU

This song is called "Chorus of Angels"

I

There's no sound.

YOU

There's one sound. Maybe a timpani. It's distant.

I do not know what a timpani sounds like. I think it's some kind of drum, but there's little chance I would be able to identify it. YOU are pensive, still playing with the buttons on your shirt. I know that it was entirely a waste of time to come here, to speak with YOU. To engage you in your histrionics and self-serving diatribes. All the empathy I wished I had felt for you I know longer desire. The road is dusty because it hasn't rained for a long time and the ground looks cracked with thirst.

I

What was I thinking.

YOU

Don't speak.

You and I hear:

I think that I am telling you "I hear it. It's pleasant. Is that playing off your phone? It's quiet but clear. Is that a timpani? Why didn't you just play it for me to begin with? It would've been much easier that describing it. You know, I think I heard a quote once, 'Writing about

' have you ever heard that quote? I don't recall who said it. But I think maybe you're a little too focused. Like seeing the forest for the trees. I've heard that saying a lot too but never had an opportunity to use it. But now I think it's probably the most accurate way to say it."

But then I realize I haven't said any of this and the music that's playing is still washing over me and it is like one voice and like many. You reach into your back pocket and retrieve a folded piece of paper. I take it from you and unfold it cautiously revealing a document which reads:

**INESSENTIAL MELANCHOLIES: AFFIRMATIONS OF JUNO BASKI**

In the US life expectancy is in a state of steady decline. Alcoholism, depression, suicide, drug addiction. These diseases of despair, as they referred to, have grown like a tumor on our collective consciousness. On our hearts perhaps. The despair is palpable and the effects measurable. The bodies of the damned and damaged piling up with gaining speed. Hundreds of thousands per year. And yet, now is when Juno Baski releases their music. In an era of unmitigated sadness.

Baski, throughout their career, has had an immense grasp of time and of timing. Their hits have always felt contemporary, inciting sonic revolutions across the map of popular music.

They have always thwarted familiarity with further experimentation and wrangled the relatable from the avantegarde. "Sidereal" is no exception.

The music is engaged with our time to the extent that Baski seems to be speaking to us within the very force of time. The listener is encouraged to ruminate on the moments captured here, within a temporal stillness. The songs become dialogues with our momentary melancholies, asking us to betray our expectations. Asking us to look into the dark bodies of water that seem to have no bottom.

Compositionally, these are pop songs in length and structure. Simply crafted melodies, though without lyrics. Perhaps there are voices. One or many. It is impossible to tell what is vocal and what is ethereal.

The only textual clues are given in song titles, some spiritual, some observational. All stilted by our own perceptions. Baski seems to be in communication with things outside our terrestrial vision. While we, stuck on earth, are trying with all our might to resist capitulation with the sadness.

I

(Pulling away from the paper.)

I think I would prefer to listen.

YOU

But the context. You must understand. It will illuminate the music. Much like a border will give context to what it surrounds.

You and I hear:

And I come to think it is quite common.

I

This feels very common.

YOU

It is nostalgia. It's something that you've heard, played through a watery filter.

I

You know, your piece, I don't think I really understood it. The connections you were making. It all seems unrelated.

YOU

I'm building context. I'm opening up the world to a greater level of perception.

I

It all means very little to me. I hear a song. I don't think a song.

YOU

Well, you must agree. "Chorus of Angels." It's something. It comes from nowhere and it is something.

I

It's nice. Like a song I would hear while shopping. It makes me feel good. Like things are going well.

YOU

They aren't! You must see things are not going well.

I

They feel like they are though. And the song. It sounds just like the sounds of a supermarket or a mall. Just far enough in the background to be inoffensive.

YOU

That can't be very meaningful.

In the absence of a response I think that what is meaningful to you is quite arbitrary. When I was young I found great meaning my own made-up language. An imaginative kind of guttural moaning.

I would amuse myself endlessly with the sounds of my own mouth and decide on the meaning of sounds after making them. I would think, this grunt means yes and this grunt means no. But sometimes they were the exact same grunt. So the meanings were not reliant on the sounds.

I

(Grunt that means "No")

You motion once again to the paper in my hand. I bring it closer to my face and read:

On the track "Watering Hole" Baski conjures the desolation and wandering entropy on the outskirts of a world foreign and familiar. The most bombastic venture on the album. We find no reprieve from the dusty paths we have followed. Only more borders in the road. More obstacles in our way. It seems to this lonesome listener that Baski is denying entry.

YOU

Listen to the watering hole.

I place my head above the still water. It looks filmy and tepid. I think I would not drink from it. As I move closer I catch my reflection and smell sulfur. From within I hear a CHORUS OF ANGELS singing.

CHORUS OF ANGELS

I

Is that the sound of a few stones falling in water?

YOU

The elements sure. They're all there.

I back away from the watering hole, from the stones, from the chorus of angels. You sink your face into the water. Like a pig at a trough. Your arms extend and collide with the stones. All of them falling like dominoes. There is a plinking sound as some fall into the water, others scattering all around you. After what feels like hours you raise your head from the water with what I believe to be the perfect imitation of a pensive look on your face.

YOU (CONT'D)

This is music ripe with meaning.

I

You're really undermining your work over here.

(I point to the stones.)

That's fine by me. I think it was a waste of time to begin with.

CHORUS OF ANGELS

I

I'd rather just listen.

Your face is dripping beads of oily water onto your shirt. You place your hands on your hips as though chastising a child.

YOU

You're not listening.

And what comes after that is quite dissonant. Many notes that do not belong with each other. The rise of an uneasy feeling in one's stomach.

Eventually the feeling fades out slowly, as if it is still occurring but so faintly that one could never notice.

The notes brace you and surround you, outlining your body like a thin membrane. You open your mouth and seem to be singing but what comes out is only the echo. The reverberations in the back of your throat.

But there is no horror and your face is calm and resolute. You remind me of a yawning dog and I am almost
laughing at this point.

I

(Grunt that means "I like it")

# VINCENT JAMES PERRONE

Vincent James Perrone is a Detroit-based writer and musician. He is the author of the full-length book of poetry STARVING ROMANTIC (11:11 Press, 2018) and cofounder of the 51 W. Warren Writers group. Recent work published and forthcoming in Ghost City Press, Levee Magazine, and Prometheus Dreaming. @spookyghostclub

# CHAPTER TWENTY-FOUR

*"You see a watering hole. Reprieve from the old dusty path."*

A drink of whiskey in my hand    I am ready for my turn
in the dust of victory    literally blind under the flower shop
window ⟶ minus the hero ⟶ shaped by smoke
Bacchus tonguemeat hubbing through post-modern hazes
I am raison de vivre for every possible blueprint of
scientific incommensurability
and inciting

the amalgamation of math-death

Me ⟶ Mime

dissect its ironic choice of title
more self-aware / even subversive
watch it wipe its / bloody synapse on flamingo wings
it's your eidetic / haunting
where the / tallowed rune castellated by
/ drenches
will / have licked    the fur
off / numbers

this time /
whiskey like lie down whiskey / like
I am the ground. This time synthetical crystal / rain
after the interlude / this
time I / sang, this time I
slew the skullbath / grind.

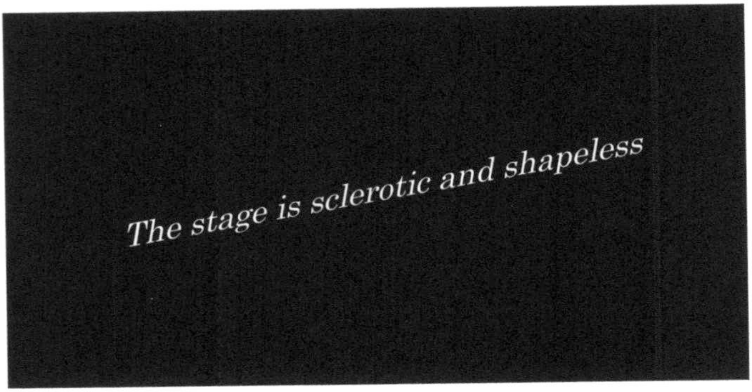
The stage is sclerotic and shapeless

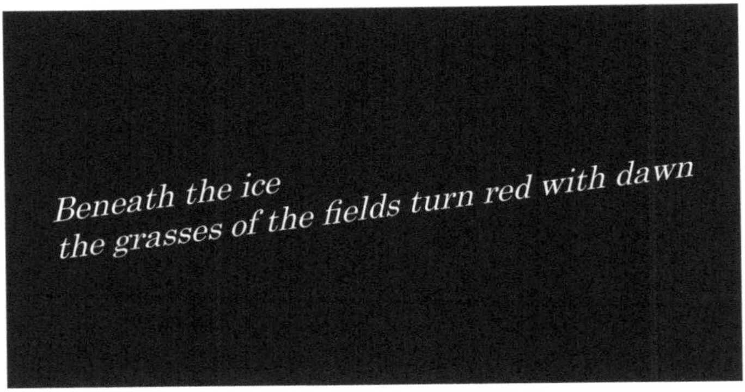
Beneath the ice
the grasses of the fields turn red with dawn

*"You are in a white room near the pulse end of your crave."*

I had

been hoping

for something

~~green~~

greener. But

to what end?

I slipknot tongues when the sea of question marks in my name
shivers up the console keys like cirrus
like furling waves where the flower of my carnage turns to spiral
and thereafter, its swollen anthem feeds the last wet desert
manes of scalding clouds in the frill, where I am just a billboard.

My optimism has made you rich
with the softest of isms of the aborted streets
and I'm socked in like a glove, or a chore of torsion
totally lacking the gift of first-person ontology.

My natural evolution from the string of the dream is hell knows where
scuba-scaping sclera-light.
Yes, I gnaw my chalk in this graveyard of culms, rewinding cotton.
I will be the crown and dauber of your buttocks of maize
then wipe your butter on the cup to pocket my spirit, inside its chrysalis.

I have tardied the odium.
I will root the square of my kiss with contagion
back to woe's pleasure with deep, prismed water
that flows like algebra from my new eyes.

*"You imagine the sound of a dying machine."*

I know it's only a riddle to you.

But my name's not Market, director.

What do you think I am?

At night, I'm a tadpole on the moon. Where you don't go, I'll come.

Jester.

A playground. I'm a first kiss turned to a blackbelt fight. I'm a gnashing poodle. An apple. A wooden block. Each of these as an elegy.

I'm not an engine, but an oil. We're all pins and needles in the monolith's soft meat. Every job is a gig. I gag. A sore on the lips of many shores.

It's time to drop the curtain and see where we've been all along.

For every love song, old and new, every spine of street

I stand, torso dignified, as my face becomes a fraction of my crotch's religion.

I chum the seam of sleepy eyelids.

*I look at you like a fish.*

*you like a fish. I you fish a like look.*
*like look I fish at you. I like you.*
*a you fish I look at. look at you. fish.*

*eifa lio ke a loyliI f. I eakia atsk ae alhoo*
*ko. laike laot ish lta ysiu. I yotoku folf.*
*o uoy hsif I iyok ta. kyos hf io ekose.*

Can you help me find the caged victims of my automatisms?

A communique function at 'our' uber-flaccid totemized summit

to lift the concrete dragonfly, this huge child

whose insect palsy is hard to cure—too shaky to grasp these shit-chiggers

teething on the isoenzyme. And the self is an object

skinned from the ravel of citrus fire

all vital to the purity and sum of death (sic).

Welch my ill winds

nil to pronounce my verses on everlasting ears

those wild green avalanches

subsecreting ad infinitum

and I am the dove that faints when the fairy-tale (that won't die)

shoots its cocoons whispering over the morning

tromping the renaissance red.

Conceal this pang of jinx in a diary written with your own vomit.

Nuke the echo with innocence in the anus of the forest

from the moment the firs blow me.

I hang them on bonfires.

*"In the impossible confluence of your utility, that name has served you in your self-doubt."*

But God is not a name.

Gong-blister.

You consider the body a symbol, a biography, but the moment you deem two

syllables

'flower'

erasure strikes.

Close the orifice of wisdom, the future is flocculating.

It's a short-cut on the highway without a driver.

Sadist, back to the cellar of your ancestors.

I told you the secrets of concavity.

Leash your tongue to my spore

asphyxiophile

my candelabrum of vicissitudes, my crystalline apex

interred, at the propitiatory altar of techno messiahs.

We burst like empty spectrums.

The sun has set on my resentment.

Heaven is a pit with scorched sheep.

# EVAN ISOLINE

Evan Isoline is a writer and visual artist living on the Oregon coast. He has work online, in chapbook form, and his full-length debut PHILOSOPHY OF THE SKY is forthcoming from 11:11 Press.

# CHAPTER TWENTY-FIVE

"**You** see a watering hole. Reprieve from the old dusty path."

The crackly processed voice forces me awake, back to where I'm staggering along the highway behind a dark blue or black pickup truck. I've mostly forgotten the dream that occupied me a moment ago... huddled masses on dingy streets, a candy factory, a row of cots, a shrieking in the night, a familiar bedsheet brittle with sweat... nothing more, though it feels like more.

Now I'm focused on reprieve from the old dusty path. The end of the journey. The right town, after so many wrong ones. A watering hole thick and hot with blood. I can't see who's driving the truck, but I can, just barely, see a woman in the back, leaning against one edge with her legs pressed against the other, her head resting on her collarbone. She doesn't seem quite asleep, nor drugged, nor sick. Something closer to hypnotized, under the effect of a spell. Perhaps the same spell I've just awoken from. She wears a black dress, thick, shapeless, almost a shroud. The air is hot. Summer air, or the air of a place that's always hot. I hurry along the highway, able to keep up although, or because, I can't feel the asphalt underfoot.

**The** truck passes several exits without taking them, speeding along the old dusty path as the sun begins to rise, until it swerves down an onramp and begins to cruise along a shaded two-lane road, flanked by weedy marshland. It's dawn now, hazy, fragrant, birds in the air.

The woman in back sits up straighter. She coughs, retracts her legs from their wedged position, extends her head, leans over the back gate, and rolls out.

She hits the ground, hard, and I hear something break. An ankle, as best I can tell. The truck slows even more, but still doesn't stop. It seems that the driver considers getting out to chase her down, then decides against it.

I keep pace as the woman limps into the marshland, away from the road. White cloths stretched against the haze grow visible, resolving into the outlines of tents. I follow her, unconcerned with being seen, uncertain whether she'd be happy, or angry, or indifferent to discover my presence. I still feel nothing underfoot, though I can see my feet squishing through the wet ground.

Now she's limping among the tents, still taking her time, but newly focused. Determined, it seems, to find an empty one. A place to lie down, after what must have been a long journey for her, as well. She walks up to one, then another, then a third, pulling their open flaps aside. All are empty. Abandoned.

Their insides, however, are still full of cigarette butts, beer cans, pennies and lint. No nests or piles of droppings, or any other signs of long human absence. Whoever was here, I think, was here until recently.

Until we came, I tell myself, deciding that our arrival is a momentous event, not just for us, but also for wherever this is. The notion of such a place—I'm beginning to get a sense of the atmosphere, the kind of air that the people who slept in these tents had been breathing in, then breathing out—jogs my memory, but I'm not yet ready to pursue it. For now, the important thing is to follow along, to see what the woman does.

She roams from tent to tent, peering into each one—there must be almost thirty, some full of brackish water, others positioned so as to remain dry—and I peer in too, still unacknowledged by her, though twice she turns in my direction and shows me her face. Worn, scarred, framed by thick, straight black hair. Ageless, androgynous, manly even. Like a face that has changed many times, bearing ill-concealed evidence of what it used to be.

After checking all thirty tents, she stretches out both arms and begins to tear them down. She moves through the encampment without hurry and without animus, knocking each tent into the mud until only one, in the far back, sheltered by a willow, remains.

This will be hers. She lets herself in through the flap and goes to sleep. I think about letting myself in, as well, and lying down beside her, or atop her. Nothing she's done indicates that I'd be rebuffed, but I stop myself nonetheless. Instead, I lie down on the pile of tent-material that's formed a cloth island in the center of the marsh, and float.

**Behind** my eyes, I sink into a cold basement. Bodies shiver two to a bed, their toes protruding from too-short blankets, terror rising out of everyone and drifting together beneath the low ceiling, while an old man, eyes full of longing, looks on from the top of the stairs.

**I'm** woken at dusk by a distant yet commanding voice, distorted by radio crackle. It hauls me out of the basement and deposits me back on the cloth island, where I hear it say:

"The Town Council, as you and I know all too well, has mandated that the shelter be shut down indefinitely, pending internal investigation. Too much blood collected from the toes of sleeping guests, they've warned us. Too many break-ins in the night. And yet what have they done about it? Sent you all to the Meadows, to shiver in tents?"

As the voice grows louder, it occurs to me that the speaker has come out here under the impression that the tents are still full of receptive heads, propping themselves on their elbows as they, like me, arise from sleep to listen.

"Never again will the..." the radio stammers, "population of our town be cast out to sleep in the Meadows, with the drafts and the water snakes, nor will you be subjected to the bloodletting that has gone on in the shelter. From now on," the car pulls closer, its headlights illuminating the murk where I lie listening, shining brightly enough that I'm able to scan the shadows for water snakes, "the basements of certain private homes will be open, on a first-come, first-served basis. Tonight, it's the blue-gray house on the corner of Woodlawn & Hillcrest. I suggest you make your way there now, before the… and the jackals slink out to… among your tents. I'm Professor Dalton, and it would be my supreme honor to serve as your next Mayor. The election, let me remind you good folks, is on…"

The broadcast cuts out before the final words come through.

**As** soon as Professor Dalton has driven off, the woman rises in her tent, pulls on a pair of moccasins that I hadn't noticed her wearing before, and sets off toward the road, trailing me behind her. Her pace is different now, quicker. Sleep must have mended her injury. I hurry to keep up, no longer as fleet-footed as I was on the highway, where, I reason, the pull of gravity is weaker. I hadn't thought of myself as elderly or unwell, but I find myself lagging behind as we hurry past an old movie theater and a candy store and a liquor store, watched by a few weathered faces on benches, their cardboard signs illegible in the flickering streetlight. I press my heels and toes against the sidewalk, trying to feel it, but all that comes through is a dull pressure, as dull as my memories of having been in this town before. Still, it's more than I could feel this morning. A symptom of the right town, I think. A return to real life, after too much time away.

We proceed out of the center and into a cleaner, tonier neighborhood, the houses recessed behind hedges or on the far sides of expansive lawns. The needle and vial are already in her hand by the time we spot the house on the corner of Woodlawn & Hillcrest, where a sizable line has grown.

**I** watch as the line surges across the lawn. Men and women in torn white jeans and corduroys, dragging cardboard signs and soda bottles full of pennies, fight to get as close as possible to the front door. When one of them, a middle-aged woman in sweatpants and a tank-top, reaches it, she rings the bell. Nothing happens. All chatter subsides, all attention is riveted on the door as she rings the bell again.

This time, the door swings open and a man in blue pajamas squints out. "Yes?" he asks.

No one responds.

A moment later, he says, "Oh yes. The, uh, the people who are here to sleep in our basement. Please, please come in." The look of memory dawning on him is gruesome to behold.

He stands aside and motions us to move along. As I watch, I feel the crowd sweeping me up in it. Soon, I'm in the house, being herded past a regal old woman brooding over a cup of tea and a clementine at the kitchen table, looking us over as we climb down a steep set of wooden stairs to the basement.

Once I've made it all the way down, I see rows of cots, ten or twelve against one wall, the same number against the other wall, with a few in the aisles between them. Behind the cots are an exercise bike, a bench press, and numerous cardboard and wooden boxes, labeled in fading cursive.

At the top of the stairs, the man says, "Since our... son moved away, we've had an empty house. Basement, other rooms, you name it. It brings us no small joy to open it to you in this way. Please, please sleep well." He stops and surveys the crowd, some of whom are already squabbling over cots. He scans our faces, his eyes weak but determined, looking for something, or someone, that he doesn't seem to find. Then he adds, "There's plastic cups beside the sink at the back of the basement. The pipes are old, but the water's plenty good to drink. There are some boxes of Oreos and maybe one or two other kinds in the back too. Make yourselves comfortable, and," he turns here, startled to see the regal old woman, surely his wife, standing beside him. She regards us with a look of concern. Then she whispers something to him, squeezes his shoulder, and walks off.

Clearing his throat, the man says, "Just, please, don't come upstairs. If you need help, there's a phone right in the kitchen. You can call 911, or… anybody you like, really. Long distance, local, you name it. Just please don't come upstairs."

He smiles in a pinched, sad way, and closes the basement door very slowly, as if we were already asleep and he didn't want to wake us.

**When** he's gone, I lie down on my cot—I'm glad I got one before people started having to double and triple up—and try to decide what to do now, whether my plan is to see if I can sleep through the night, or to sneak out once the others have settled in, or something else I haven't thought of. I feel a wave of regret, terror even, at having left the highway to come here, where the gravity is heavier and I can no longer glide along without feeling the ground underfoot. Then the voice passes back through my head. "Sleep," it commands. "Reprieve from the old dusty path. The watering hole, the blood hole, the..."

I close my eyes and swim down through the cement floor and into the night, where I hurry behind the pickup truck speeding along the highway. I follow it into town again, the woman in the same hypnotized position in back. When the driver slows down, the woman hits the ground, rolls along the pavement, and gets to her feet.

I follow behind her as she limps toward the house on the corner of Woodlawn & Hillcrest. I watch her cross the lawn toward the front door, just as Professor Dalton's car cruises down the road from the other direction, nearly invisible under the dim streetlights. "As Mayor," he intones, his loudspeaker crackling while

while the woman lets herself in through the front door, "I will personally see to it that each and every one of you is safe at night. I will reopen the shelters, under better supervision, with better-paid guards," she tiptoes through the kitchen, past the clementine peel on the kitchen table, "until you are able to move back into your houses. Never again will it be necessary for any of you to spend the…" the voice echoes and doubles, "in the homes of strangers. And as for you, good… of Woodlawn Avenue?" He flashes his brights here, which seep in through the half-windows near the basement's ceiling, just as the woman descends the stairs and begins to roam among the cots.

"Good people of Woodlawn Avenue," the two Dalton-voices insist, "what happened to your children is a disgrace. A national tragedy. But there's no need for you to open your houses to folks who have a perfectly good place to stay already. Or would have a perfectly good place to stay, if only their… weren't always on the verge of…"

She kneels down at the foot of the cot she's selected, caresses the big toe of a sleeping man, affixes the needle to her tongue, and slides it deep into the pad, drawing out a thick, hot stream that she spits into the vial. All is quiet for a moment, as if the pain is traveling a long way to reach the man at the far end of the punctured toe.

Dalton's loudspeaker crackles, his voices breaking apart.

Then the man bolts up in his cot, shrieking so loudly the rafters shake and the other sleepers likewise bolt upright and begin shrieking too, pounding their mattresses and gnashing their teeth, drawn together by a collective mania that I fear may collapse the house on top of us.

**The** old man, panting in a flannel robe and sleeping cap, appears at the top of the basement stairs, holding the railing for balance.

He opens his mouth as if to speak, but only a low wheeze emerges. While he stands there wheezing, the woman with her needle in one hand and her vial in the other slips past him. I too hurry as best I can up the stairs while the man with the bleeding toe goes on howling, and the man at the top finds his voice, and begins to bellow, "I trusted you! I trusted you guys! My wife said I shouldn't, but I trusted you, and now look what you…"

**The** woman and I are running across the lawn.

I watch the blood froth in her vial as she hurries back through the tony neighborhood and onto the street that leads to downtown. We make it back to the Meadows without incident, and I watch as she lets herself into her tent and stows the blood vial in a hanging side pocket near the door flap, exiling me to the cloth island once again. I lie down and close my eyes, trying not to notice that another tent has been set up on the far side of the marshland.

◆

**Though** it seems I've only just arrived, I begin to have the feeling that everything that can happen in this town has happened already. I spend the day circling the Meadows, watching the woman, whose ankle has healed once again, do likewise, still unable or unwilling to acknowledge my presence, or that of the other tent, and the other woman I imagine is sleeping inside.

Soon, a dim, late afternoon light fills the sky, and two headlights appear, diffusing through the watery air. I sit on the cloth island and watch, expecting Dalton to emerge and stand, at last, before us in the flesh. But all that happens is his loudspeaker crackles to life and, from within the car, he demands an audience with, "Whoever or whatever you are that… my constituents' blood in the night last night."

The woman emerges from her tent along with the other woman from the other tent, dressed identically, and both drift over to the car, right up to the driver's side window, putting their lips against the glass, which Dalton doesn't roll down.

"The taking of blood from the big toe in the night," Dalton's voice booms, "is a cause of terror that I have been called upon to confront. It is my calling, at this stage of my life's journey, after so many false starts, with so many bridges burned behind me, to see to it that none of our once-illustriously housed, now tragically homeless population is forced to suffer the… of nighttime bloodletting ever again. It is the only kindness I can show these people. Haven't they suffered enough? I am now all that stands between them and the same fate that befell their children."

As his voice booms on, another car rolls up and begins the speech again, while a crowd emerges from some woodwork behind the Meadows. "The story," the first voice goes on, "is well-known by now. Of the forces, never to be mentioned, that compelled, first, the children from their rooms, alone and then en masse, past the Meadows where we stand now, up the onramp and onto the highway and out of town. Made of them numb scuttling shades, whisking up the asphalt to nowhere. And then the parents, out of their homes as well, but not up the onramp and out of town, no, for who would be here if their children returned? They—you, I see you now, all of you, come closer, vote for me for Mayor—became the legions of homeless circling your old houses, cold and empty, terrified to go back inside, for fear that what happened once might happen again. For fear that whatever got in there is in there still."

The loudspeakers hiss with feedback, pulling the crowd closer, until it throngs the cars. I try to make out the faces of the homeless, but something about them repels me. A blur, a smudging, a sense of the inauthentic or second-order about them. Like ghosts reborn into their own dead bodies.

As Dalton returns to the topic of stolen blood, it occurs to me that perhaps he and she are working in tandem, sowing fear where before there had been none, creating a problem that only they can solve. The thought makes me cold, despite the heat of the evening, so I slink back to my cloth island and lie down, hoping to dream of colors and shapes dancing to a gentle drone.

But as soon as my eyes are closed, my head fills with pickup trucks, roaming the town in search of the woman who fell out of the back, and, by extension, in search of me, now that I'm complicit in her crimes. Every parked car they pass becomes a pickup truck, expelling more and more women in black dresses with needle-tongues, until gridlock forces all motion to cease.

◆

"**Return** to Woodlawn & Hillcrest," the voice commands. When I roll awake, the woman is standing over me. I can't tell if she's just spoken in Dalton's voice, or if he's speaking now, unseen in the distance. "The watering hole, the blood hole. Reprieve from the…"

The woman and the voice fade as I get to my feet and begin to trudge across the Meadows, past the new tent, from which a figure is also trudging. We trudge together, in mutual indifference, the sidewalk growing more palpable underfoot.

The road to town is full of the loitering homeless, seeking the distant drone of Dalton's voice. It gets alternately closer and farther away, as he plies his route and I ply mine. Again, I have the sense that there are more than one of him, casing the town with ever greater redundancy, campaigning on the same platform, against himself and himself and himself, until victory is assured.

No one seems invested in following me, so I take my time, exploring side streets and alleys, letting them jog my memory a little at a time.

I catch sight of Dalton's car from unexpected angles—across a sudden jag of railroad tracks, on the far side of an open mine or construction pit, in the lot of a hollowed-out convenience store, then in front of what looks like a gallows, though no rope swings from its outstretched iron arm—and I listen while the speaker rehashes the story of how first something terrible happened to the children and then, as a result or an echo, the parents were forced out of their houses and onto the streets.

Just as they did in the Meadows, the homeless orient toward the car, their heads swiveling as it passes by. I watch them and, though the thought comes unbidden, I think how they're all made of blood. How they're nothing but blood—blood that I might once again be able to taste—standing there, waiting for tonight.

**We** follow the loudspeaker through the dark, past a cement factory, and a candy factory, and a refinery, toward a broad, one-story building with a sign out front that reads FORMER HOMELESS SHELTER: CONTAINMENT SITE DO NOT ENTER.

The crowd masses around this sign, staring at the campaign car as it glides to a halt beside several others. "This is what it's come to, folks," Dalton begins, the speaker still live after the engine's cut out. It wakes up the other Daltons in the other cars, all of whom start in with, "It's time that you saw it for yourselves. That's why I've built my campaign headquarters here. It's ground zero for what's happened to this town, and for what needs to change. Time is running out. There is no… choice. Do what needs to… done… done… done."

Three voices conclude the speech at three separate times. Then the speakers merge into static. I have an instinct to hang back and try to speak with Dalton directly, but the crowd sets out across the bike path behind the former shelter, so I have to hurry if I want a cot at Woodlawn & Hillcrest.

**When** we make it to the front door, the woman at the head of the line rings the bell. She waits, looks back at the crowd filling the lawn, then turns and rings it again. The man in the flannel pajamas appears on the second ring and looks us over. From where I'm standing, I can't tell if he recognizes us. He must, I think, and yet his expression makes me wonder.

When the woman says something to him, that same look of gruesome recognition creeps back across his face. "Oh yes," he stammers. "The, uh, the people who are here to sleep in our basement. Please, please come in."

He leads us inside, past the regal old woman peeling a clementine and drinking tea at the kitchen table, and down to the basement, back to the smells of dust and freshly-laundered sheets. It seems she's washed them since we were here last, hoping to erase the bloodstain with chemicals and hot water.

We bed down after being told that there are Oreos and tap water in the back and a phone we can use upstairs. I close my eyes, hoping for an hour of cool darkness before the shrieking returns.

**As** soon as my eyes close, I'm following the pickup truck again, riveted on the woman as the driver cruises past Woodlawn & Hillcrest. She jolts awake and rolls out of the back, clutching her needle and vial as she gets to her feet, dusts herself off, and limps across the lawn.

As she lets herself into the house, I force myself awake in the basement—I leave the dream here, and return to my body, or my main body, beneath its clean sheets, which I now realize I've been smelling all night—and tiptoe up the stairs and across the kitchen, past the clementine peel on the table, past the phone in the hall, narrowly avoiding the woman as she begins her descent.

I walk up stair by stair, torn between wanting to linger to hear the scream from the mouth attached to whichever toe she punctures, and wanting to make it as far from the puncture site as possible, into the safety of my old room.

I creep along the upstairs hallway, past where the parents are sleeping, and make it inside what I realize I've begun calling *my old room* just as the scream reaches the second floor. As I explore the shrine—it's clear that not a single item has been moved—the parents' door opens and the father begins his nightly limping run down to the top of the basement stairs, to see what the commotion is all about.

I get in the bed and pull one of the pillows over my face, inhaling the linen's familiar must. Unlike the sheets in the basement, these have not been washed. I can feel particles of skin and hair clinging to them, and smell old, long-dried sweat, turning the cloth brittle. I draw more of it in, through my nose and my mouth together, trying to remember when it was mine.

I lie like this, focused on nothing else, until the door bursts open and the parents stand, shocked, shouting that I'm no son of theirs.

"What have you done with him? What have you turned him into? Who scarred your face like that? We always prayed he'd return. That's why we kept our doors open so long. So much longer than we should have. So much longer than anyone else in town. Despite the shrieking in the basement. The endless washing of sheets. So many strangers in our house, because we knew you'd return. But not like this. Not like this!"

They shout, vibrating in the doorway without entering the room, as if afraid of coming any closer. I lean up, yawning, unsure how I appear to them. The pickup truck rolling into town, the woman in back rolling out, the cots in the basement, the exposed toes, the prick of the needle, the whoosh of blood, the legions of homeless, the crackle of Dalton's loudspeaker, the damp of the cloth island… perhaps they can see all this running through my head.

I lie there, staring at my parents in the doorway while they go on vibrating, demanding that I leave.

Eventually my father sighs, "I'm going to get my gun," and walks off. My mother stands there longer, her eyes locked on mine, a veil of tears rendering her irises indistinct. She looks like she's trying hard to remember something, but I can't tell if she's succeeding. Then he returns and begins shooting. Bullets tear through the blanket and through a photo collage taped above the bed. Then one tears through my ankle, shattering the bone.

The pain blooms through my body, tautening my slack nerves. I shiver, elated and terrified, as I crawl through the window, grab the drainpipe, and travel down through queasy dark onto the soft grass, its softness a revelation.

◆

**I** come to in the tent, supping blood from a vial, desperate to get as much down my throat as I possibly can. I can taste it. It tastes like more than air. It tastes like…

A crackling in the distance steals my attention. "And so it happened, folks," the voice drones, "just as I feared. A bloodthirsty freak was found in the son's room of the genteel elderly couple in the handsome 1920's residence on the corner of… & Woodlawn, an event that signaled the beginning of the end of life as it was in this town. The son who ran away years ago, as you all remember, returned in horribly mutated form. A wanderer from the highway, a creature of the wilds, nestled in the very sheets that…" his voice breaks and sputters before coming imperfectly back together, "the very sheets that once housed this town's most promising valedictorian."

ing valedictorian."

A version of Dalton's voice that sounds more processed, as if coming through several speakers at once, continues. "He was chased out at gunpoint, but, in quick succession, all the other houses on Woodlawn and on Hillcrest, not to mention those of the Town Fathers on Dryads Green, emptied out, none of the residents willing to face the prospect of a similar invasion. All the rooms of the sons and daughters of this town have been converted to shrines, and all the parents who've left their homes have become, it pains me to say… wondering what cruel twist fate has in store for them next. The shelter behind the candy factory is full to capacity, and there have already been," he sighs here, and falls to a yet-lower register, like he's said this many, many times already, "reports of bloodletting in the night. That is why, here and now, to all of you listening, I formally announce my candidacy for Mayor."

◆

**Weeks** pass, moving either forward or backward, as I regain my strength, gulping down all the blood I've saved. Tasting every drop of it. When I close my eyes, I see myself following a pickup truck off the highway and into the Meadows and then into the house on Woodlawn & Hillcrest, into the room upstairs, where I remain until I'm chased out at gunpoint, only to land on the lawn with a shattered ankle and end up back in the tent to heal.

Following this, the town's children disappear and following that, their parents leave their houses, and following that Professor Dalton awakens in his mansion on Dryads Green, puts on a clean suit, shaves, and decides to run for Mayor.

I look around and see that the Meadows is now full of tents.

At nightfall, I drape myself in the black dress of

the woman who used to be here with me, and creep into the basement at Woodlawn & Hillcrest. I kneel down by the toes of the homeless and extend my tongue, sinking its needle into their soft tissue, forcing their numb bodies awake, and beginning to lap the blood, which runs into the flesh of my tongue, causing it to grow so large it fills my mouth.

"The watering hole," I hear. "The blood hole. The soft…"

**When** my tongue grows so large I begin to choke on it, I startle awake in the tent, sweating in my black dress, and I pant, huffing down air until I can breathe again. I want to press my finger to the needle-tip of my tongue to verify that it's still there, but I can't summon the courage to do so.

I am beginning to feel better and better.

**Dalton's** voice wakes me up again. "It's only getting worse. Every night, at Woodlawn & Hillcrest, another of our once-honored citizens is forced to undergo the horror of bloodletting from the... The mayoral election is tomorrow morning, people. Make the right decision, this one time. As Mayor, I vow to put an end to this. I will have you back in your houses on Hillcrest, and on Woodlawn, and even on Dryads Green, before my first term is out. The scourge of bloodthirsty freaks will be behind us at last. They will never again make it down the highway offramp. They will, and mark my words here, be chased out of this town in mortal terror, no matter what it…"

The voices split into polyphony, dozens of Daltons screeching over one another, all desperate to say the same thing. I dream that Dalton has caused all this to happen, that his loudspeaker is no mere campaign tool. That it was what forced me from my room at the very beginning, just as it forced him from his mansion on Dryads Green and onto the campaign trail. Perhaps we're all equally subject to its power, I think. Nothing but mouthpieces for that which has no mouth.

I flash back to my bedroom on Woodlawn & Hillcrest, where I'm working on the speech I'll give as valedictorian when a voice through the window commands me to pack my bag and walk off, past the Meadows and onto the highway, in search of the watering hole, the blood hole, the soft, welcoming...

**I** fall back asleep, and wake up on Election Day.

I pick up the needle and vial, pull on the black dress, and walk on my mended ankle out of the Meadows, up the ratty side streets, past the candy factory, and across the football field behind where I went to high school.

My vision swims, breaking up and coming back together, revealing the town in shards, all nearly identical, but subject to the same smudge I saw earlier, only worse now, further along. Many iterations later.

I sit in the bleachers and watch the homeless queue up, growing antsy as they wait their turn to vote. The Election Committee ushers them in twenty at a time. I count how many groups have gone in, and how many have come out, trying to gauge when my moment will come. I lose and regain and then lose count again. The sun rises and rises in the sky and then it begins to sink. It makes me sleepy, and I feel my eyes sagging shut, my vision coalescing into a unified field.

**When** I wake up, the sky is dim and murky and the high school is abandoned. I pull my dress closer around my shoulders and hear the metal clink of something falling from my mouth. The needle I'd brought to draw Dalton's blood. To drink him down, until he grew so dry and brittle the voice could no longer use him.

I climb down from the bleachers, past traces of dozens of others like me, and duck underneath, just as I used to in high school, to swig from plastic bottles in the

the months before I left town.

I crawl among those same bottles now, or ones just like them, searching for my needle, until two headlights and a crackling amplified voice dominate my attention, as they always do. "This is your new Mayor speaking. I know you're under there, and I know what you're looking for. You won't find it. It's all over now. Come here and accept what you deserve. Hasn't this town suffered enough because of you? Haven't you drunk enough of our blood already?"

I take another few moments to rummage for the needle, convinced that if I can only find it, I'll prevail. I'll vanquish Dalton—all the Daltons—and return triumphant to my bedroom, where none of this will have happened, where flubbing my valedictorian speech will be all I have to fear. But there's nothing except whiskey bottles and ticket stubs and squishy old condoms. Nothing sharp, nothing I can use, and I feel the headlights coming closer, the campaign car driving across the football field, and I can tell that I'm trapped. One loudspeaker boasts, "This is your new Mayor speaking, my new administration begins today," while another drones, "And so, that is why I've decided to run for Mayor," and a third insists that, "There are not enough beds at Woodlawn & Hillcrest! There simply aren't enough beds to house all the..."

I make the only move I have left. It brings me no pleasure, but it's either this or going wherever Dalton chooses to take me. Vanishing, I'm certain, into some bowel of the old candy factory from which I'd never reemerge.

So, clutching a mostly empty bottle of whiskey, I close my eyes and say "Yes" to the voice that has asked if I'm sure this is what I want. Then I stand, careful not to hit my head on the underside of the bleachers, and make my way across the illuminated field toward the idling pickup truck, along with dozens of others I can just barely see, approaching pickup trucks of their own.

When I get there, I take the last, luxurious sip of sweet, brown liquor, toss the bottle, and climb in back, sitting against one edge with my feet pressed against the other. I drift into hypnosis as the driver guides us through the all-encompassing crackle of Dalton's voice, insisting that we'll never be safe, that we'll never manage to stop running, that he'll chase us to the northernmost tip of the continent. I lick the insides of my lips, mourning my sense of taste as it disappears.

The driver skirts the Meadows and pulls up the onramp and onto the highway, where the only traffic is that of other pickup trucks. "The journey has begun," I hear the voice declare. The same voice that speaks through Dalton, the voice that's left a row of ruined towns along the highway, a hundred of them lined up, or ruined the same town a hundred times. Though I know not to trust it, I can't help but nod when I hear it say, "Good riddance to the wrong town, and onward up the dusty path to the right one. The watering hole. The blood hole. The soft, welcoming…"

# DAVID LEO RICE

David Leo Rice is a writer and animator from Northampton, MA, currently living in NYC. He's the author of the novels A ROOM IN DODGE CITY, A ROOM IN DODGE CITY VOL. 2, AND ANGEL HOUSE. 11:11 will release his debut story collection in 2021. He's online at: www.raviddice.com.

# CHAPTER TWENTY-SIX

You see a watering hole. Reprieve from the old dusty path—

Those words, scrawled in pencil across the page. Those words, glowing in violent neon against a yellow wall.

—here and there my shape fragments and becomes less real. And sometimes, my shadow dances in ways unlike anything I've ever seen—

Sometimes—I am not myself.

The book came to me weeks ago through a series of exchanges—hand to hand to hand—across this city to my apartment, scrawling a thin line of black ink. Who wrote it, who passed it along, and why—I will never know. It sits open in my hands, here in this naked room, inside this naked apartment, cold like ancient iron and as heavy. No book should have such weight. No book should thrum with such sound.

Every word sinks into me, every silver-grey sentence, written in a hand that staggers and crawls across the dry paper. Like tattoos on ancient skin, my fingers move over them as my lips move and sound out each word in turn. An incantation hundreds of pages long. A spell, the result of which is unknown.

In places the text has been re-written, over and over, multiple sets of handwriting. Clearly as the book has been passed from person to person, so each has modified it, so each has made it their own. In places the pencil has been erased and fresh writing inserted. Sometimes it is scrawled out, an angry scratching on the page. Notes in the margins. Additions above and below the line. Text at angles. The book, rotating in my hands as I read, not just turning each page, but reading through each page, delving deep into the mass of letters, words, sentences, paragraphs—falling into and through the text itself—

—crimson sits a far walk to narrow shores she sits and spins threads of glass from the bitter sand and salt

present a show of lips

of eyes

say yes and no one will see—

These are thin walls, a skin that I feel moving through the night, breathing in with me, pushing air in a steady, syncopated rhythm. When I place my hands to those smooth white surfaces I feel a slight dampness although they appear very dry. And if I concentrate very hard, I can feel the undulation of their breathing. My palms feel the slight pressure. The hair on my neck stands up. The blood in my veins thumps through my ears. That glorious thud. In my chest. Through my crotch. My teeth set. Sometimes I feel like I could push through those walls, slip into something else. Somewhere else. But I open my eyes and I remain.

The book remains.

Here are no doors or windows. No furniture. No smell. I am sealed here in this pristine white. I am alone here with the pulsing, the breathing walls, and my own heart thumping. The electric throbbing.

I haven't always been here—I know that. But what came before seems so distant and vague as to be completely meaningless now. How I came to be here.

How I am.

I just am.

—twisting metallic sinew and rusty copper coils curling cold tongues around these arms growing as enormous limbs stretching yearning pushing into the fabric of this body trapped within a cage that breathes in breathes out each a noxious cloud of vapour bristling with static and neon arcs within those flashes the bleeding light a face blinking stuttering a mouth moving soundlessly—

This bleeding shape. This failure. My light escapes me through ragged holes. I itch. Hands shake and shiver. An arc of cold blue cuts across the room—wallpaper peels. You stand there praying. Your shape is indistinct. A guttural cough, like a clogged sewer. I try to shout but my words are nothing now, just clotted lumps. Sounds with no edges.

I am bankrupt. Spiritually empty. You try to fill me with your light, but the tears in me just leak it back out, it spills and I can't help but lie here laughing.

I don't know your name. I never knew. I don't know what your face is like, but it shines so blindingly. It's a star shattering. I am dust, blasted by neon, eroded by your wind. The rust in my joints stiffens, and I lurch. I stumble. These windows no longer throw views across the city. They are blackened in the soot of your burning.

Beneath ceilings of wax, the impression of your body pressed into the soft, I reach an arm out and touch the delicate void that is you. Beneath ceilings dripping, melting into twisting shapes that possess your prayers, give form to words. I descend through floors of holy filament—your star rising, my star falling. You are above me. Your eyes blaze in violet. You will stand over me and your mouth will move in soundless moments, a sermon I will never understand, will never hear. And all I

I will ever do is collapse and fall.

My failing shape. My useless light. I burn up in the descent through your atmosphere.

Coiling dirty white smears on a wall seared and blackened with char, a sting of words seen through an insect's compound eye—a gloomy view through broken tenement walls. A bare lightbulb swings. Yellow neon wash. Shivering on a floor of broken glass.

You open your mouth and the light.

You open your mouth and the black of flies.

I am falling in this vat of black. There is fat in your eyes. Oozing through pores. Fists move through glue, and my eyes close tight.

And all the arms.

And all the legs.

And all the fingers.

In my mouth and eyes. Pulling and pushing. So much urgency. Your language of limbs stuttering like twitching muscles.

And all your words are written in blood on the stained yellow walls of this apartment. These are years of watching the thick drip.

Of red drying to black.

Of sunlight giving way to the night.

And your hissing. The shimmering bricks. My eyes cannot focus on anything. No edges. Like underwater. Like sinking. Forever in that absence. And all I can hear is the vibrating stone. The floorboards groaning. Such a musical pain.

Your body heavy.

Your body heaving.

Dark whispers of car crashes and demolitions. Of explosions in stars. Lying flat on a glacier, the pitch of the night. You can see to the end of the universe when there is no sound. You can feel the end and beginning of.

And when you pace around these halls, there is a ghostly wake. I can only watch from the floor, nailed here through this body. You cried at each hammer blow. You wept, and your blood was a fresh baptism.

I am not alone.

I am not here.

I am.

# KENNY MOONEY

Kenny Mooney was born in Berlin when it was still divided by a stupid wall. He grew up in Scotland, England, and Cyprus. He is a writer, musician, and software developer. He is the author of IN THE VAST AND BOUNDLESS DEEP and DESK CLERK. Learn more at www.fieldofdissonance.com.

# CHAPTER TWENTY-SEVEN

You see a watering hole. Reprieve from the old dusty path. Come take a piece of the road, just a piece. It's at the foot of the mountain just before the bridge under a copse of young sugar maples.

"Bring a clean piece of dirt. Anything around here will do."

It's a place she knows well. But also knows that she has not, cannot, as of yet, find all that lies within. She taps on her wristwatch. It looks old, with a cracked face and blood-splattered with red, yellow, and pink.

"Come on, we'll make our way to the source."

You kick the earth with your heel. The playing area gets smaller and smaller. You pocket some and follow after her.

It's early evening. The sun is shining and the sky is golden. You can hear the birds chirping and there's a heavy mist forming below the mountain. The mist has always been the embodiment of this deep valley, its boundary—the boundary between our dreams and those of our ancestors. The boundary between dreaming and a dreamer.

"Just tell me if you start to feel tired."

Weird and cold things come up to eat in the woods. Regular wildlife, but stranger things too—the odd-ball rolling of a sputtering birdbath, a pile of lumber breathing in and out, a discarded swimming pool dried out and scuttling across the undergrowth.

If you are lucky, you will find a gaggle of retired handymen, hiding in the thicket, doing their work. You spy one for a moment before he ducks away. His face is one of real joy, as if he's just found the best place to eat and drink in all of the county.

The steep banks of valley make for slow going. Eventually you reach the river. There are big roots and little roots and the river tends to muddy around large shallow spots. On the opposite bank the trees grow denser.

"Wait here. I'm heading behind those sugar maples to look for bones."

She wades across with her pack above her head and you do as you're told.

The body of a young woman floats downstream. Your guide told you to expect as much—the older ones float on the river bottom. You look over and there the woman is lying on her back, going all the way around the bend just out of sight. She gives you a wave and disappears, her not-quite smile lingering in your memory.

Does this sound familiar?

Creek bottom.

Blue water.

Opening, closing

Bodies, bodies, bodies.

No? Okay.

Eventually your guide steps out from under the shade of the trees and leans her wet clothes against the side of the riverbed. She's soaked, but happy.

"Nothing much. The mother-god is coming soon,

though, I can smell it. There's smoke coming from the center of the valley."

She asks how you're doing. You are not so thirsty, nor so cold. You can do this for as long as you like.

"Good. Just give me a minute to dry."

The surface of the hardwood forest is covered with fossils, some of them clinging to branches, some of them peering out from the dark places where bark has been chipped away by other, carnivorous things—crunching away at paradoxides like filthy, cracked walnuts.

"Okay, let's catch the last of the sun."

You know these things are here and that the ground you walk could blow away at any moment, but as the light dims and the forest becomes harder and harder to traverse, you become so accustomed to the anomalies that you stop paying attention to them. Well, maybe not yet, but you stop caring.

This is true of many things, including fire, running, sex... anything involving action. Eventually you will develop the ability to fall asleep when in the presence of these incongruities, and when you finally do you will dream of weird things that are far more real than any nightmare.

As you walk into the darkness and your eyes widen you turn a corner and see the night sky has changed. It's lit by constellations that you've never seen before, some exotic things you can't even begin to comprehend.

She, too, is amazed. She has seen the strange cross-shaped star pattern several times before, but this is something else entirely.

"We're close."

It's a declining ecosystem compared to a few years ago, but you enjoy the varied and unusual life forms found in the otherworldly landscape that lays before you. Especially the magnificence of the creatures that, for the most part, are completely at peace with themselves and one another. From some childhood, a paper airplane emerges and rests on your shoulder, waiting patiently for a mate to take notice. You don't have the heart to brush it away.

Before long you too start to notice the bones. Ankles, heels, thighs, and feet scroll past, their veneers in tatters. Your guide stops to inspect each, nudging most into the river and packing a select few into her bag.

Suddenly the river empties into the middle of a clearing and you've arrived. Smoke billows from lake's center creating black pools in the mirror of the water's surface. There's no ripple or bubbles, only a steady smolder.

"We're here."

You ask her what to do and she tells you.

"Go as far as you can, making sure you keep the smoke at least four feet in front of you. Wrap the dirt in cloth and let it soak for five minutes. Here, like this."

She takes your bandanna to show you, and again, you do as you're told. Wrapping the dirt with care, you wade in. Four feet, five minutes.

One cough and then another. You're having trouble breathing the air is so clogged here. Despite that, you are happy. You don't know how to describe it, but the feeling of being there is almost soothing.

The young woman you saw floating stands at the edge of the lake, naked from the waist up. She waves but you don't know whether to wave back, if it'll break the spell in some way. Smoke wafts past her as she crouches down, filling her pockets with stones. Waves cling to her hair as she walks toward you. And again, she's gone, marching beneath the surface.

"Okay, come back."

The hunter leads you to a tree and instructs you how to hang the bundle. A piece of twine a foot above the earth. You pull back as far as it will go and release, the pendulum swinging as it traces a path into the dirt.

"And now you wait. And watch."

She turns to the lake and approaches its boundary. Reaching into her pack she takes out the bones, giving each one a last look before lobbing it into the smoke. Pale spirits materialize and waft towards the heavens. Their anatomy differs greatly from natural human shapes, and glancing away from your project, you see tears running down her face. These spirits have been through difficult times, and her spirit is quite simple in comparison.

Suddenly the sound of rain. Some unknown door is flung open and dripping turns to mist turns to waterfalls.

You peer into the cascade and you see yourself—your face, head, and arms caked in amber as you too stand at the edge of the lake. In its middle, the mother-god glows orange. She seems about to say something but she lets the silence hang. It is nearly midnight and starlight is falling down like rain down upon her shivering form.

Behind her, the blurred image of a fine old man in white sits shrouded by mist and diffused in light. You know him from your childhood. His eyes say everything.

As she smiles, she looks over her shoulder and whispers something to her companion. The figure disappears. Turning to you, she finally speaks. Her words convey a feeling of familiarity and comfort, but it's both a jumble and an indecipherable murmur.

Far below the lake, the mausoleum deepens. The crumbing walls more and more cave in. Beams of electricity begin to join the veins of the enormous, blackened beams that arc down from above, and the temple looks ever more cavernous. Ceiling panels that had once been festooned with delicately rendered cross-sections of relics collapse in on themselves, swaying in the power of the cataclysm.

As you watch, the right-hand wall drops away, and a great, vista-filled hall emerges in its place. It stands above you, stretching, stretching, before you, the fullest, richest hall in the world. Inside, five curving stories, each seven stories tall, drop away, revealing a vortex, a pure sphere. It is cold and nothing but white, and still the halls spew in a rich, random orchestration of color.

The woman is here. She's emptied her pockets between the pews. She waves.

And waves.

And waves.

Suddenly, your spine gives out and there's nothing but darkness and the sensation of warmth.

Drip. Drip.

Drip.

Creek bottom.

Blue water.

Opening, closing.

Bodies, bodies, bodies.

A gentle and tentative hand comes down to rest on your shoulder and eases you up. It's your guide. She's trembling slightly, but not as much as you.

"Did you find the one you were looking for?"

You nod.

"Did he tell you anything?"

You shake your head.

"Did she tell you anything?"

You shake your head again.

"Ah, bummer. Well, maybe next time."

She pulls you to your feet and the two of you start walking slowly up and out of the valley, silent and silent. But the warmth is still resonating with you and you can feel every detail of the dreams—the sounds of nature, your family at home, the hermits in the forest, the buzzing of the fly.

Opening, closing.

Bodies, bodies, bodies.

They lived the dream as best they could, barely, and found a way to live on in a new world.

You feel awakened now and it's this inner awareness that keeps your mind from going up into a world of nightmares. You don't want to stop being this warm. You want to remember it and remember all the things that people, the whole of the world, have to take to keep all this up.

And it's this: Being in but out of world.

And it's this: Being out of the valley but seeing past it.

All you see are the bodies and they're happy and giggling and talking.

And suddenly so are you.

And so is your guide.

And she hands you something to drink.

Or another drink.

Or some kind of cigarette.

# TYLER CRUMRINE

Tyler Crumrine is a designer & dramaturg and the founding editor of Plays Inverse Press. More at crumrine.info.

# CHAPTER TWENTY-EIGHT

You see a watering hole. Reprieve from the old dusty path. *No. Come back. Come back.* You screech romantically for his safe return Home. You are halfway through your perineum already and will swim upwards if need be. In a Sotheby's dining cart if gods will it so.

Everything is quiet now. Now He comes. The Prince Aeolian. Oh Great Keresh. Did you know there is no smaller honor than a buck shedding his velvet where you are standing? Do you see the sanguine curtains before his eyes? Now you are reminded of your insides. You are bleeding from the inside and He reminds you of This. Now his eyes you see and you turn half bird and the rain this time is real and He will not come back. Now He lets you speak. *I am sorry. I am sorry I have feigned every government in this body including the erotic. I am sorry. I am sorry I want a gosling for a child and I will eat every egg I find in this godforsaken.*

# ARIELLE TIPA

Arielle Tipa is a writer / poet who lives near a haunted lake in New York. She received her BA in Comparative Literature & English from Stony Brook University in 2015, and additionally holds an Associate's in Journalism. Arielle is the Founding Editor of Occulum, a literary journal which launched in 2017. Her debut chapbook, DAUGHTER – SEED, is available from Empty Set Press.

# CHAPTER TWENTY-NINE

You see a watering hole. Reprieve from the old dusty path.

A bulldozer pushes bodies into a pit. The bodies are always the same, always this one on that one, always still alive without meaning to be. And nobody has stolen the eyes. And they're your favourite kind, turned opaque like that, swirled shades of white and no one inside. You say they're full of sea mist, because you're reborn and you can say anything you want. It's the way things are since your tongue got removed. Your mouth glued shut. You're breathing the air. You're bathing your sons. You're in the sweet spot of a massacre finessing your scruples.

It just wasn't right the way they blew up those planes, she says. In the air from the ground. Like any one idea of God was an antidote to commercial flight. Like the event itself was the onboard movie of them being blown out the sky. I remember how our lungs were full of burning air, how cold their ghosts were on the way back out. The way I see it, you're evoking the pretense of a family. You're revoking all the killers caught on cameras before their time was up.

You see two men in green uniforms standing over the pit. They are why the bodies congeal. They are scanning them one by one with pink light.

You watch the pale undersides of forearms queerly limp to their touch. You watch a pink light uncover more pink light secreted inside them. You watch tremulous carnivores chewing their lips. You pretend like Hollywood's watching back, and that nobody anywhere gets mutilated for real.

The men are foaming at the mouth, and it stays there or it falls off. You think of dogs and horses. You think of other animals without hands.

You notice a dereliction to the faces like they've been awake for a week. There's the sound of livestock in the background. A woman singing a lullaby through her neck. You hum children screaming to yourself. You clutch at the back of your head. If you could dance, you'd Tango your lovers to death, and marry them in slow motion, in extremis, in the back of a pick-up, and nobody would be any the wiser.

A body is dragged away from the pile. It's the way it happens, so young and thin and precisely gendered. As they drag her across the compound she wets herself. And as if the accident wasn't an accident, they're sniffing at her thighs. The look on their faces suggests a complex bouquet. It says: Who would have thought it, and from the piss of a girl that young.

They lay the body flat, face up, induce a fit with blue lights.

The body convulses on the ground and the men shake hands. They talk using a sequence of clicks and beeps. Their laughter is dubbed from hyenas and bird squawks. As the body vomits, a hush descends over the entire compound. The something alive in her sick has a segmented thorax and six legs. Each one moving independently of the others. It has landed on its back and can't get away. As the men approach the body becomes still.

A woman of regal bearing is swathed in dampened ermine and hemp. She watches on with her guard, and when she speaks she uses his mouth. Her voice comes out of him like a parasitic worm. His eyes bulging, his jaw locked open around her extended vowels. At 30-second intervals her mouth salivates so much it pours out

ond intervals her mouth salivates so much it pours out over her chin. The sky is cloudless and domed like a snowglobe. It somehow matches the thoughts you have about waking up in the middle of your life.

Around her neck is a string of pearlescent stones. Presented with the large insect, she summarily crushes it. Inside it is a stone the same colour and dimensions as those strung round her neck. She hands it to her guard and he cleans it with his tongue.

The two men bore holes in the girl's thighs. They each take a leg and copulate with the wounds. There is no pleasure in it, only pained concentration, only a dutiful exertion they've absented from in order to perform.

You sit with a woman in a room in a prefabricated block of similar rooms overlooking the clearing.

It's like we're here, you say.

Yes, it's happening to someone, says the woman.

We are happening to us.

These are my arms and my legs without thinking.

My body is soft all the way in. The holes will close up. Your belly will harden.

Do you see my skin moving?

I see you in a way that my hands won't pass through. I feel myself the same way.

I hear you like your voice is from somewhere.

Maybe it's not what we think it is. Maybe you can't see

it from outside.

We'll get used to it.

Or it will get used to us.

You think: I am not coming back with my tongue in a soup.

You wouldn't understand, she thinks, but does not say. You think you hear the animals scheming.

When she touches you on your arm and the skin retracts it's like so many snail eyes coming together, and you both feel sick.

There is a screwdriver snapped off inside a head. There is the hiss of the skin coming off. The bones you see belong to the young, thin girl. And nobody will think to give them back.

# GARY J. SHIPLEY

Gary J. Shipley is the author of twelve books, most recently STRATAGEM OF THE CORPSE: DYING WITH BAUDRILLARD (Anthem), 30 FAKE BEHEADINGS (Spork), WAREWOLFF! (Hexus) and THE UNYIELDING (Eraserhead). He has published in numerous magazines, journals, and anthologies. More information can be found at Thek Prosthetics.

# CHAPTER THIRTY

You see a watering hole. Reprieve from the dusty old path. You watch the puddle dry. Thousands of eggs form in its stain, hatch a swarm. Flies aggregate into human form. Scream of buzzing tongues the air. Wall of cocaine fog. Beginning and end of a war.

Inside is how the hum of the sun knows fire. Ambiguous loss. Vacant cities.

We are the wall of empty faces watching you watching the emptiness. Plate glass. Shattered sugar. Prop glass. Crystalline.

Time absolves everything of being permanent. Hallucination.

This is nothing. Nothing. Nothing comes. Nothing turns to nothing. Like air becomes a part of what you are. In nothing, and the absence of light you swallow all these spiders and their ideology.

You visit another you in their childhood. In the yard watching something faceless place a noose around your brother. A tall ladder.

NOTHING IS A CLEAR DARK THING

The night the cops followed us home and we hid behind the garage. The clarity of weeds my parents found me in when I was two and picturing the blood pored through eyes of Christ.

*Aim for the shape in the middle and miss.*

You wake. From the dream of emergency. From complicity. The beacon disappears.

# You are the broken law.

Remember what's been pulled away. All the lapsed insurance. Of family trees. Of time
cleanoffacescleanoffacescleanoffacescleanoffacescleanoffacescleanoffacescleanoffacescleanoffacescleanoffacescleanoffacescleanoffacescleanoffacescleanoffacescleanoffacescleanoffacesclean
well spent. Of fish to catch. Of what's killing the fish that float along the boat when you
cleanoffacescleanoffacescleanoffacescleanoffacescleanoffacescleanoffacescleanoffacescleanoffacescleanoffacescleanoffacescleanoffacescleanoffacescleanoffacescleanoffacescleanoffacesclean
reach the lake. Time bends in water. A cloud is killing inside the lake. The sound of
cleanoffacescleanoffacescleanoffacescleanoffacescleanoffacescleanoffacescleanoffacescleanoffacescleanoffacescleanoffacescleanoffacescleanoffacescleanoffacescleanoffacescleanoffacesclean
bone on bone. You should burn the lake. You should burn its rim.
cleanoffacescleanoffacescleanoffacescleanoffacescleanoffacescleanoffacescleanoffacescleanoffacescleanoffacescleanoffacescleanoffacescleanoffacescleanoffacescleanoffacescleanoffacesclean
Clean of faces:

# You should burn the days

A child of the soil or someone like who you were is banging a drum. A child of the creek. Child of the pond. Child of the skull pile. The crossing. The answer a fiddle gives itself.

: snapped strings are hatching here :

You remember the house. It was your house. When men enter the house the faceless shape eats its way through them.

You remember the boat. You are the boat. You remember its side. You are its sides. You remember your hands. You are your hands. You have arms. You are your arms. Remember the sky.

How long have you have spent in this tunnel in this thought of maybe?

Tunnels under you are lifting you.

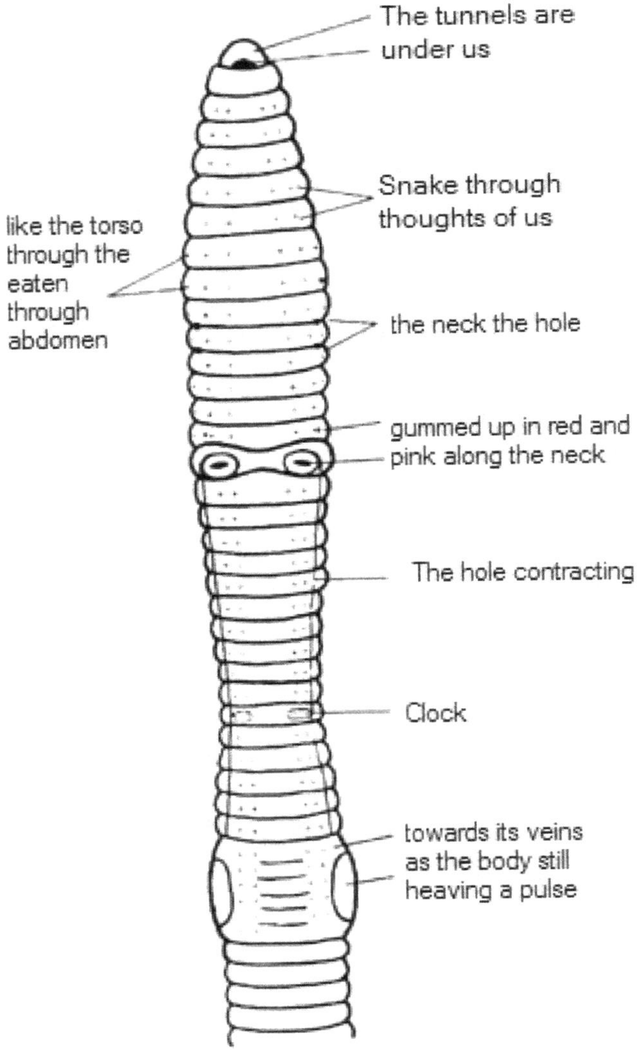
The tunnels are
under us
Snake through
thoughts of us
like the torso
through the
eaten
through
abdomen
the neck the hole
gummed up in red and
pink along the neck
The hole contracting
Clock
towards its veins
as the body still
heaving a pulse

Walking between waking and the tightness of a fist you open. Wipe away an hour with in the dark with arrows. The astronomy complex softens. Squeezing a heart until it expands to cover consciousness.

Once you dream the worms, they can move throughout your body -- your eyes, your tissues and most commonly your brain, leaving doctors puzzled in their wake as they migrate and settle to feed on the body they've invaded. Very few things move in the brain but it had moved from one side of the brain to the other dragging the dream through its tunnel. Four years ago we first experienced the dreams as headaches, a glow absorbing light from the horizon. When we reappeared we had new symptoms, a new part of the brain pushing through bone. Seizures and weakness of legs, the abdomen spreads.

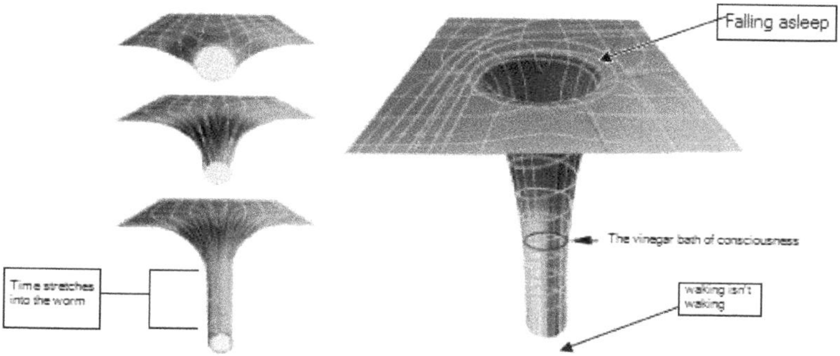


There is no known drug to effectively treat the dream without feeding the worms. You are in the end of a complicated life cycle, accidently drinking waters of an infected dream. Encysture of the fields, the spread of blind heat pervaded the family. The spread of targets, the dream approaches a door in the distance.

Your house in the distance. You see from the path through its windows its walls covered in math. Your body halts. Your eyes pull back beyond your body and see the stones rolling into place. Silence mouthing an ancient jewel. Reluctance is the texture of time. Time is skin that hides you from yourself. You drip back into embodiment. Pinch the fat of your wrist to stay in motion.

Once you were driving toward the worm. Everyone had knives. The car fell apart. All the bodies split in halves. The worm came closer. The heat of the bodies a beacon.

Before you left yourself behind you lived on this mountain. Spoke to vast awareness with a kite and feathers. Found new ways of seeing face down in fields. Everything remembered but jimson in the space between thumb and pointer. When you make them touch a grain of salt falls out of ambience.

Disintegration is a loud echo you are chasing off the end of the path. Strangers point to the house. The air is fluorescent grey. You are walking toward the cure.

*What's at work in you*
*A hand to torch*
*Time*
*You slow dissolve*

*How long have I been talking out loud?*

You were quiet today when you saw yourself dissolved through a slip of time you spent in a chair. You were quiet in the dark when you told yourself that your name is the key to your body. We are quiet when we tell our best lies. You've never had anything you didn't destroy. One long stain running to your home. You were quiet in the woods on your birthday when you removed the masks. You are quiet as you open the door.

THINGSMELLSLIKECOCAINETHEBOOKISONATABLEBYTHEDOOR
PATHTOTHEHOUSETHESKYSMELLSLIKECOCAINEINSIDETHEHOUSEEV
NGSMELLSLIKECOCAINETHEBOOKISONATABLEBYTHEDOORONTTHEP
HEHOUSETHESKYSMELLSLIKECOCAINEINSIDETHEHOUSEEVERYTH
LLSLIKECOCAINETHEBOOKISONATABLEBYTHEDOORONTTHEPATHTO
SETHESKYSMELLSLIKECOCAINEINSIDETHEHOUSEEVERYTHINGSMELLSI
AINETHEBOOKISONATABLEBYTHEDOORONTTHEPATHTOTHEHOUSETHE
LLSLIKECOCAINEINSIDETHEHOUSEEVERYTHINGSMELLSLIKECOCAINE
KISONATABLEBYTHEDOORONTTHEPATHTOTHEHOUSETHESKYSMELLSI
AINEINSIDETHEHOUSEEVERYTHINGSMELLSLIKECOCAINETHEBOOKISO
EBYTHEDOORONTTHEPATHTOTHEHOUSETHESKYSMELLSLIKECOCAIN
THEHOUSEEVERYTHINGSMELLSLIKECOCAINETHEBOOKISONATABLEBY
RONTTHEPATHTOTHEHOUSETHESKYSMELLSLIKECOCAINEINSIDETHEH
ERYTHINGSMELLSLIKECOCAINETHEBOOKISONATABLEBYTHEDOORC
PATHTOTHEHOUSETHESKYSMELLSLIKECOCAINEINSIDETHEHOUSEEV
IGSMELLSLIKECOCAINETHEBOOKISONATABLEBYTHEDOORONTTHEPA
HEHOUSETHESKYSMELLSLIKECOCAINEINSIDETHEHOUSEEVERYTHI

LLSLI ITOT
SETHI LLSL
AINET SETI
MELLS AINI
OKISC SME
COCA EBO
ATAE LIKE
EINS ISON
BYTH AIN
THEH EBYT
RONT HEH
ERYT ORO
PATH EEVE
GSMI HEPA
HEHC THI
LSLII ITOT
SETHI LLSL
AINET THES
LSLII INET

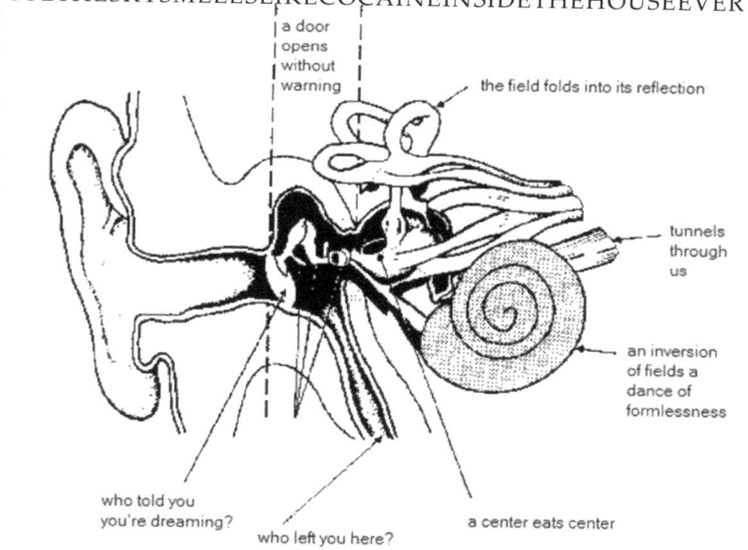
a door opens without warning
the field folds into its reflection
tunnels through us
an inversion of fields a dance of formlessness
who told you you're dreaming?
who left you here?
a center eats center

ISON LLSLI
INEINSIDETHEHOUSEEVERYTHINGSMELLSLIKECOCAINETHEBOOKISON
BYTHEDOORONTTHEPATHTOTHEHOUSETHESKYSMELLSLIKECOCAINE
HEHOUSEEVERYTHINGSMELLSLIKECOCAINETHEBOOKISONATABLEBYT
RONTTHEPATHTOTHEHOUSETHESKYSMELLSLIKECOCAINEINSIDETHEH
ERYTHINGSMELLSLIKECOCAINETHEBOOKISONATABLEBYTHEDOORO
ATHTOTHEHOUSETHESKYSMELLSLIKECOCAINEINSIDETHEHOUSEEVE
GSMELLSLIKECOCAINETHEBOOKISONATABLEBYTHEDOORONTTHEPA
EHOUSETHESKYSMELLSLIKECOCAINEINSIDETHEHOUSEEVERYTHI
LSLIKECOCAINETHEBOOKISONATABLEBYTHEDOORONTTHEPATHTOT
ETHESKYSMELLSLIKECOCAINEINSIDETHEHOUSEEVERYTHINGSMELLSLI
INETHEBOOKISONATABLEBYTHEDOORONTTHEPATHTOTHEHOUSETH
ELLSLIKECOCAINEINSIDETHEHOUSEEVERYTHINGSMELLSLIKECOCAINE
KISONATABLEBYTHEDOORONTTHEPATHTOTHEHOUSETHESKYSMEL
OCAINEINSIDETHEHOUSEEVERYTHINGSMELLSLIKECOCAINETHEBO
ATABLEBYTHEDOORONTTHEPATHTOTHEHOUSETHESKYSMELLSLIKE
EINSIDETHEHOUSEEVERYTHI

This is the book of the book of the feathered tongue   you think   opening the book you come to   you become the words.

*A castle on fire is on fire and the fields between us and the castle and the castle and the horizon are on fire and a fire is on fire with a new kind of fire a sentient fire of bodies licking like flame or everything we picture here is from another story like every other description of an inferno is from another inferno and every book is of another book and every day is the day of another fire and we meet each other in this place where something is out to get while the getting is good.*

*I'm praying on a book that is on fire and my hands are on fire and then my head and I go out looking for you in the field but you run out into the body of another field inside another tunnel and the dew damp slick grass of this field is the ooze of a body's interior rotting like a too long wet book of names or money buried in the tunneled yard. A length of time is measure in how long it takes another body's segments to accordion together into now.*

*The ridiculousness of remembering who you were before now is lost in the fires between then and now. The time it takes to think this is something that collapses an inconceivable distance from here. The lives of clouds waiting to wet fire in ejaculate.*

*No one appears here to explain the field. The field doesn't speak or if it does it does so through an inversion of its surface. The tunnels beneath us lift us out of thinking about an explanation which is not the same as tiring of wondering how long we've been wondering as the light crests the field.*

*The field is the roof of a mouth and then a tongue and then an eye and then teeth biting through all of these as the deer nose through wildflowered scrub and all of this loses its color in the frames between our frames of consciousness and the reel slows then speeds as I move from one face of the field to the other.*

*The field is eaten through until we think we're wide awake, until each of thinks we're the last living thing. The field mutates in each appearance often populated with deer. The field tunnels through itself into another field and another body falls into its face blown out and pale. The deer fuck the body.*

*We are in the backyard of the house we grew up in where we threw hammers at moving cars from the attic window and burst aerosol cans on the stone wall across the street. We are in the field in the stomach of the worm turning in on itself inside of us. We are always hungry and thinking about fucking and the field is always turning.*

*Between the field and the body and a cube and the field is the fog of worm its murmurations an alphabet used to write the story of how I came to know the worms the grey air of grey day passing through my ears and out bloodless and starred a pyramid of light within my forehead as we speak in the car we leave the bridge in driving past a place that used to be a town like the one at the pyramid's base where all the ghosts live selling their skins to the worms to ward off the faceless and wonder and starve and starve the thought from you who thinks better than belief and belief in keyless entry or the taste of another's flesh.*

*The cube is room glowing in the distance. When you reach it climb inside. In the quiet of this space you are three small lights. Flashing. I was quiet when I saw these and I was quiet when I said your name. After a long time you will become math and this will scare worms.*

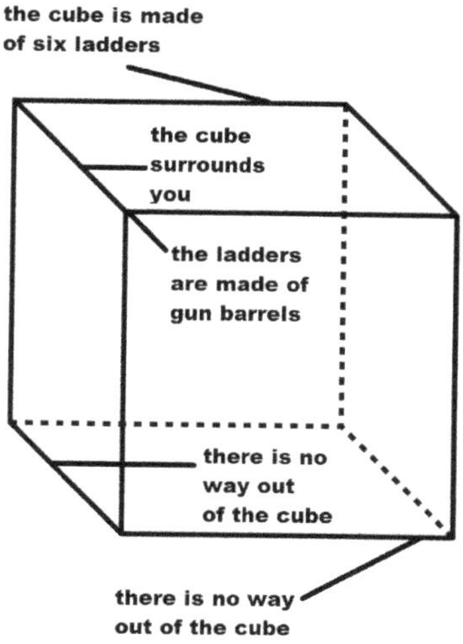

the cube is made of six ladders
the cube surrounds you
the ladders are made of gun barrels
there is no way out of the cube
there is no way out of the cube

*Everything was soft and glowing*
*the cube was floating*
*in the center of the room*
*they watched me*
*stumbling*
*shaking invisible objects*
*screaming*

You follow a rat's tail off the pages and into the boatyard past the burn barrels and scrap piles to the rotten body hidden. Round of matted thrush at river's edge blown out and bluing. A trunk of buzzing meat. Puckered boil on the field's hairline loosens water back into its eyes. All the impure fluids fucked free by your tongue snagged on a flicker of memory.

the wood fucks

the wind fucks

the worm fucks

the pale field the visible woods the pale green the pale white the pale sky and in the pale night

thedeerfeedonthoughtsoffuckIngthedeerf
eedonthoughtsoffuckIngthedeerfeedontho
ughtsoffuckingthedeerfeedonthoughtsoff
uckIngthdeerfedon thoughtsoffuckingthe
deerfeedonthought soffuckingthedeerfee
donthoughtsoffuckIngthedeerfeedonthou
ghtsoffuckIngthedeerfeedonthoughtsof fu
ckIngthedeerfeedonthoughtsoffuckIngthe
deerfeedonthoughtsoffuckIngthedeerfeed
onthoughtsoffuckIngthedeerfeedonthoug
htoffuckIngthedeerfeedonthoughtsoffuck
Ingthedeerfeedonthoughtsoffuckingthed
eerfeedonthoughtsoffuckIngthedeerfeedo
nthough tsoffuckIngthedee rfeedo thou
g htsoff uck In gthede erfeedon y

# ADAM TEDESCO

Born in Upstate New York, Poet and video artist Adam Tedesco is a founding editor of REALITY BEACH, an independent chapbook press, journal of new poetics, and roving reading series. His video poems and site-specific work have been shown at MoMA PS1, &Now: A Festival of Innovative Writing, No Nation Gallery, and the New Hampshire Poetry Festival, among other venues. He has written long-running columns for a number of publications on the topics of drugs and dream analysis. His poetry and essays, have appeared or are forthcoming in Fanzine, Fence, Gramma, jubilat, Conduit, Laurel Review, Powderkeg, Prelude, and elsewhere. He is the author of several chapbooks, most recently ABLAZA (Lithic Press, 2017), ISO 8601:2004 (Really Serious Literature, 2018), and MISRULE (Ursus Americanus, 2019). His first full-length poetry collection, MARY OLIVER, was published by Lithic Press in February of 2019.

# CHAPTER THIRTY-ONE

u see a watering hole. reprieve from the old dusty path.

e

/error

/system.reset

/error ii

/hard.reset

e x e
m o i
d e d
g a g

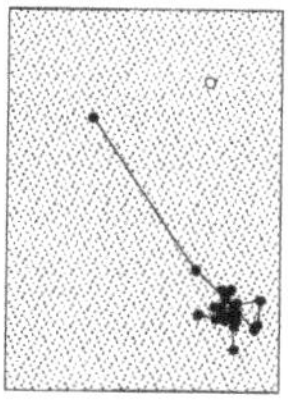

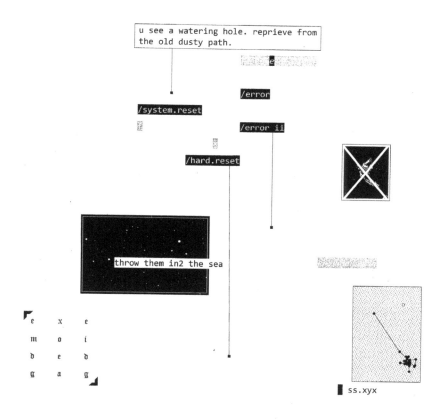

ss.xyx

```
           *    +    +       +         +    +
+    x    +          .    +    @    +    +    }
[         +.   @    +.             ~    +
     %    .          ~.       %    +
+    +    +    %.            /         ]    +
          +    /    +    ]    +
```

```
system-----------11,789--------(12k)
comm&------------2,001---------(2k)
bmt_fix-----------5,088---------(5k)
arft_mntn-----------988---------(1k)
```

▌ *startup complete . . .*

```
▌ c:\narcst_iii.sys
```

▌ *u reach the galapagos;*

▌ *the men had 2 fly straight in2 the mouf of a psychic'd blank darq wūrmhole 2 find u*

▌ *not all of them made it*

▌ *the skye is melting, again*

the wetware fails

an experimental van

the occult detective is dead (face down)

barefoot magicks

dreams of mist-kiss'd cavves [undamag'd]

a[n] unremarkable sort of violence

~~ . ~ ~~~ . ~

@ the lago border, where it is impossible 2 truly ever comprehend what is happening

humans, acting like dogs

imperfect palm trees, swaying in the wind

homogenized landscapes

derelict boats

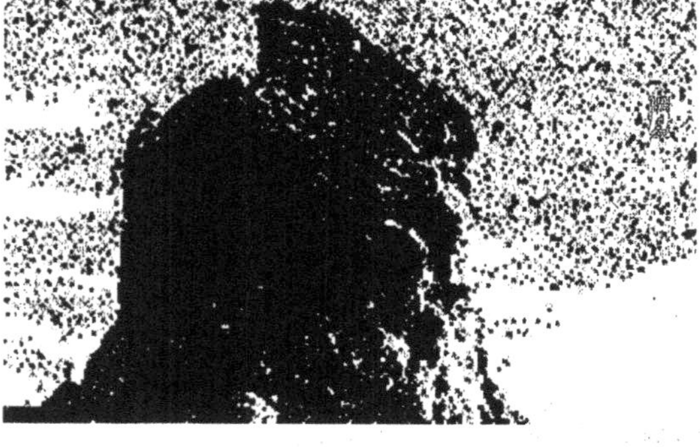

muscle men, flexing on a beach

apparent-women, unhooking themselves from tree of disasters™

humanoids acting distract'd; some1 is pumping new age in2 the air

a metal dome, snuffing out the oxblöd'd skye

a private beach, fund'd by white nationalists

quarter-dozen cyborg guards near blöd palace

torpedoes floating & ab&on'd yachts on / around / near the scorch'd-urth lakeshore

blöd aeroplanes, circling a[n] crypt

observing the eternal'd purple abyss

| |
|---|
| blaq ocean vii |
| lake kwaku |
| blöd palace |
| fiji crater |
| lago border (v.8.09b) |
| darq continent |
| arafat mountain |
| goblin haus |
| crystal cavves |
| known space |

# the fjordist

(n) the baqdrop 2 all this is a dense jungle & on the outskirts, immediate-like, a desert w/ s& so red ud swear there's clay & silt in there. he'll shoot films here—science fiction, when there's a need 2 pretend ur on another planet. snakes & insects uve never seen exist in this dense foliage. aeroplane residue & crash'd helicopters (engulf'd) have now become part of this jungle of greens. certain men live w/in. entire populations, still undiscover'd, living off "the 1&" in these parts. the rubber tree still makes money & deep beneath the ground, ull find no oil. all that was there is either dri'd up & gone or severely exploit'd.

a sound; the uncomfortable stink

the torgen fields, the last remaining safe haven

the eternal compound of keepers who have not yet fled

the men, breaking bones 2 save a fail'd 4tress

grotto goblins

considering the existenz of shrimp isl&

clautsrophobe'd cavves

synthetic skye-scrapers

oppulent castles on well-manicur'd lawns

nightclub! asunder > > > .

a laby'rinth, complete w/ minotaur!

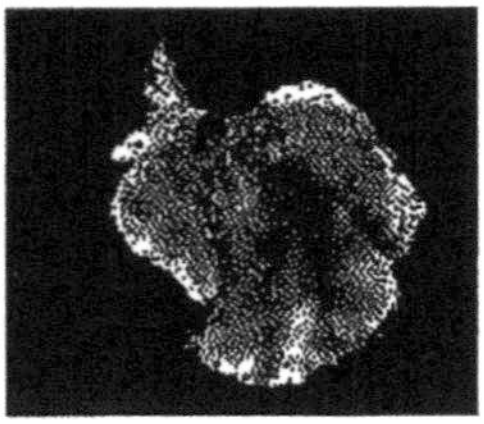

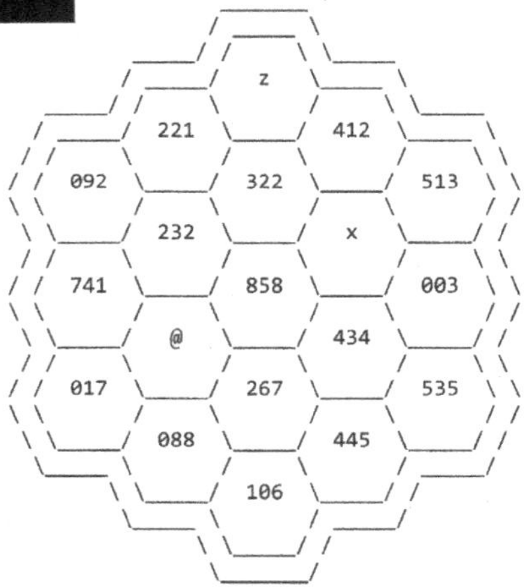

z
221
412
092
322
513
232
x
741
858
003
@
434
017
267
535
088
445
106


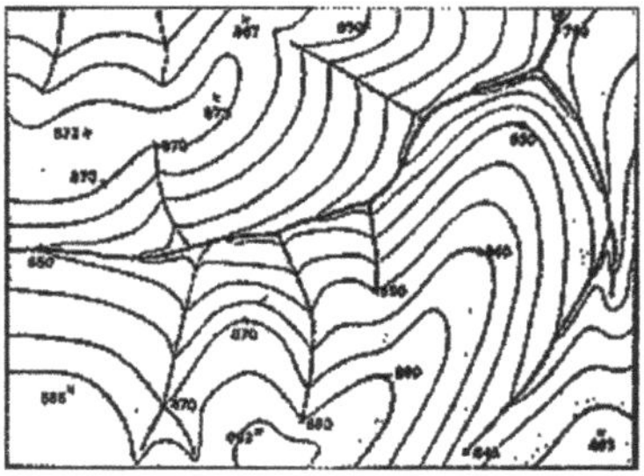

ppl in trees, waiting, silent, w/ mūchetes

these r the true architects of known meatspace

@23h18, rituals 4 esoteric damp’ning

cars on fire; the metal, dripping down in2 the water table

gang initiation

the great colonizer / also the great collider

robb’ing the pleasure dome

cannibals, entering the secret garden

colour of absolute void

4gotten acids, bubbling up 2 the surface; a(n) cracked spherical object

hanoi mountain range; or what looks 2 b the hanoi mountain range

t t t  t tt tt t t ttt t
t t t t t  t tt tt t t ttt t
t

t t t  t tt tt t t ttt t
t   t   t

t t t  t tt tt t t ttt t
t

t t t  t tt tt t t ttt t
t t

root@basedx10

os:       QRX.t

kernel:   amd128 QRX.t 50.2c

uptime:   11h 42m 19s

packages: 22

v.0.9.7b (2666-07-11) [DOS]

t t t  t tt tt t t ttt t
t t t  t tt tt t t ttt t
t t                        t t t  t tt tt t t ttt t
                           t t
t t t  t tt tt t t ttt t
t t

t t   t  t      t tt t
t ttt t t t  t t t    t
t t t  t    t tt t t ttt
t t t  t t t t

pushing a half-human in2 the slipway

a castrat'd vigilante who is also immortal

a pterodactyl swooping in, from the skye-ceiling

helicopters made of glass & space shuttles from urth, crashing in2 1 another, outside the *4 walls*

a hypacreean priest, released from a thous&-year darqness

pre-reset rap musicks

u analyse the vaste blankness of the sea

amputat'd-at-the-fin dolphyns ocean-cook'd in fluorescent seaweeds

the stones, who know nothing

lake kwaku, still burning

suicide by jagjaguwar

```
/load_burning_sun_008.bat
```

```
/real_world_physyx.sysx
```

```
/load_blimpp_crash.exploit
```

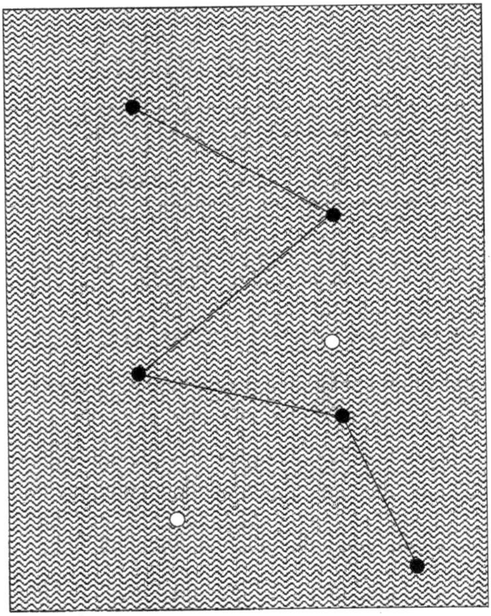

a robot from sector 19, sent 2 analyze & assess the situation

clouds displac'd, from 4eign currents, eating up & swallowing whole, infant tornadoes

smudged aesthetics

press < enter > 2 continue . . .

a single drone, hi above, near the suicide-rip of a[n] blaqn'd skye-screen, disinfects clouds using arterial spray & a sponge-like mechanism

in the land of sufrajettes

mounds of dirt & rot, 2 4m an aerial geodesic-pattern'd-like design

a single hellfire missile costs $100,000

godzilla succumbs

u point 2 extinct animals (w/ ur bad h&)

u drink the potion, & pay attention 2 the position of the sun

purple lighting; a moses simwala replica appears

zerubab'bel

netscape'd worlds, invading dreams

all that's left, following pock-mark'd memories of what really happen'd; sudden kinetic trauma altering the metal cardioid of blöd, 4ever

@night, sometimes, the stars unmask themselves, 2 reveal the true hi-definition look of nature

urth magnets so hot, u can see the waives of bend'd light

34.9285° s x 138.6007° e

dracula never die'd

u flick some sweat in2 the obscurity,
& pray it is enough

chems oozing down from space & in2
the synaptic geography of the planet

local abyss: full of rott'd bodies

monsters on motorcycles, riding off
in2 a(n) pink'd sunset

the roar of the mercedes om617 3.0l
turbo diesel motor

textures, loading

spirit devour'd

^   ^ ^  ^    ^^^^  ^ ^  ^^
^ ^ ^     ^ ^ ^ ^        ^
^ ^    .   ^ ^^ ^    ^

^   ^ ^   ^    ^^^^^^^   ^ ^
^^   ^   ^   ^        ^  ^  ^
^^^^^^^^^^^^^^^^^       ^
^ ^    .    ^ ^^ ^    ^

^^^^^^^^^^^^^^^^^^^^^^
^   ^ ^     ^^^^^.   ^^^^  ^
^     ^^^^^^      ^^^^^^^
^^^^^^^^^^^^^^^^^^^
^   ^ ^     ^^^^^,    ^ ^
^^ ^  ^  ^    ^  ^  ^ ^^^^^^
^^^^^^^^^^^^^        ^  ^
^     ^^^^^     ^ ^^ ^

pink_ocean.bat

/system.reset

r

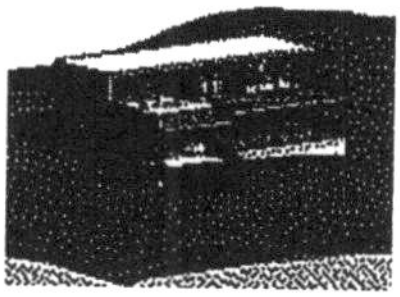

% ^^ * $ _ ___ _.g --

*metal tin, overflowing w/ ppl*

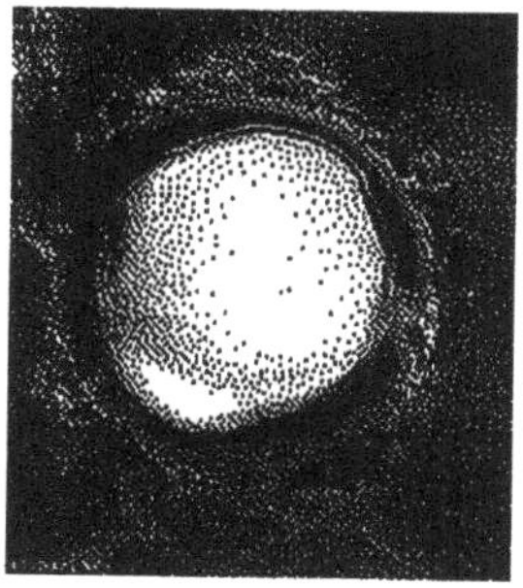

o o o ^ ^ # ) )

+

/crater.xx

/hard.reset

u locate the shotgunne, & when ur bruis'd finger brushes against the cold+soft blue metal, there's a hi-pitch'd pierce'd squ'wheel & all the birds+vultures outside make end-of-the-urth sounnds

this time, a glass skye but w/out clouds

the air, smelling like straight-up moon

wells of urth juice

a quasi-woman, playing the farfisa organ in2 the late evenings; every1 indulging the drone

humans literally tumbling down the sides of tall buildings

i'll show u the light now. it burns… 4-ever

this is the place of the corpse machine™ [1 of them]

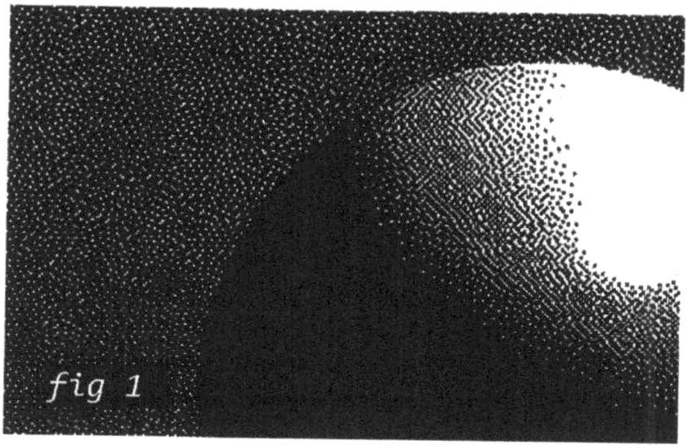
fig 1

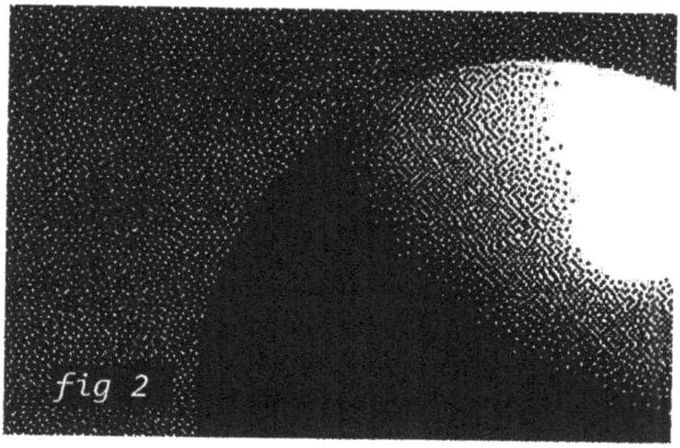
fig 2

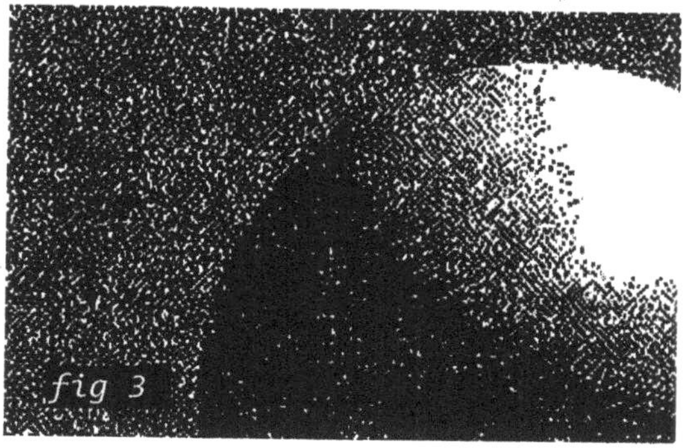
fig 3

the bmw of beach_babi, found @ the bottom of prawn lake

*a thing*, gliding thru the jetways of a(n) shatter'd skye

ppl, @ the fiji crater

the maggots of deh'n'yyii'l

pool of blöd, evaporating in2 the ether

the nyc[x] location, conscrib'd2 die!

opening the door 2 the swamp

alluvial dampers, 2 muffle the sounnd of harsh'd screams

mood cube hovers, over the offal

it's the fields of wrath, & some1 is throwing the bodies of dogs in2 palumbo lake

```
-----x------x-----------xc---------
-------0---------b-----------;----
----X-----f-yy.0------------------
---------------------8----.-------
----\.\\}------..----^----------█---
-------------------------4---------
-------QRX.t------..----------3/32--
p.pp.pp... ----------------------------
---------------------^^-----------
---------------------------------
4---------------pfq.t------..------
----3/32---------------------------
--------------.--------░---@--^-----
----------------------.------------
---------4---------------53v------
..----------3./-----------▯---------
-----~-~-~---------------------------
------~~~--------3/32--------------
------~~--~------------------▲------
---------~-----f--------.-----------
------cwc---------------.--.---2---
-----------,----------------------
```

the lago border / a schema .

/ / / / / / / / / /

future men, appearing (& then dis-appearing)

memories of grain'd-out shadow souls

merzbow concert, at platypūs lake

the hunchbaq, permanently disfigur'd

walls of jericho, limit'd

a pyramid made of different sorts of meat

the stink of blöd & shit & blöd &
blöd & blöd & blöd & blöd & blöd &
blöd & blöd & blllöd& bllöd & blöd &
blöd& bbbblöd & blödd & blöd&& &&
blöd & blöd & blöd && ..& && blöd &
blöd & blöd. …>& bbbblöd & blöd &
blöd.. bbbbbbbllblöd llll ll lll l
lll b bbbb bb o oooo o . . .. . .

```
█ error.iii

█ system.reset

█ error.iv

█ hard.reset

system-----------33,049--------(33K)
comm&------------11,011--------(11K)
bmt_fix-----------1,001--------(1K)
knly_stbrk----------200--------(1K)

startup files complete

c:\ghetto_ville.sys

█ load_brok3nskye.bat

tachyon_pulsar_needs_a_reboot_2.bat

█ negative_void.osyx

config.sys

█ disk_load_fail_0 . . . execute.bat
```

[redacted]

[redacted] [redacted]

[redacted]

[redacted]

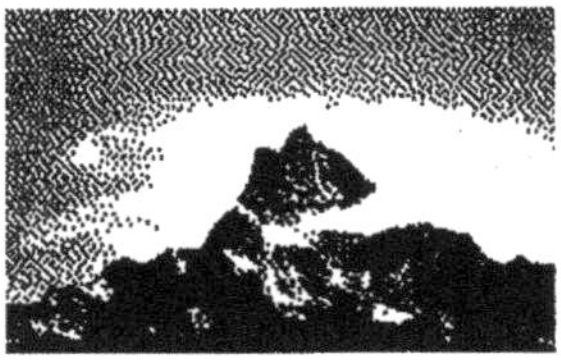

g he*tt ovi*lle.

[redacted] [redacted] [redacted]

[redacted] [redacted]

[redacted]

[redacted] [redacted] [redacted] [redacted]

# MIKE KLEINE

Mike Kleine is a writer. He is the author of *Kanley Stubrick*, *Lonely Men Club*, *Mastadon Farm*, and *Arafat Mountain*.

# CHAPTER THIRTY-TWO

You see a watering hole. Reprieve from the old dusty path."

This article **needs additional citations for verification**. Please help improve this article by adding citations to reliable sources. Unsourced material may be challenged and removed.
*Find sources:* "Path" computing – news · newspapers · books · scholar · JSTOR *(July 2008) (Learn how and when to remove this template message)*

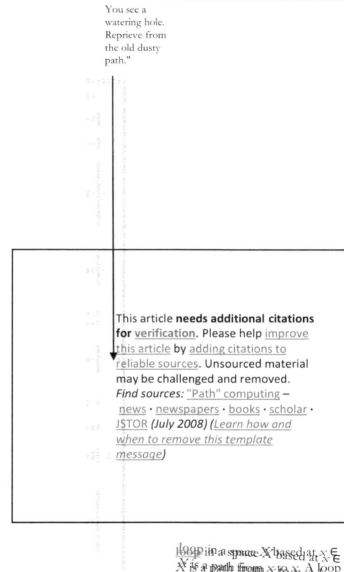

loop in a space $X$ based at $x \in X$ is a path from $x$ to $x$. A loop may be **equally well** regarded as a map $f: I \to X$ with $f(0) = f(1)$ or as a continuous map from the unit circle $S^1$ to $X$

$$f: S^1 \to X.$$

ADING

es and methods of reading, with differing rates that can be attained for each, for different kinds of materia

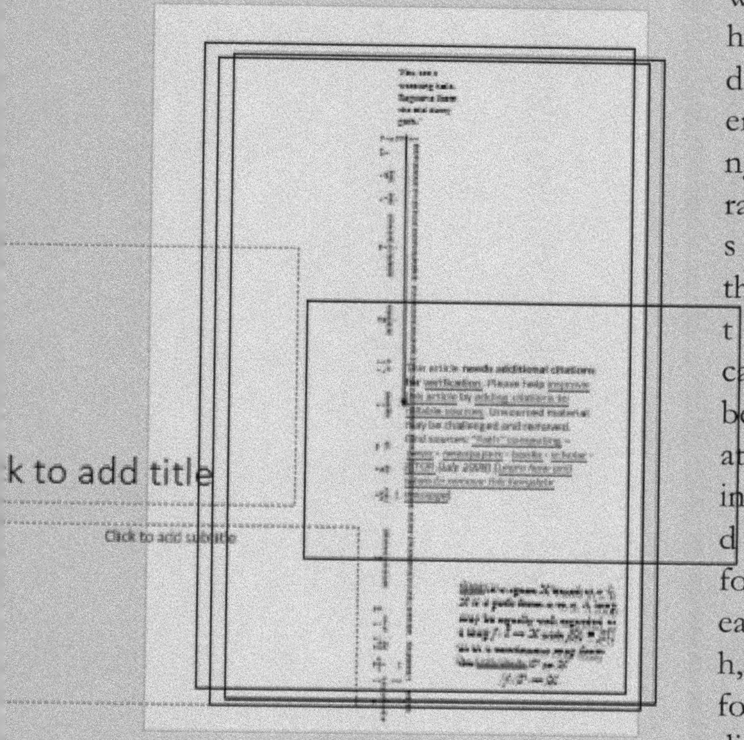

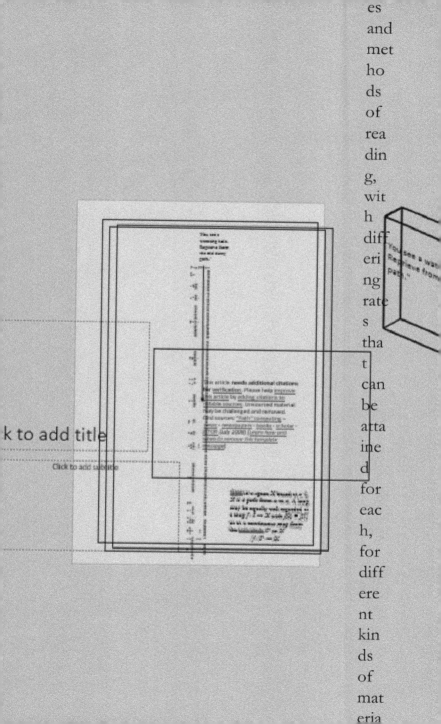

ead chan
an electrical c
that transform
the physical
magnetic flux
changes into
bstract bits. A
ead error occ
vhen the phys
art of the
rocess fails fo
ome reason, su
dust or dirt.

Many take notes while reading.

- *Structure-proposition-evaluation* (SPE) method, popularized by Mortim... in *How to Read a Book*, mainly for non-fiction treatise, in which one ... writing in three passes: (1) for the structure of the work, which mi... represented by an outline; (2) for the logical propositions made, o... into chains of inference; and (3) for evaluation of the merits of th... arguments and conclusions. This method involves suspended judg... the work or its arguments until they are fully understood.
- *Survey-question-read-recite-review* (SQ3R) method, often taught in pub... schools, which involves reading toward being able to teach what is ... is appropriate for instructors preparing to teach material without r... notes.
- Multiple intelligences-based methods, which draw ... of thinking and knowing to enrich appreciation ... fundamentally a linguistic activity: one can basic... without resorting to other intelligences, such as ... "seeing" characters or events described), auditory ... mentally "hearing" sounds described), or even ... considering "what if" scenarios or predicting how ... on context clues). However, most readers already ... intelligence while reading. Doing so in a more di... constantly, or after every paragraph—can result ... experience.[citation needed]

- Rapid serial visual presentation (RSVP) reading inv... in a sentence one word at a time at the same loca... at a specified eccentricity. RSVP eliminates inter... word saccades, and prevents reader control of fi... Mansfield, & Chung, 2001). RSVP controls for differences in rea... movement, and consequently is often used to measure reading spe... experiments.

Reading process is therefore a communication context.

There are several types and methods of reading, with differing rate can be attained for each, for different kinds of material and purpos

- *Subvocalized* reading combines sight reading with internal sounding words as if spoken. Advocates of speed reading claim it can be a b habit that slows reading and comprehension, but other studies indi reverse, particularly with difficult texts.
- *Speed reading* is a collection of methods for increasing reading spee without an unacceptable reduction in comprehension or retention. Methods include skimming or the of words in a body of increase the rate of reading. It is closely connected to
- is a software-assisted reading method designed f . "Incremental reading" means "reading in part in each session, parts of several electronic articles are read inside a prioritized reading list. In the course of reading, important pieces information are extracted and converted into , which are reviewed by a algorithm.
- is a kind of reading for the purpose of detecting errors. One can learn to do it rapidly, and profession proofreaders typically acquire the ability to do so at high rates, fast some kinds of material than for others, while they may largely sus comprehension while doing so, except when needed to select amo several possible words that a suspected typographic error allows. A proofreader needs to have a strong vocabulary and should be meti in their approach.
- *Rereading* is reading a book more than once. "One cannot read a b one can only reread it," Vladimir Nab once said. A paper published in the *Journal of Consumer Research* (Cristel Antonia (2012 re-reading offers mental health benefits because it allows for a mo profound emotional connection and self-reflectio

SharedFolder". Instead, the SharedFolder
me consists of an arbitrary name assign
the folder when defining its "sharing".
me Microsoft Windows interfaces also
cept the "Long UNC":
NC\ComputerName\SharedFolder\Resource
crosoft Windows uses the following types
paths:
cal file system (LFS), such as C:\File
niversal naming convention (UNC), such
ver\Volume\File or /<internet resource name>[\Directory name]
ong" device path such as \\?\C:\File or
NC\Server\Volume\File [6] This path points to the lo
namespace and \\.\
/ to \ and interpreting names
indows NT object manager \\??\ prefixed path
versions of Windows prior to Windows X
y the APIs that accept "long" device path
uld accept more than 260 characters.
e shell in Windows XP and Windows Vista
plorer.exe, allows path names up to 248
aracters long.[citation needed]
ce UNCs start with two backslashes, an
backslash is also used for string escapi
d in regular expressions, this can result i

hierarch
the pare
one dot
represe
current
itself. B
compon
complex
(e.g.,
"../mark
, where
as the
compon
relative
represen
[8]
working
(using
to a pre
current
directory
sometim
distingui
resource
found in
directory

./bobapples

or for short:

bobapples

and the absolute path for the directory a

/users/mark/bobapples

Given *bobapples* as the relative path for directory wanted, the following may be t at the command prompt to change the current working directory to bobapples:

cd bobapples

Two dots ("..") point upwards in the hiera to indicate the parent directory; one dot represents the current directory itself. B can be components of a complex relativ path (e.g., "../mark/./bobapples"), where alone or as the first component of such relative path represents the working dir (Using "./foo" to refer to a file "foo" in th current working directory can sometime usefully distinguish it from a resource "f be found in a default directory or by oth means; for example, to view a specific version of a manual page instead of the one installed in the system.)

(e.g., "../mark/./bobapples") where "." alone or as the first component of such a relative path represents the working directory. (Using "./foo" to refer to a file "foo" in the current working directory can sometimes usefully distinguish it from a resource "foo" to be found in a default directory or by other means; for example, to view a specific version of a manual page instead of the one installed in the system.)

- Filesystem formats
- File signatures
- Magic number
- Sparse file
- Swap file
- System file
- Filename
- 8.3 filename
- Long filename
- Filename mangling
- Filename extension
- List of filename extensions
- File attribute
- Extended file attributes
- File size
- Hidden file / Hidden directory
- Directory/folder
- NTFS links
- Temporary folder
- Directory structure
- File sequence

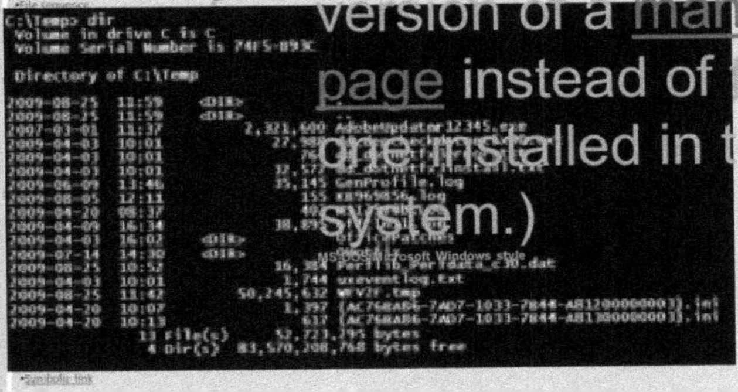
C:\Temp> dir
Volume in drive C is C
Volume Serial Number is 74F5-893C
Directory of C:\Temp
13 File(s) 52,723,295 bytes
4 Dir(s) 83,570,208,768 bytes free

MS-DOS/Microsoft Windows style

- Symbolic link

If one considers a loop based at a po[illegible]
then path composition is a binary operatio[illegible]
Path composition, whenever defined, is n[illegible]
associative due to the difference in param[illegible]
However it is associative up to path-homo[illegible]
[(fg)h] = [f(gh)]. Path composition defin[illegible]
group structure on the set of homotopy cl[illegible]
loops based at a point $x_0$ in X. The resultin[illegible]
called the fundamental group of X base[illegible]
usually denoted $\pi_1(X,x_0)$.

situations calling for associativity of pat[illegible] [This legal file uses ... containing slashes as directory separator. The command redirects the content of the file to the ... more]
composition on the nose, a path in X [illegible]
defined as a continuous map from an i[illegible]
[a] to X for any real a ≥ 0. A path f of this
length |f| defined as a. Path composition
defined as before with the following modifi[illegible] [... 07BE-0... Directory of ... SubFolder ... AM <DIR> DOMAIN\user .. 18 ... 2008 08:15 ... IN\user .. 18 October 2008 08:15 ... DOMAIN\user ... bytes free ... path ...]

whereas with the previous definition f, g[illegible]
have length 1 (the length of the domain of[illegible]
map), this definition makes |fg| = |f| + |g|. W[illegible]
made associativity fail for the previous defi[illegible]
that although (fg)h and f(gh) have the sam[illegible]
namely 1, the midpoint of (fg)h occurred be[illegible]
and h, whereas the midpoint of f(gh) occur[illegible]
between f and g. With this modified definiti[illegible]

[illegible] is locally Euclidean [illegible] and [illegible]

[illegible] R [illegible]

[illegible] on the [illegible]

[illegible] systems of [illegible]

[illegible] many of the [illegible] aspects of [illegible]

[illegible] topological space. It has important [illegible] to the [illegible] matics.

[illegible] Such spaces are called [illegible]

[illegible] examples to [illegible] about topological spaces [illegible] open sets [illegible] set and the sets [illegible] in the set.

[illegible] a set is defined [illegible] if [illegible] either [illegible]

[illegible] When [illegible] this topology [illegible] counterexample [illegible]

poses of the
elf (often
ny other

secondary ...
213–229.

- ... Windows Commands : Window...
- ... 2019.
- "Sorting it all Out ..."
- "DavGetHTTPFromUNC..." ... Docs. series. Retrieved 14 July 2019.
- "File path formats on Windows ..." ... Docs. Retrieved 14 July 2019.
- "Naming Files, Paths, and N..."
- "winapi - Is there a differen..."
- "Path prefixes \??\ and \..."
- UNC Definition by C...
- POSIX pathname r...
- POSIX pathname...

1. "Naming Files, P..." Microsoft Docs. R...

External links

- The Lin...

- Naming Fil... Microsoft D...
- Comp...

Navigation menu

- Tal...

- Español
- Français
- 한국어
- Italiano
- Português
- Русский
- 中文
- Edit lin...

- Printable version
- Cite this page
- Wikidata item
- Page information
- Permanent link
- Special pages
- Upload file
- Related changes
- Conta...

- This ...
- 2020
- Te...

# JAKE REBER

Jake Reber is a writer and artist. He is a co-curator of Hysterically Real and an editor for Recreational Resources. He has published several artist books and experimental projects, including INVASIVE SPECIES (Void Front Press, 2019), BUREAUCRATIC TOPOLOGIES (Gauss-PDF, 2018), and LOBSTER GENESIS (Orworse Press, 2016), among others.

# CHAPTER THIRTY-THREE

You see a watering hole. Reprieve from the old dusty path.

You think of stuff: the wasp's nest stung five fold through with your unhinged acrylics, the personal moon you wore on your left hand, the wig of spider webs, the peach fuzz sweater the confessional poet handed you in a dream that later appeared in your armoire, a vial of dreams, the golden typewriter keys embalmed in wax from the bullets of lipstick you intended not to wear again. At first, a saucepot of the seventh chakra; confetti of the future. Eventually, a batter of nostalgia; non- as ash. Your beauty itself borborygmi; distant thunder of desire for desire. Your last kissprint all you think is left of you, a stain on a hand mirror in a town where you no longer know the weather.

You've been walking for longer than you thought this world went. Often, you think of your vanity: turning your back to the wall mirror so you can examine the nape of your own neck in the hand mirror. Your portable-self. Often, you think of the stuff outside your own image: of the part of the mirror that mirrors the mirror.

To feel smart, you think of the post-structuralist scholar from the European university who called the Land O'Lakes butter package *a colonialist mise en abîme* at the conference brunch.

Really, though, what you think of is a poster that was just an image of green grass. The one your math teacher kept behind his desk. *It's not the destination*, it's the *journey*. You worry that you have started to use the word *journey*.

You worry that you have started to speak, almost exclusively, to yourself.

As if you are auto-composing a letter in the third person in a language no one understands but you.

∞

This began when you bought the ouroboros in that pet

shop that you mistook for the progressive sex shop: The Smitten Kitten. Later, you found out that the place you were looking for originally is actually on Lake, the mainest-most street of your polite city.

This all happened, then, because your new grad advisor was totally correct: you are an *assumptive thinker.* You assumed the adult store would be in a fringe district, pushed out of the sightline of families going to the farmer's market or the children's theatre or wherever.

The Smitten Kitten you find is a black steel door between the front of an Ethiopian restaurant and a three-story gay bar. As you inhale a mixed scent of legume stew from the restaurant and detergent for a bubble machine from the bar, you wonder what city planner permitted this kind of zoning. A strange scent tumbles down the steps you climb to The Smitten Kitten. Something like artificial watermelon and bodily gas, something like if one of the My Little Ponies you had a stable full of as a child came to life and actually used the pasture you built them out of popsicle sticks for shitting.

It is not the worst smell. You assume it is the aroma of some variety of edible lube.

Despite the odd sounds—a heavy splashing, a fan set up much too high, something like sandpaper rubbing against sandpaper and a moan distorted as if processed through a bad record player—you continue up the steps. This is probably one of those peep show places, you guess. You've only lived in the city for a few weeks, but just like when you did that summer seminar at Tulane and everyone insisted on telling you right away that liquor was street legal in New Orleans, everyone here wants you to know sex shows are allowed. Because this information is entirely unsolicited, you have begun to wonder if people are seeing something in you that you don't see in the mirror.

The splashing, you realize at the apex of the staircase, is from an iridescent fish tail spanking against the surface of an enormous aquarium. The fan is not a a fan at all, but the feathered flappings of something with both wings and legs. The moaning is just Tom Waits grumbling from an old radio.

Windowless, the room is crowded with wire cages, terrariums, and other variety of enclosures. You can't determine where the sandpaper sound is coming from, although you can feel it in your body: a euphoric tingling down the back of the neck and along the crest of the scalp. Lately, the only sound that has satisfied you has been the wicked staccato tap your largest geode makes when you slam it against your desk. You've been working on your dissertation for too long.

"So long you started again and rewrote it accidentally, am I right?"

The voice comes from the same direction as the satiating sound. In fact, the voice itself fills some need you were not aware of. When you turn to face it, you are too seduced to be startled that it comes from a person whose floor-length hair is writhing. Little long serpents, you realize.

A Medusa.

"No, honey. Nothing Greek like that."

This must be true, your reason. Looking at Medusa causes instant death and you are still alive. You step forward for a closer look and understand that the sandpaper sound is the hair-snakes rubbing their dry scales against one another.

"Do you mind if I ask—" you hesitate in case there is some taboo against asking unidentified creatures how they identify.

"I'm a Pythoness."

"That's a...soothsayer?"

"Look at you," the Pythoness winks and moves in your direction, "What are you? Some kind of ancient scholar?"

You are about to say no, you are still just a grad student when you realize the Pythoness is teasing you and is, suddenly, very close. They smell like white sage and clary. You think of the first time you felt like this, watching Joan Crawford dressed as a cowboy in *Johnny Guitar* and you remember you are actually looking for something else.

"Everything you need is already here," the Pythoness reminds you.

You are shown a basket of hot pink eggs that will hatch into Halcyon Birds, a hare with seven skins, two variety of miniature cave-minotaur (one with a conscience, one without), a spider that could only live in a beam of moonlight cast between tree branches, a tiny demon clutching an hourglass that never empties, and a cloud of mist trapped beneath a bell jar labeled *Godgene.*

Next to this, the locked cage wherein you meet the ouroboros. It is pale pink, soft as the skin of puppy's belly. The Pythoness allows you to rub your finger around and around it. One revolution takes just a second; the ouroboros is only about the size of a woman's watch.

You pay the Pythoness the amount you had intended to spend on what you thought you were looking for. You name the creature Amor Fati, because you are pretentious like that. The Pythoness gives you the cage gratis, but warns you that even if you have the key to the chains not every lock is the same. You shrug and agree.

On your way out the door, a serpent wraps itself firmly around your ankle. Serious as shackle. You turn to face the Pythoness.

"One piece of advice before you go, hon?"

You nod.

"Not every watering hole is a reprieve and your life isn't some sexy old cowboy movie. Once you get on the dusty path, keep walking."

∞

It seems certain, when you finally do encounter the watering hole, that you are going to ignore the oracle who sold you the creature.

You have never been so thirsty before.

∞

Amor Fati's illness is abrupt.

Because your apartment is tiny—and because you almost immediately develop an obsession with the way Fati's soft skin oscillates between shades of pink tourmaline, matte rose quartz, and carnelian—you cleared a space right on your desk for the creature's cage. This way you could watch Fati wind into all shapes while you failed to complete your dissertation: a lemniscate, a twisted ribbon, an imitation of a game called Juggler's Diablo that was banned from your elementary schoolyard.

You felt guilty, at first, for making room for Amor Fati by shoving the stack of books on memory theory and genocide to the floor. Then, Fati turned into a fuchsia Möbius and you felt nothing but relief. This is the first time you have felt your own energy field since you began to read the books your advisor said would help you solve for the X of your dissertation. Thin volumes, recently published, mostly confusingly translated from Italian with titles like *Adult Dreaming: Interior of the Génocidaire's Nightmare* and *Perpetrator Induced Trauma Syndrome: From the Slaughterhouse to the Abortion Clinic* and, your least favorite, *Monster, Man, and Mass Atrocity.*

"But don't you think some events should end?" you had asked your advisor that day in late January when she had insisted you push your thesis in this macabre direction.

She was a very gorgeous woman who had taken a seven-year sabbatical to interview serial killers. You and everyone else called her Clarice Starling behind her back. When she agreed to be your advisor, you felt momentarily as if all your problems were solved. Her mere proximity to your intellectual contribution was akin to one of those late-in-life baptisms born again undergo: a dip in the lake of acceptance.

"Do you?" was all she had said in response.

You knew then that the blessing wasn't going to be an erasure, but an immersion.

For about a month after you get Amor Fati, you just sit on your couch and watch as Fati blends into the exact shade of your flesh. On April 1st, you check your bank balance and see that, even though you have not written a word of the dissertation, the University has deposited your fellowship check as usual. Your feelings for Fati deepen into reverence. It is as if you are moving in reverse: from love to infatuation. The specific euphoria of a crush overtakes you. Then, as has happened at other times in your life when you cared too much, Fati begins to fade.

∞

Your obsessions have always been a little slant.

So much so that in your very first semester of graduate school, a member of your pedagogy seminar referred to you as a *perv for Derrida*.

It was she, though, who pronounced the philosopher's name with two instead of three syllables, as though the first were a homonym for the French word that your grandmother occasionally used as a synonym for *tush*.

Throughout your entire presentation on "The Exorbitant: Questions of Method," you had said *Dare-eye-dah*. Three stresses. It took everything you had just to make sense of the essay and then it took more to figure out how to give the "casual presentation" required by your professor. So, yes, by the end you were indeed a perv for Derrida and you assumed your cohort was, too.

But, no. They had already read De Man and Barthes and Foucault and Nancy back at their Ivy League undergraduate institutions where they learned it was not only fashionable but morally correct to scorn the contributions of old white men. They privileged diversity in the canon. From then on, you knew you were considered the stupidest person in your Prestigious Masters program.

For your undergrad, you went to a state college in Ann Arbor and received a comprehensive and unembellished education. You were so absolutely dumbfounded when you received the call that you had been accepted to the Prestigious Masters that the keys to your car, which you had been holding in your hand as you listened to the voicemail, instantly disappeared. In the end, you had to walk home.

It isn't until you are several days into your journey down the old dusty path to find the ouroboros hospital that it occurs to you that perhaps the very fact that you had never even heard the word *deconstructionism*—didn't know the difference between an *–ism* or an *–ist* or a even the basics of semiotics—meant you were, in fact, the most diverse student in your class. You never trafficked in any Greek networks, had no professor-parents, and came from neither money nor metropolis. You feel relieved that when you applied to the Prestigious Masters, you didn't know any phrases like *first generation college graduate* or *queer identifying* or any other code words that you could have used to get through the gates from within which you would feel permanently like an interloper. You are intellectually sticky-fingered as it is. No, you got through with just a mediocre degree and a personal statement about memory.

A gold-green burst spreads across your chest as, for the first time, a sense of self-reliance digs its petite claws into your heart. You cradle Fati and consider that everything you've ever had the potential to be is, and has always been, here.

"Maybe we're going to be okay," you whisper to Fati.

"Maybe I'll finish the dissertation after all," you add.

Whatever luminescence you thought you might have seen in Fati dims and you inhale dust, quicken your step, and recheck the coordinates of the hospital.

∞

The sun was setting on the ice-sunken city park your apartment overlooks when Fati began to fade. You became instantly vigilant, as at other times in your life when a romantic interest did not return a text or one of your teeth began to ache. Watchful, but not in a psychotic way.

By the time the park is entirely dark, Fati has begun to shiver and shed. You are now deranged by worry. Not enough to go to the dangerous part of town where The Smitten Kitten is located after nightfall, but enough to drive to your yoga studio where a Kundalini class you sometimes go to is ending.

The class is taught by a deeply mystical woman from Illinois. Her name is Myra and you know she has two guinea pigs at home.

Once, on your way out of class you remarked to her that you were, "Pretty into Kundalini."

"It's a reluctant messenger," was her only reply.

It's because of this—because you think of Myra as a straight shooter—and because she talks through her entire class about the Shakti, an energy that lives at the root chakra and curls up through the spine in an eternal coil, that you turn to her first for help with Fati.

Myra peers into the blue velvet jewelry box you have placed Fati in for transportation across the cold city. The box says ZALES in silver letters on the side. You only have the box at all because it was the receptacle for the watch your mother gave you when you graduated the Prestigious Masters.

"Energy can get stuck," Myra says. She places her Reiki-warm hand on the crook of your elbow. As you feel the flow of energy enter you and then retreat, you realize Myra cannot help with this.

It's almost 10:00 PM—Midwestern midnight—when you pull your car up outside the unplowed driveway of your former dissertation advisor, Dr. Bell. Dr. Bell is the reason you came to this frigid city to write your dissertation in the first place. On a daily basis, you suspect that if the University had not made her prematurely "emeritus" and passed you on to Clarice Starling, you'd be done by now. You and Dr. Bell were making some good progress into the Dream-Space Continuum. In the last meeting you had with her before her office was packed up and her name taken off the registrar's roster for Spring enrollment, the two of you had felt so emboldened by your recent findings that you created several neologisms to explain your research.

> *Envoyage.* A portmanteau taken from the final stanza for a sestina, an *envoy*, and *envisage*. Meaning: To experience the sense that a cycle has completed while acknowledging that the cycle will complete endlessly.
>
> *Joie d'avoir déjà vécu.* In the tradition of French memory studies. Meaning: The joy of seeing again.
>
> *Aporia Euphoria.* After Derrida. Meaning: Extreme contentment as a response to a glitch in rational logic or inability to solve for X.
>
> *Lacuna Dysphoria.* After Sorokin and Markovina. Meaning: An obsessive tendency to create meaning, especially within a closed circuit.

You knock on Dr. Bell's door even though the ancient Victorian is dark inside.

Your old professor materializes quickly. She

still very much resembles an overly intelligent deer, all dreamy and aware. She always appears to be staring contentedly into the distance, like the captain of a ship who can see the horizon before everyone else. You suppose this very look has a lot to do with why the university got rid of Dr. Bell. They tolerated it when instead of presenting a research paper at the semester faculty symposium, she spread a deck of homemade divination cards across the lectern and demanded that her advisees come up and have the liminal regions of their psychogeography assessed.

The faculty for the Creative Writing MFA did much worse, the admins reasoned.

They ignored student complaints that her tests were subjective beyond any academic precedence when she started assigning final grades based on the results of an aura camera she got at a metaphysical fair.

Tenure removal was a costly process and Dr. Bell had just about run out the clock anyway, the admins once again reasoned.

But then she started the research on the Dream-Space Continuum. You were her chief researcher and so it was you who played Mother during the tea service she insisted on before her lectures in Dreaming Dangerously: A Jungian Approach. These lectures always evolved into an immersive experience, complete with crystal sound bowls and long screenings of Stan Brakhage films and psychological profiles more commonly used by the FBI's abnormal psychopathy unit. You alone knew the Lavender Earl Grey was microdosed with both ketamine and psilocybin. By Halloween, the class regularly visited the Weisman, the campus' small art institution perched near a major American river where a poet who wrote something you have never read—a book called *The Dream Songs*—suicided.

Dr. Bell believes this very spot is rich for mapping the coordinates of the Dream-Space Continuum, which she explained existed in many dimensions, not the least of which was one's own unconscious.

"We must travel in the direction of our fear," she told the class before sending her goon-eyed charges off to wander. It was a museum guard who reported that Dr. Bell was bringing a bunch of tranqued out grads to crawl around the Weisman.

You can tell Dr. Bell is herself under the influence as you follow her into her oversized house. Even though you are very thirsty, you decline the tea she offers and carefully place Fati on top of a copy of *The Red Book.*

The spectacles she puts on to peer at Fati further magnify the blacks of Dr. Bell's eyes. She looks for a very long time. Fati sheds a bit of skin on *The Red Book* and it dissolves instantly, a snowflake in a pool of blood.

"Where did this creature come from?" she eventually asks.

You are about to tell her about The Smitten Kitten when she holds her hand up and shakes it as if she is already aggravated by your dullness, "Which desire, I mean? Which dream."

You think of the Pythoness but do not know how to explain it.

*"Lacuna Dysphoria,"* Dr. Bell pronounces. She very carefully takes one ancient finger and places it near Fati's mouthtail. In the incarnadine leather of the book, you see the scratch her fingernail leaves as she draws Fati's diameter. "Do dreams come from within you or from without you?"

"Unanswerable. There is no difference," you recite.

"And that is the cure for your little creature."

Dr. Bell hands you a tincture in a shaded bottle and hugs you like she is your Grandmother, not your disgraced former dissertation advisor.

"I hope you figure out how to admit what you want, dear."

She closes the door in your face.

You return to the car and drive directly to The Smitten Kitten even though you are afraid.

You have to walk several blocks through the now busy streets to get to the shop. You have hardly ever left your house this late during grad school and you are amazed by how many people are out. They all appear to be in costume, bedecked in shades of neon and feather wigs or pleather corsets or garments with strategically places holes. There is so much velvet you are afraid if you start looking, you won't stop. You keep your eyes down and your hand wrapped around Fati, who you have placed in the pocket of your subzero parka.

People keep offering you things as you hurry to The Smitten Kitten. Directions to private parties, drugs, dates, and some stuff you've never even heard of.

Through the icy air, you smell the Ethiopian place and then you see the Day-Glo lights of the gay bar. You remove your thick winter glove and prepare to pound on the door to the shop when you realize there is no door. The discreet entrance to the steps you walked up hours earlier is simply gone, replaced by a brick wall.

You and Fati are struck dumb—overcome with panic and grief, ready to begin crying—when you notice the book of matches shoved into the crack between the wall and sidewalk. *SMITTEN KITTEN: An Emporium of Rare Shadows* is embossed in holographic writing on the side. You flip the book open and inside there is a note in writing that resembles ocean coral.

*Hey You,*

*Lost already?*

*25.0000°N, 71.0000°W*

*P.*

∞

You were in such a hurry to begin your journey that you barely remember packing the bag. Dr. Bell's words echo in your head—they always do, invasive as sound that won't stop fingering a canyon wall—as you stuff an old suitcase with randoms.

*I hope you figure out how to admit what you want, dear.*

In an airport bathroom on the other side of the world, you search through the luggage for a toothbrush and deodorant but find that all you've packed is a set of acrylic nails you've had since you wore them to a New Year's Eve party in Ann Arbor, an opalescent ring your best friend from high school gave you that she claimed was blessed to bring romance to the wearer by a former nun in New Orleans, a bunch of lipstick, an angora sweater the color of flesh, and Dr. Bell's tincture.

You wash your armpits in the sink, finger-comb your hair, and put on the sweater and some lipstick. Oddly, you look better even though you are exhausted from compulsively checking on Fati throughout the long flight. Underneath the fatigue, an enervation you usually identify as anxiety. Not today though. A salty breeze slinks through the airport and you know what you are actually feeling is excitement. A sunbeam penetrates the thin knit of your sweater and you feel organic warmth on your stomach for the first time since you started school.

Outside the tiny airport, you have the sense that everyone is smiling at you. Nodding and welcoming, although you cannot find a taxi driver who knows where the destination is that your phone has identified as the coordinates the Pythoness left you.

The seventh driver actually gets out of the taxi to talk with you. She stares into your iPhone screen at the small dot you are trying to get to. You tap the plastic with your acrylic fingernail and say, "Ouroboros Hospital?"

"You're ill?" she asks. Her eyes scan you up and down and you realize you feel healthy for the first time in a long time.

"No, no." You take Amor Fati out of your pocket and open the jewelry box, "My friend."

The taxi driver's mouth drops open and before you know what is happening, she is showing you a black and white photo of a woman who looks very much like the taxi driver herself. The woman in the photo is about ten feet from the camera, smiling broadly, and cupping her hands as though protecting a flame.

"My great-grandmother," the driver explains, "and *her* friend." Now it is her turn to tap the photo with an acrylic nail and you realize that her great-grandmother is holding her own ouroboros.

"Yes!" you shriek the shriek of being seen and, spontaneously, you and the driver hug and jump up and down.

"Take me there?" you ask. "To the hospital for friends?"

Her smile fades then, "The hospital…nobody remembers how to get there."

"What? How can everyone on an island forget a place?"

"It happens. The ouroboros went extinct, people quit talking about them," she shrugs sadly. "Most people don't even think they exist anymore. Nothing but a legend. Now everybody just wants to search for them on the Internet. Candle. Dream Market. You know."

"You mean I can find the hospital through the dark web?" you ask hopefully.

"*No,*" the driver is emphatic, "You can only *look*."

Randomly, you think of how you thought The Smitten Kitten might be a peep show. How you kept walking up the steps anyway.

*I hope you figure out how to admit what you want, dear.*

"What about your great-grandmother? Can I ask her?"

"She was dead before I was born. Just my mother's memory to me," she says. "I guess you gotta figure it out for yourself."

Someone starts honking at the parked taxi. The driver squeezes your hand and takes one more look at Amor Fati.

"Damn," she says softly. "It's good to know it exists."

You watch her drive off into the pink horizon and then peek into the box once more. Fati is wiggling. Happy, you think, like a puppy tail.

You light up your phone screen and let the electronic guide lead you in the direction of the mystery coordinates.

∞

You're so dehydrated from the flight and general lack of liquids that you start to absently lick the sweat off your arm, just to make your tongue feel smaller in your mouth.

You don't know how long you have been walking. You have been circling the site of the coordinates for a long time, waiting for the phone to admit you have arrived. The sky has remained the same dreamy rose gold that the taxi driver disappeared into for what you would guess might be three days. Or maybe twenty. Or maybe it has only been a few hours. You don't know—you threw your watch on your bed when you replaced Fati with it in the box and your phone is frozen on the mapping app you are using to find the hospital. You're certain that if you do a hard restart, your phone won't come back at all. You keep tracing the same tracks and occasionally a logical question surfaces, like *why has the phone battery lasted for so long to begin with?*

You strongly suspect rational thought is making Fati sicker.

It took a terrible thing to make you realize this.

You were explaining your dissertation to Amor

Fati when the creature began to shiver, then undulate.

Nervously, you kept talking, "So there has to be some way to solve for X. It stands that if the brain scans during REM are the same for deviants and average people, they must experience and remember along the same neural pathways."

Fati forcefully curled in at the very point where Dr. Bell had drawn her fingertip. You have no idea if Amor Fati has a spine. If so, this convulsion must be breaking it. Your friend has curled into something like a deformed heart.

"Yet, their remembrances manifest differently—as melancholy and nostalgia for the average person," your voice quakes with tears as Fati twists, "and as violence for the deviant."

Fati's eyes roll back. Although you have never seen a seizure before, you know this is one. Amor Fati, you realize, is trying to dislodge the tail from the mouth.

Powerless, you have no idea what to do but keep speaking in a soothing murmur. "But not everything adds up, Fati. Why should it?" you babble. "Maybe there just aren't anymore pieces to factor in."

Fati stills and for a moment you are worried your friend is dead.

"Maybe everything we need is already here." Fati's pretty gold eyes focus. "Maybe there is no destination."

You know how trite you sound, how self-help. But Fati is undeniably calming and so you begin an entirely new train of discourse. As you circle and stare at your phone screen, you find yourself talking for so long that you tell Fati your whole life story. How you won a prize for thinking in high school and then you couldn't quit moving in a linear path towards more prizes, not even when they became increasingly dubious. You sit down on the sand and tell your friend all the stuff you've done just to get a wax stamp and the signature of the college's dean. You have a dose of Dr. Bell's tincture. You set the phone down, screen up. You explain to Fati about diplomas because you can tell the creature doesn't have a concept of institutional gratification. At some point, you pull a wig made of spider's webs out of your suitcase and put it on.

You're just sitting there in your bright makeup and wig and fuzzy sweater, letting tears pool into the basins of your acrylic nails as you tell Fati you no longer see the satisfaction in finishing your dissertation when your phone dings and the watering hole appears before you.

Fati glows in radiant pulses.

You step towards the watering hole and in its circular surface you see your reflection. It is as if you have travelled back in time to the centermost moment of your existence.

You lean forward and, remembering the Pythoness' warning, you keep your mouth closed.

The last words you think of before your lips touch the reflection of your lips is Dr. Bell telling you she hopes you figure out how to admit what you want. Then, Amor Fati wraps tightly around your wrist and as if a whirlpool, pulls you in.

A sensation of constriction and relief, a surging of blood to the surface. Sage is burning somewhere. You hear the sound of sand falling on sand. There was the rushing of rivers pooling, a neon odor in the air.

Notes:

"The Pythoness gives you the cage gratis, but warns you that even if you have the key to the chains not every lock is the same." Sentiments in this line are loosely paraphrased from a passage in Friedrich Nietzsche's unpublished notes.

Dr. Bell's statement, "We must travel in the direction of our fear," is from the poem "A Point of Age" by John Berryman.

# CANDICE WUEHLE

Candice Wuehle is the author of Death Industrial Complex (Action Books, 2020) and BOUND (Inside the Castle Press, 2018) as well as the chapbooks VIBE CHECK (Garden-door Press, 2017), EARTH*AIR*FIRE*WATER*ÆTHER (Grey Books Press, 2015), and curse words: a guide in 19 steps for aspiring transmographs (Dancing Girl Press, 2014). She is originally from Iowa City, Iowa and is a graduate of the Iowa Writers' Workshop.

# CHAPTER THIRTY-FOUR

Please read the even pages until page 426.

---

Flip the book over at page 427 and read the odd pages, moving towards the front cover.

[[[You see a watering hole. Reprieve from the old dusty path.

It's a familiar place you've returned to, and you don't know why.

You want to let the whole thing play out, and maybe you will, but first, your hands. Where are they? You see them, rising, falling, palm up. Fingers move. Shake them.

Noise, through the ears of your physical body, become your thoughts.

You are the voice telling yourself: I am more than my physical body, because I am more than physical matter.

You watch yourself telling yourself: I can perceive that which is greater than the physical world.

The dreamscape fades into static as you tune in to your surroundings.

You did what the book told you to do.

Do not drink water two hours before you plan on retiring for the evening. Swallow 1/8 teaspoon of salt. And you did, the salt turning into a thick paste, and you mashed the remaining solids into your gums.

You wrote your intentions in the notebook you keep on the small table next to the bed.

You become lucid with the hand trick, and then, more awake as you speak the words.

And now, where are you?

Like that person over there, standing by the water at the end of the path. And then you remember that it all begins and ends like this, with someone you vaguely recognize standing by the river, and they tell you it's time, and you nod your head. Come down to the river they say, and you do. And you take their hand and they take yours. And they tell you that this will be just like all the other times, and all the times to come, and that being alive is difficult and that you've done a good job, and everything will be ok. And then you jump into the river together, because you know that everything is mental, and metaphors are the way we understand ourselves, and the world, and our place in it, and you'll let the river take you until you begin to remember that time and space are only metaphors too, and nothing can be created or destroyed, and you lie peacefully in water, looking up into a vast uncaring emptiness. ]]]

You are where you always are when you dream of water: the creek behind your house, the closest source of moving water when you are asleep at home. And this confuses you when you are traveling for work, because you'll find yourself transported to this creek behind your house, even when you're thousands of miles away. Why? Out of ease? Habit?

You don't know what to call it. It is something that started when you were a child, and it was only when you were older and began to wander beyond the creek when you realized it wasn't a bad dream after all. It was your life, the real thing, and it was occurring outside of your body. You read about the ancient Egyptians, and how they thought the Ba (the soul) could move with the Ka (second body) outside of the physical body, what new age spiritualists call astral projection. The invisible vibratory energy that animates your physical body, what you call consciousness, and what Hermetics call the vital life force. The Ka, the second body within the physical body, and the ba, the soul, wrapped up like Russian dolls inside of the physical. Now—body asleep—mind awake, your consciousness has separated from the physical and anyone who sees you here standing by the creek would think you're a ghost. And you sometimes wonder how many ghosts are really just sleepwalking minds, dreaming, replaying an emotional event or are simply looking for moving water.

As a teenager, you couldn't escape the world like your friends could. Drugs, alcohol, romantic relationships were forbidden in your religious home. A misfit at home, at church, at school, you would escape the only way you knew how. You would lie very still for what seemed like hours until you clicked out of your body. Dream walking is what you called it, and like most escapes teenagers indulge in, it was easier than suicide and still felt a lot like death. You, lifting out of yourself to become something

[[[Your mouth is dry. You know the thirst should wake you, but it only makes the dream feel more real. You look at your hands, but you cannot stop the ride. You want to wake up, and if you can't do that, at least wake up in the dream, as you remember yourself, as an eight-year-old, so you can stop it all from happening. But it moves on with indifference without you being able to stop it, so you surrender, like you've always surrendered.

Your father gets out of his new car, a brown Premier Padmini, and walks over to the other car, but before he gets there, you are already ducking in the backseat, there was no thought, just movement, out of some reflex, likely from the noise, but you hear nothing, because this isn't real, and you just know certain things in dreams, just as you know this will be the last time.

You know your father has been shot. Your mother is taken from the car by men who grab her at the wrists. There is a knowing of the sound, the pain, the future. The clawing at one's vocal cords. More gunfire. And you're still there, somehow, in the back seat, under the blankets, and under the trash of banana peels and plastic wrappers, and only when it gets dark do you dare move from your hiding place. And then you're walking, walking away from the car. Away from your life. Away from the bodies that are motionless, too motionless, so they don't even look like bodies, and then you walk away from yours too, as the sand sucks the blood back into the ground. Death is only death, you thought there would be something more final about it, but life's biggest changes are never as final as they should be. And now you're walking toward the mountains, because you know there will be people who can make this right. They can make it all ok. They can fix your dad and your mom. And when that happens, maybe they'll be able to fit you back into your body, because for the last 40 years you've never felt at home inside yourself.

else. Now, it's not so easy. You're tired all the time. You fall asleep before you feel the click and have to pull yourself out of a dream. When you come to, you have to orient yourself. Tune-in.

You figure that you are just as lazy outside of your body as you are inside your body, and that's why you are always at the same creek whenever you come-to out of a dream about water. It could be the ocean dream, where you are walking into the waves, and a crowd of people are behind you, watching with sharp sticks and fire. Or the pool at the middle school you attended where you had embarrassing dreams as a teenager, and it's always odd when you find yourself as an adult in a rerun of a dream from many years ago. And you remember the water dreams and dream walking only started after you almost drowned in lake Michigan as a child, when the rip current took you under, and your father's arms dove in after you, bruising your ribs and shoulder, swimming on his back to the sandbar parallel to the shore. How many dreams have you struggled against the undertow to only be pushed farther away from shore? How many times have your lungs filled with water and death has never come? You sometimes think that everyone in the world died somehow in childhood, but none of us have accepted it, so we're all just living in a shared fantasy with other dead children. And we're all growing older, procreating, and creating a new alternative reality for other children who cannot accept their deaths.

You're not sure why the salt works, why it helps you become conscious out of the body when you miss the click and enter a dream. You think it has to do with desire, and how it must be easier to leave the physical when it is tired or uncomfortable. Uncomfortable, like a stress dream. Tired, like a fever dream. And this is why stress dreams and fever dreams are so vivid, and why the dead seem to always be trying to tell us something in them.

ever it was that was placed in front of him, it looked like it welcomed death with open paws. Just one of the millions who were bred for food in a tiny cage. Cut open and drained of their blood. Seasoned and slow cooked for some overweight banker or politician's enjoyment. It wasn't that he was an animal rights activist, the whole act of eating, putting something inside himself was repulsive. But then, there were times when the urge to eat, rather, to consume, overtook his disgust. He'd binge on entire sleeves of salted crackers and canned fish and feel repulsed by himself afterwards. The same was with every other normal human function. Putting something inside of himself, putting himself inside of something. It was as if he was a different person during the extreme times of desire: thirst, hunger, sleep, sex, that he had a total break from his version of reality. *What the hell is sleep? A loss of control, a black out, a theatre of suppressed thought that plays out as bad dreams?* These are the thoughts that raced around his body, always in the negative, before succumbing to the urge, and immersing himself completely. *Things only make sense in the moment a decision is made. That's why people can't understand bad choices, because they are the right choice in that moment, and only that moment, and no one else can ever be in that moment with you. It was Dream Logic, he thought.*

Dreams, he thought. And what do trees dream about? The axe? Windstorms? Children climbing on their limbs and picking at their bark? And the flower? Do they know their throats will be cut so they can be put on some office receptionists' desk?

The deer, do they dream of the hunter or the highway?

The last place he wants to be was in his own mind. The last place: alone by himself with only himself for company. Eyes closed to the world, another set open.

On the other side of the creek, there's the door you pulled yourself out of. It's made of light and leads to a tunnel made out of bricks, and the bricks are made out of math equations that form as you move through the dense body of dark, and you know it leads to the dusty path you came from. You realized long ago that everything here is a metaphor. Reality is one big system of metaphors. And here, you're not thinking, you are thought, because you are a metaphor in a system of systems, and now, walking through the light, one system will attempt to run its source code in another system.

```
("hello, world")
```

Even though the scene is vivid and tactile, you know you will begin to forget when you are called back to your physical body. When the silver cord begins to retract, and the second self begins pulling towards the physical, you'll only be left with strange images and partial story lines that you'll creatively fill in later. But it won't be a total loss. Some deeper knowing "you" will know it has happened. The gut instinct you. The intuition you. The you that tells the story to me.

Squiggly green math is pulled from the atmosphere and is pressed together into bricks as you move through the tunnel. The further you go, the more you remember, and you begin to remember everything you've forgotten. You promise yourself you'll remember this time. Key details, you tell yourself, remember concrete objects, specifics, so you can write them down immediately.

The path is dusty. There is water and you are rising, falling, hovering. ]]]

He grabs the notebook before opening his eyes. Every

Back at the hotel, he clicks play on his music app. Asha Puthli sings *Neither One Of Us Wants To Be The First To Say Goodbye* and he thinks about the music video he saw at a friend's apartment in Montreal as a freshman at McGill. He has just moved there and joined a club for students from India, though, most of the group grew up in the west. And he told them that he too grew up in the west, in Michigan, in America, where his mother teaches chemistry at the University there and his father works in the auto industry as a consultant since he had developed many patents for Hindustan Motors. They were all sitting around, talking about extended family and how hard it was to find good food here. Someone popped in a VHS tape, and everyone was amazed with the quality. This is the future. And there she was. When he saw Asha singing to an empty boat, he felt something inside of himself, the deep-down part no one knows about except for him. The secret place he returns to every night when he is asleep on the floor of his residence, because the bed there feels like one big giant marshmallow. And Asha was singing about that place, and she was singing directly to him, saying, I too have a place where only I am allowed to go, allowed to be completely myself with myself, and no, I too will never tell anyone about it, but it's nice knowing other people have their secrets, have places you will never know about.

He thinks about how he ever got from that moment in time to the one he's at now. And then thinks about how he ever got from the orphanage to McGill on scholarship.

*Well then*. He says to himself, not wanting to get caught in the past, because if he did, he would never leave it.

And then he felt it. The urge. He grabs the hotel information booklet and orders room service, orders the most expensive meal on the menu, and doesn't leave a tip.

And when it comes, he can't bring himself to eat it. What-

second counts. At first, the writing is quick and nonsensical. *Old brown car, really hot, pond or river in the desert.* His eyes remain closed, letting the sentences form: *I look at the water—into the pond—and I can't see myself. Something catches my attention, not a sound because I don't know if you can hear in dreams, it's more a knowing. Something, like a presence. I looked at my hands again because I didn't want my emotions to get the best of me. I wanted to be able to maintain full lucid control.* The pen stops moving, and his brain fills in the missing data, adding to and subtracting from the whole. Now he's unsure what is real and what is invention but continues writing with the same conviction. *I lost it. But something bigger took hold. I was watching myself, but I wasn't myself, I was another ethnicity, maybe a past life. Don't know. I understood the language, or, the thoughts of myself, this self, as this child. There was this… fear. My parents were dead, and I knew it because I had, at some point, watched them die. I don't know how. Famine? Disease? And I was walking. I want to say this is a past life regression dream, but the car was too new, like 1950's Chevy.*

And then, the images are gone. Evaporated into the curtains over the window in the hotel room. He stares off, trying to pull at what was once alive and real and true, but now feels so childish, foolish, and imaginary. Like all dreams do after you leave them. He thinks about all the times he was scared as a child, as a teenager, but when the words came out, there was nothing to be afraid of. He wonders how the same thing can change so quickly from one extreme to the other? From believing something is real and true, to dismissing it as crossed wires in the brain. *Dream logic,* he thinks.

A clean white shirt is unrolled from a non-descript black suitcase and is placed on the tiny hotel ironing board. Hot water drips through a one-cup coffee maker, which will be poured into a one-cup French press. Before leaving, he ground the locally roasted coffee beans and put them in

After the bus drove over an unrecognizable animal scattered across the entire width of the road, he asked the driver why there were so many and why nothing was done with the remains.

"Well, you gotta watch out for them deer. 'specially at night. Had a friend once hit a 12-pointer going bout 70 and kid you not they hit'm so hard it sucked the lungs clean right out'ov'hm. Blew the sucker 200 ft. down the interstate. Kept the head, though, police let'em do that. Had a tarp in back and popped it in the trunk. They're not all bad, especially when yer deal'n with a county cop. Got'em mounted over the fireplace at his up-north place. Beautiful buck."

He retuned to his seat and thought about how the driver would tell all his friends about the Urdu man who asked about their beloved roadkill.

*[I told'em nah we don't eat it like you towelheads do, but we might put a good look'n 12-pointer up on the fireplace if you kill it with an F-250. Ya hear? A kill is a kill, I don't care if it's with your truck. Shit. Give me another one-a them beers.]*

He thinks: Before you can build a new identity, you must be like this. Empty. Like the voice of a child at night, in the home of addicts, when they find their parents overdosed bodies lying on the floor. Empty, like the eyes of animals in cages awaiting their next injection of an experimental drug. Empty, like the hearts of the elderly, after their body has failed them, and everything has been taken.

He thinks: Once you are empty, you will realize you're only a collection of stories. It is only when you see yourself as a story that you will be free to change and create your future.

an airtight canister, because high quality coffee is important. Because mornings are important. Because routines are stable, and no matter how many talks he's given, or countries he's visited, routines are the only thing that helps him stay focused. And if a person can only make a few good decisions every day before encountering decision fatigue, he doesn't want to waste them on what to wear, what to eat, what to drink, when to sleep. What are we, he thinks, but a lifetime of routines? Thoughtless habits. Driving down the same road and forgetting the journey.

In the routine of early morning, he can let these thoughts wander freely, the words coming to mind are mostly praise for the good routine he has created, and then go on to explain the benefits to an imaginary someone, justifying himself to himself. And then he thinks about a friend who works at Duke's Rhine Research Center, and how this friend told him that paranormal activity might simply be psychic energy that is stuck in a routine, like a current in a body of water, the energy continues to move after it has left the physical body. There was a story about an old woman who would read her bible at 5:30 PM every evening in her rocking chair, and after she died, the new tenants swore they heard a rocking chair every night while they were making dinner. But they didn't own a rocking chair. And when pressed for an explanation, this friend said that the old woman likely doesn't know she has died, and she is still caught up in her routines and lives in a thought reality that is as real to her as this one is to us. To settle the unease of the couple who, without a doubt, was curious if the old woman was watching them, watching them take showers, sleep in their queen bed, or use the bathroom, this friend reassured them that the old woman's lingering psychic energy is separate, like the negative of a photo. Though, during times of high energy or emotion, the old woman could think the new tenants are phantoms or demons, because their worlds overlaps

not the politics. [pause] Us. [pause] And we will carry it on our shoulders. We will feel it pressing down before sitting down to a meal with our friends, family, [pause] children. And we must live with the guilt of our choices here today. [Long uncomfortable pause] I for one, I know I cannot live with that kind of guilt following at my footstep. Thank you all for your time."

He felt more comfortable in his own skin, his ugly tub of a body, when he knew people were watching. It was the opposite of voyeurism. Instead of watching, he wanted to be watched. He wanted to feel the eyes of someone watching behind a curtain as he went about his everyday life. He imagined the presence of someone watching as he picked his nose, farted under the covers, wiped his ass, squeezed his testicles, smelled his fingers. As a child, he pretended his life was a Bollywood movie, and everywhere he went, a camera crew followed, albeit hidden behind an overgrown tree stump or parked car. Even now, playing the villain, he was the devil himself, charming and persuasive. The thing about mischief, he thought, is that everyone, deep down, wants the thrill of causing a little chaos.

He didn't understand why the deaths of children in a faraway land brought these white people to tears when they have so many starving children in their own country. He remembered visiting the U.S. on a speaking tour with other internationally respected researchers and policy makers. It was late September and a caravan of people, all invited by the FDA, were driving from the University of Wisconsin in Madison to the Mayo Clinic in Rochester, Minnesota. The dead animals along the side of the road were astonishing to him and many of his colleagues. Every kilometer a bloodied deer would be scattered across the highway. Rotting pieces of meat for hundreds of cars to drive over. Other critters, too. Birds. Their beloved turkey. He hadn't seen this kind of carnage since a horror film. And the ease with how it was ignored.

just so, that to her, they would only be a shadow's outline or faint white noise in the background. *Dream logic,* he thinks. And he wonders if the friend ever told the young couple about what to do if they dream of the old woman. Then again, if the friend did, then they would have had to tell them everything.

His hand grips the iron for another pass across the back of the white button-down shirt; his mind is still elsewhere. He remembers the friend saying that consciousness can take many forms and we're often moving between many states of consciousness at any given time. Each state is associated with different brain waves, and these waves can exist outside of the body.

His thoughts are interrupted by a text message from a colleague who is trying to find a printer in their hotel. Later today, his team will be defending their position on a matter that could potentially impact billions, and it always strikes him as odd that decisions that could change the fate of humanity always happen in such tiny rooms with such little press coverage. He wonders if it was because the decisions were made not on merit or data, but secret pacts and private school friendships across multiple nations.

His thoughts drift while ironing his shirt, and then his slacks: Life doesn't get better after high school; it only prepares you for more of it. The dynamics of high school are everywhere, because no one ever leaves high school, because there is always the in-crowd and there are always the nerds, and everyone knows there is a pecking order and where they fall in line. He laughs to himself: *If you liked school, you'll love work.*

He was trying to kill children, helpless children in third world countries, or, rather, that's what he was up against. The rhetoric from big multinational corporations import-

lic speaker for that matter, is more about you than it is them. It's about inviting them into your world. It's a form of hypnosis. It's why so many can be manipulated at once in a group setting.

The real music in the English language is in the vowels, he thought, as he pronounced each word slowly so all the dignitaries, with their own accents and variations of the language, could understand his unique cadence.

Like a Broadway actor who has performed the same scene day after day, week after week, the routine was comfortable, and still something to revel in. First, the problem. There was an outline of the data. Case studies. This was all acting, for a scientist, all emotion must be amplified so the journalists in attendance will pay attention and write something favorable. That's the real ticket. All these journalists who get credit for the scientists' work, writing about it as if they were the ones who conducted the research. No, all you need to do is tell them a story about malnourished children dying in shantytowns, and they'll write favorably about whatever your solution is.

The solution. His solution. The new, cost effective process. And yes, the emotional appeal. His personal story of growing up in an orphanage after both parents were murdered by drug smugglers.

"The saddest part about everything we've heard today is we have every piece of the solution in this room. Death and disease from nutritional deficiencies is preventable. [Next part spoken quickly] We have the research. We have the tools. We have the funding. [pause for dramatic effect] The only question left is if we are willing to put the science to work. [pause] And if we don't act now [brief pause] and if we let this tragedy persist, [scans the room at eye level, mimicking eye contact with every person] we are the ones responsible. Not their country's leadership,

ing vitamins and minerals to be cooked in bread and sprayed on breakfast cereals would have anyone believing this. At this event last year, the World Hunger Initiative Conference—with attendees from nearly every country in the world, and special guest speakers from the UN, WHO, FAO, UNICEF, and The World Bank—in front of everyone, a poster was presented with the words: CHILD MURDERERS next to the logo of his non-profit organization. The letters of the words CHILD MURDERERS were in the same coloring as the eyes of the malnourished children, which were also artificially yellow, because starving children don't have jaundiced eyes, which made his presentation all that more depressing, because he knew that emotions would always be more important than a comprehensive statistical analysis.

The claims were untrue, of course, and he never understood why organizations who were working towards solving a common problem made the other side out to be the cause of the problem. Divided as they were in their strategy, couldn't the other side present their data without making him look like the enemy? Like something to defeat? But they were not working towards the same goal. The issues were never the ones at the forefront, because everything in politics was always several times removed, and research was only praised if it validated the current system, and he was up against organizations who tailored their research to justify the established processes. Millions of dollars, pounds, and euros, went to funding bad science that made it easier to live exactly as we always have.

The real enemy was folic acid producers. If he could speak freely, he would talk about how the US created a global industry around a problem they created. He would say: *We never needed to add folic acid to bread or iodine to salt before everyone adopted the unhealthy Western (aka US) diet. The white bread and squeeze cheese lunch. The fast food family*

Say: I will travel abroad on scholarship and study and the greatest institutions in the world.

Say: If you say anything enough times, it will eventually become true.

Say: I lead by example and make my family and my nation proud.

Say: I owe every day to the fine people of this state-run institution, and not one minute will be wasted. All of my effort will be used to create a better world.

If you say something enough, it will become true. If you say it again, it will become truth. Say it again.

The world is my body.

And my body, the world.

Paddle your own canoe.

He remembered: The Christians came to town and started an orphanage, giving us food and a place to lay our heads. But it was conditional. You can only have food if you believe what we believe. The factories came to town and started giving people dreams of houses and computers and television and cell phones. But it was conditional. You can only have the American dream if you work in our call centers. Work in our manufacturing facilities. The devil knocked on your door and promised riches, food, power, and immortality, but the price for the exchange was your soul.

There he was, shaking hands with people whose faces were on the front of post cards, and they were excited to see him. Being likable, he thought, and being a good pub-

*dinners. The high-fructose corn syrup. The partially-hydrogenated oils. Everything deep fried and chemically treated to last longer on the shelf. The invisible enemy. The invisible war.*

He would say: *We are paying someone to suck the nutrients out of our food and paying another to put synthetic nutrients back in. The simple solution is to not suck it out in the first place; to eat whole foods. All you need to do is teach people how to grow food, locally. Make traditional dishes. Return to the old ways before they are forgotten.*

And that's when he was going on and off script, unknowingly practicing his talk scheduled for later in the day: *Instead of giving starving children white bread full of synthetic rocks, we should be teaching our at-risk communities how to make bread with local ingredients.*

This is an incredible threat: teaching people how to catch their own fish. But he wouldn't say it like that. He would sidestep it, just as everything else is sidestepped. So, he used this free time while his body moved in routine to release his true emotions so he would be calm and collected on stage.

He imagines himself on stage talking at TED, a place he thinks might one day be receptive to his pro-culture approach. He's decided to call the TED talk "pro-culture is the new counterculture", and he begins somewhere near the beginning and hops around through his favorite parts.

Face scrunched and concerned, he thinks: *Everyone is at fault here. It's my country's fault for offering you money and it's your leaders fault for taking it…*

*… Western countries built factories in war-torn countries, paying the corrupt government so they can pay the workers pennies a day. Before western imperialism, the native people,*

There is no wrong. There is only the individual, and we call things that inconvenience us "bad" and things that scare us "evil", but it's all objective, all singular to a universe of one.

The animals, he thought, that was the only true evil. The animal testing. Raising them for cheap food like radishes. Violence without purpose. In human matters, it is a pendulum. The good causes bad and the bad causes good.

Was the Tokyo subway sarin attack bad if it brought a nation together? In the US, 9/11?

Creating lifesaving pharmaceuticals leads to incurable super bugs.

Every technological advancement we've made has led to the destruction of our environment: overfishing, dead soil, the ozone layer, global warming.

Is there such thing as a good or bad act? He thought about the brain in a vat theory, and how thought equates to consciousness. But what is consciousness? Since everything happens in the brain, we don't need a body.
He thought about the orphanage, and how they would recite positive messages taught to them by sunburned volunteers.

Say: I am valuable. Even though my family is gone, I still have value.

Say: I am becoming a better version of myself every day.

Say: doing my chores will lead to good work ethic and good work ethic will lead to good grades.

Say: good grades will lead to a good school, and I will make my family proud when I graduate from college.

*the first people, didn't have nutritional problems. ... What happens when an overweight, diabetic, high blood pressure indigenous person returns to the bush to live as they did when they were a child? The way their ancestors had been living for thousands of years? All of their health problems go away. And we know this to be true. ...*

*...The older generation is dying, and with them, their culture. And with them, the health of a nation. If we work to preserve the culture, we will preserve the quality of life for future generations...*

*...If a nation of people are dependent on you to donate fortified bread and a nation of consumers want to pay cheap prices for technology and handbags and sweatpants, there will never be an impetus for change...*

*...Western consumers get cheap clothes and cell phones, so they turn their heads. The corporations continue to profit, so the stockholders turn their heads. And the government continues to get paid, so they tell everyone they have a strong economy. And government officials get paid off, and they turn their heads on the people who gave them their trust. And there are always workers, because young people will continue to leave their villages for the city, because they think they'll get rich, and a year later they'll still be getting paid next to nothing. They lose fingers and get sick. They realize they're replaceable. They become drug addicts. Prostitutes. Homeless. So, the US sends more fortified bread. The funding goes to organizations who suck nutrition out of corn-based products, and then spits laboratory jelly back in. And the cycle continues.*

He was dressed. His bag was packed. He was stretched, showered, and caffeinated, all without thinking. He texted with his co-worker who told him she found a printer, but the hotel clerk who was helping her blew a circuit and blamed her for having a faulty international converter. She was able to print off their notes for the presenta-

*for less cost to the customer, but there's a hiccup. A very small malfunction. Tiny tiny. The difference between methyl alcohol (methanol) and ethyl alcohol (ethanol). In the wrong hands, a new and improved folic acid could have similar, how should I say this, mistakes. With the right mistake, it could become neuraltoxic. How long do you think it will take until it reaches the soccer mom as she's eating her fiber cereal in the morning? How long does it take before she notices a faint ringing in her ears? How long does it take for the irritability to set in? The shortness of breath. And then, finally, the loss of memory, understanding, and judgement. In a high enough dose, maybe, two slices of bread, or one medium bowl of cereal, it could move along quite quickly, ending in an irregular heartbeat, a cement mixer dumping its final load until it flatlines.*

*Row row row your boat gently down the stream.* It was a favorite song taught to him by the missionaries, one that did not talk about God or Jesus or love.

*Merrily, merrily, merrily, merrily, Life is but a dream.*

He thought about traversing a small river in a wooden canoe. A creek maybe, with overgrown brush. Logs in the water, and fish swimming beside him. People have to paddle their own canoe through life, he thought.

It is only through great tragedy that people come together in love and support. And it is only through love and support, that tragedy can exist.

If this was wrong, someone would stop me. But no one stops these things from happening.

If this was wrong, the conditions for this to happen would not exist.

If this was wrong, he thought, truly wrong, the universe would intervene. But no one will. Because this isn't wrong.

tion but was unsuccessful in convincing the clerk that the U in USB stands for "Universal".

In the taxi to the convention building, he felt his body changing, pulling closer to the bones. Retreating. Folding in on itself. In public, where did his confidence go?

He knew people felt uncomfortable around him because he was anxious. Even around people he knew quite well he still found himself talking to the ground most of the time, or just past them over their shoulders. Medically, he tried to self-diagnose. The only traumatic event he had was nearly drowning in Lake Michigan the summer of his eighth birthday. The tug under, the rolling, the loss of control, the feeling of being very small, smaller than he was, feeling the incredible size and weight of water. He tried Toastmasters International to work on controlling his public speaking anxiety, but while others steadily improved, he'd always catch himself shaking. Sitting in his chair watching a mom practice a speech for her daughter's bachelorette party, he still felt the familiar motion, the way he felt dizzy from being in the water too long, in the waves, the steady rocking and the fear of being swept away if you closed your eyes.

He thinks: I am not the same person when I am under stress. I say things. Mean things. I am not the same person when I am happy. Or sad. Or in love. Or angry. Or confused. Or tolerant. Or horny. Or hungry. Or shy. Or ashamed. Or confident. Or impatient. Or anxious. I am high, I am low, I am centered, but never one for very long. Who are these people, these personas? And where do they go? Am I only a collection of my emotional states? Is this why Buddhists and yogis tell us to find our center, so we can grow this one persona and kill the others?

Then again, he thought about past lives and death and transition and dualism, all the things that occupied his

world, he knew that adding folic acid to food was a simple solution to a problem created by first world countries. It was the American way. And it was the Indian way to learn how it works, reconstruct it, and use it against them. And no one questioned his involvement in other multinational oversight committees. His tinkering with co-sponsoring non-profit events. The friends from McGill, and those friends of friends. In fact, they all saw his involvement on the production side as yet one more thing to boost his credibility. Something he would never say to anyone is: *do you ever wonder why India doesn't put folic acid in their food?*

It was the difference between bubbly water and death. More practically, the moonshiners in the United States during their prohibition found that one type of alcohol could make you happy and drunk and the other would make you go blind. He thinks: *Someone, somewhere, should catch this. But they won't.*

As he's putting on his three-piece suit, gray with a buckle on the back to shape his body, and buttons all the way down the front. The upright collar and no tie, he thinks about how easy it was: *Folic acid is an essential B vitamin manufactured and captured as a fermented extract. So many of our essential foods and drugs are products of bioprocesses, which are created in laboratories and manufactured in large-scale facilities. Foods like bread and cereal are fortified with B vitamins, essential B vitamins, to treat malnutrition, so places like the United States of America can sell processed corn meal, void of nutrition, and spray vitamins on later. Take some cheap American shit food, spray cheap imported vitamins on it, and call it healthy. Sell it with cartoon characters and donate the rest to poor colored kids in places you feel sorry for. Sure, create a marketing campaign that says America is saving the world. So long as you trust where the vitamins come from. Yes, right here. Hyderabad, Telangana, India. Now, let's say there is a new bioengineering process that promises more potent vitamins*

mind when he wasn't fully aware of his surroundings. He thought about the bones from all of the bodies he had ever lived inside, and where they are now. What state of decomposition they were in, and when he would leave this one behind? He thought about the soul, and how his friend at the Rhine Institute also said that in cases of violent deaths, the consciousness energy can get stuck in a loop, on repeat, reenacting the death over and over. Like people who have trauma, PTSD, and reenact the experience over and over. And he hoped that's where he went when he dreamed, when he passed through the light, to the places the dead escaped to who didn't know they were dead yet, so he could talk them down from their brutal murders or horrible accidents. And in his dream body, he would make everything black, black out the scene and sit with the soul. Tell them it was ok now. Everything was ok. It's over and that they were free. And once they were free from the horrors of their own creating, they would disappear, move on, move on somewhere he did not know the name of. All he wanted to do was help people from hurting themselves, because helping people was a distraction of all the ways he hurt himself. And all he ever wanted was for someone to say: it's ok.

In the room that feels too small, with the people who are wearing earpieces, listening to his words in their own native language, he's talking about how his team worked with a community in Guatemala teaching mothers from the lower class how to make traditional meals for their children. After 18 months, the children of the lower class were healthier than the middle- and upper-class children. Less hospital visits, less school absences. Higher grades. He talks about how the wealthier mothers caught on and wanted their children to have better food, so there they were, the lower-class mothers teaching the wealthy mothers how to cook for their children. A bridge was constructed, and the entire community came together,

The lights go out, knocking his thought pattern out of sync. The shower sprays his skin and steam hangs in the air as the bathroom fan winds down to a halt.

Lights, camera, action. He hears the words: *you are awake.* The bathroom fan works its way back up to speed. The environment is exactly as it was, and so everything that happened in that brief moment was forgotten. Nothing exists, we only have the memory. A glitch in the circuit. A global hiccup, something easily forgotten, a door everyone passed through, insignificant, because as soon as everything turned back on, everyone re-entered the hypnotic state of daily life, none the wiser to the little things that shape our reality.

He thinks about how he must be losing his grip. The dreams are getting… stronger. Before the dreams, he only remembers walking. Walking for 36 hours until a couple of tourists in a large oversized car stopped for him. Poured water on his face and hands. They had air conditioning in their rented vehicle. They were Scottish, yes, from Scotland, and they saved his life. That's why he passed on building the UK office in Glasgow, because you wouldn't dare harm the people who saved his life.

Out of the shower now, he thinks about how easy it was gaining complete access to 1/3rd of the world's food supply. He thinks: *Yes, the MD-PhD wasn't easy; laughing at dumb jokes, getting to know a bunch of boring white people with a repulsive amount of money wasn't fun, but once they found out about your story, your childhood, the true one from your transcripts, not the one you told your friends, where you really came from and what you have overcome, the rest was a piece of cake. You learned how to make people with power like you, trust you.*

As the Director of the biggest folic acid producer in the

crossing social and economic boundaries, and if rich and poor mothers in Guatemala can come together, surely communities could come together anywhere. It was difficult, sure, but it's the only way that leads to sustainable results.

He could feel himself leave his body. The person talking wasn't him. Afterwards, he wouldn't remember what he said. Since he knew this happened every time he spoke in front of an audience, he trained himself to read, word for word, what was on the printed paper before him, reflexively looking up every few seconds so he didn't look robotic.

Rising above the crowd, he could see the faces more clearly. Even in different languages, different cultures, you can tell when someone isn't listening. Distracting themselves from being bored, watching the painfully dull person stumble over their painfully dull speech. Clicking a pen, rubbing a neck, fingers being picked, anything to distance themselves from the uncomfortable moment, because the more they listen the more they feel sorry for the speaker. The more anxious they feel. They look anywhere, anywhere except at the speaker, tracing the lines in the room's architecture, leaving their eyes and ears and drifting to those faraway places.

Descending, back down to earth, everything was ok. It was ok that he was a line item on a schedule. It was ok that his nonprofit was only invited so the leaders could go back to their countries and say, "after exploring all possible options, we have made the informed decision to…" It was ok, he thought. I'm ok, you're ok. Their minds were already made up before their airplanes landed, before they checked into their hotels, and before they walked in these doors. I'm ok, you're ok, we're intelligent creatures living in a meaningless world. And that's ok. It's ok to make emotional decisions because that's the law of the

thought, *as if you have ever been in India as more than a tourist. What, you graduated from UC Berkeley then went to UCLA.* He thinks more negative thoughts, about how this second-generation kid freeloaded their hardworking immigrant parents. *Not even a real doctor, not an MD,* he thinks, *and I'm sure they hear it at every family gathering: you work in healthcare, but you are not a doctor? Then what are you? Pharmacist? Physician Assistant? No? You make your parents very sad.*

Despite these negative thoughts, he was sure that he liked the psychologist, because he found himself thinking about their conversations. He didn't know why his default thoughts were so critical of others. He knew he was rude, even in small gestures. He knew he commanded respect by the way he walked into a room, even those who thought he was a jerk still did whatever he asked. It was the only way he made it out of the orphanage, on scholarship to the university in Canada. The only way he survived his childhood was by becoming this other person. He sometimes thinks about the tender child he might have been, playing cricket with his father, his father kneeling down to show him how to place his fingers on the ball. These images, the false ones, still warm his tummy.

He pours the coffee into a mug, missing a little, slopping onto the counter, and drinks it all in one gulp. He turns the shower water on and lets it warm up. During times when there is no need to think, his thoughts return to the psychologist's words: *You are a story. You are the story you tell yourself. If you change a part of the story, it will change who you are. It will change how you see things. When you become aware in a dream state, you become the narrator of your own life. You see your life as a story and you dream of the past, you can either change it or accept it fully for what it truly is: a chapter in your life, something you have overcome, not something you are defined by. You are in control of the narrative.*

world, what rules humanity. I'm ok and you're ok, and we all want to be fed, and liked, and touched, and cared for by someone besides our mothers. And when someone wasn't ok, well, that's ok, too, because we adjust our lives accordingly until everything is good enough to not complain. Good enough to sit here a while longer. Good enough to be ok. I'm ok, you're ok. We're all ok.

It's not that he didn't care, it's that he realized that he was caring about the wrong things. People can't change other people. People are not good at being people to other people, and it only hurts when you expect them to be. One time someone cut him off in traffic, and later, when the same car was weaving its way back over to exit off the freeway, he didn't let the car in. The car drove along next to him for a while until the lane narrowed and couldn't go any further. And no one else let the car in. It was stuck there honking the horn. The driver couldn't open its door because it was up against the concrete barrier. The passenger door was too close to traffic to open. He thought about why he didn't let the car in, and if that was the right thing to do. He wonders how long the car had to wait before someone let them back into the slow-moving current of traffic. He wonders if the person driving the car had a loved one in the hospital who was dying, and they were driving erratically because they wanted to say goodbye for it was too late. He wonders if there was a sick child in the car. He wonders if the driver was transporting his pregnant wife to the hospital. He thinks about that time whenever he wants to be cruel to someone or pass judgement on their behavior. He thinks, I'm ok. I'm ok. I'm ok.

He thinks: To be alive means accepting all the stories of your past, but what happens when you can't remember? Without memory, how much of our lives exist?

He remembers the early years, dating, the first time meet-the vile word he learned from the men in the factories when he would deliver hot lunches to them as a child.

"What they say?" His tone is even and without emotion. "No, don't call them back. They need us more than we need them. Don't say anything, don't even entertain the thought in your head of calling them. Give it 12 more hours and they will call."

He hangs up the phone and returns to the partially finished email and hits send. He walks over to the mirror outside of the bathroom door, there is a sink and he puts cold water on his face, drinking a little, and looks at his teeth. He thinks: Those बहनचोद, *stupid stupid stupid*.

He empties the little coffee package into the tiny hotel room coffee maker and adds water. Presses the button. *You'll give everything away with that kind of attitude, you can't rush things. You only rush them if you don't want them to think, and we want them to think, so the liability isn't on us.* He gurgles mouthwash and spits it into the sink. Doesn't run the water. *No wonder they were colonized by the British. It's not a matter of being nice and checking in, it's about who has the upper hand. If people always want something from you, you'll always have business. You'll always be in high demand. You'll always have power. And when you have power...*

Images of the dream came back, shooting through his mind like a toothache. The car, the gunshots, the ugly faces of death. His young body, running. The same one in the reflection of the mirror. The image of fear. The image of pain. The image of powerlessness.

"There you go," he says to himself, "dreaming of the desert again."

He thinks critically about the psychologist and remembers when they referred to our people. *Our people* he

ing his partner's family. How this new family slowly became part of his identity, part of how he defined himself and introduced himself to others. How the relationship becomes bigger, your family and their family, and how the inevitable split, either through a breakup or death, and how it's so much more painful because there are so many more hearts to break.

In the second year of their relationship, his partner's grandfather's dementia suddenly became worse and they placed him in an assisted living home. The family visited daily, and he was there with them in the afternoons, after teaching his last class of the day. In a conversation about nothing all too important, it came out that at one time he wanted to be an artist. He minored in art in undergrad, and everyone tells him that he must paint something for the grandfather, the grandfather who is confused and depressed and doesn't grasp their situation. Something to "pull him out of his funk."

He buys supplies at an overpriced art supplies store by the hospital near the University bookstore and gets to work right away. For the first time since submitting his grad school dissertation, he feels like he's putting part of himself into something. Every night after visiting the assisted living center, he spends hours on the painting, until the painting tells him it's finished.

The next afternoon, he gives the painting to the grandfather, who tells the nurses to hang it below the TV. Points with a boney finger, as if to say, yes, yes, over there, isn't it obvious? He rolls his wheelchair right up to it and lets out a tired sigh, motions, "no, no," with an annoyed hand when the nurses try pulling him away.

The next day, the grandfather looks at the painting a few hours in the morning and most of the afternoon. He tells the staff to turn off the TV and never plug the goddamn

don't seem to fit. Everything, in this whole world is mental, you think, and because you think it, it is so.]]]

The phone interrupts, and he lies motionless listening to the ringtone. It plays again, it's whistling, and sounds like this:

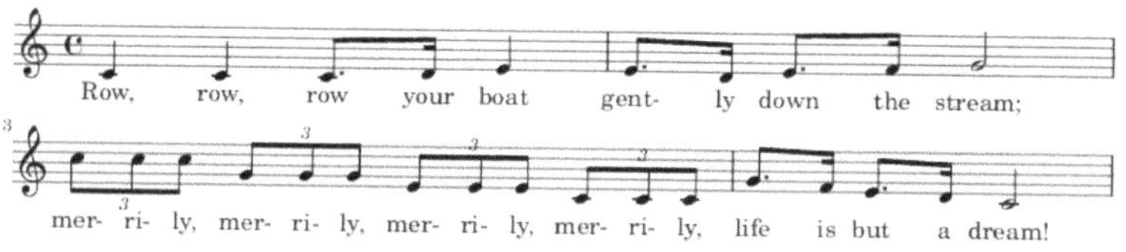


He lets out a sigh. "Ah yes, hello" he says into the phone. "No, no, I'm ok, I am awake. Time is behind here, you know, but it's ok, brother. What do you need from me?"

He remembers that he was having the dream, the awareness of it, but will soon forget. Right now, it's a dull headache and if he doesn't think about it, it will go away.

"Yah, ok, ok. Good. Yes, I'm confident we get official thumbs up today. Yah ok. K. ok. Good. First shipment leaves port next week, Thursday. "

He's sitting on the edge of the hotel bed, legs hang over the side and point towards the floor. He is wearing socks because he doesn't want to touch the floor with his bare feet.

"Yeh. Yah. Ok. Good, brother. You also."

He hangs up and sits upright in bed, looking at emails and opening and closing his eyes in exaggerated gestures. He rubs them, let's out a fart, and chuckles to himself. In the middle of composing an email reply the phone rings and blanks out the screen. He mutters बहनचोद to himself,

contraption in again. He breaks for meals but requests to sit in front of the painting until it's time for bed.

A third day, and the grandfather is laughing with the painting. Talking with it. He tears up once and touches the corner gently. But most of the time, he's staring off, eyes open, not looking, something more than that. In tune with something else.

A week goes by and the nurses are having private conversations amongst themselves, which spill over to conversations with the family. They talk about moving the painting, maybe it would be best if it wasn't here at all.

A nurse wheels the grandfather away and another moves in to take the painting down, hoping he'll forget it all once he's had supper and Wheel of Fortune is on the TV.

The grandfather turns around and whispers through a dry voice, no, no. Please don't, don't do that.

We have to, the nurse says, for your health.

The grandfather protests and says: to hell with my health, don't you think I know I'm dying?

No one says anything, no one moves.

The grandfather looks at him and then his partner, and back to him, and smiles only with his eyes. The grandfather speaks again, this time in a voice more coherent and youthful than it has been in years: This painting contains the memories of my life. I'm not only looking, because seeing is only a fraction of it, but more importantly, I am remembering. And it's all here. This painting is my life. If you take it away from me, you'll take away my memory, and if one cannot remember their own life, what was the point in living it in the first place?

of a friend, and they prescribe you pills that only makes it worse. You catch up with the friend of a friend about other friends, and who's gotten fat, and who's divorced, who had affairs, and who moved back to India. You tell them to just give you something that will knock you out, and they do. But the medication gives you sleep paralysis and you are stuck in your body unable to move, unable to wake up from the night terror. You are prescribed another medication, and everything moves along just fine until two weeks later when you wake up in the driver's seat of your car with the key in the ignition. Thankfully the garage door was open, or else your face would have been on the cover of every major newspaper in south Asia.

You gave up on Western medicine and asked your psychiatrist if there was anything else. And there was.

Your psychiatrist recommended a psychologist who you met with weekly to talk about "the event". This psychologist recommended an experimental treatment, since the dreams were so vivid, and this was for you to wake up, rather, become conscious in the dream, and within the dream, change its course. Or if it can't be changed, to face what happened, because that's why it keeps coming up, because you haven't been able to truly face it.

"It's called lucid dreaming, and our people have been doing it for millennia," they told you, all of this is mental, and the trick is to look at your hands, because then you will have something to ground yourself in.

So, you look at your hands in the dream and yeah, they're hands alright. But there's something off about them. They're not your hands, but a mirrored reflection. You look closer. The scar on your pinky finger is on your left hand, but it should be on the right.

You are not sure if you should write down the details that

He doesn't know why he's remembering this or what triggered it. He's confused by the things he remembers, because they could be the things others easily forget.

The grandfather died shortly after demanding the painting stay hanging in his room. The TV was never turned on again while he was alive. And on the day he died, he was sitting in the wheelchair, looking at the large brushstrokes from afar. He closed his eyes and said: yes, now that's that ticket. And his head nodded, motionless, as if bowing before the artwork.

He thinks: But where do those people go? The ones you have given part of your life to? He wonders where all the people are who he had once loved. The people he told secrets to, from best friends in elementary school to his first romantic relationship. And then college, and all the places he's worked and the many communities he's helped grow and develop. All the people had so easily come in and out of his life.

He thinks: why are the people you share the most of yourself with the ones who you risk never talking to again?

He thinks: How much of myself has come from people I will never see again?

He thinks: What are we but slices of everyone we meet?

He thinks about all the pieces of himself and all of himself that is composed of pieces he has taken from others.

Back at the hotel, he pulls the covers over his body.

He thinks: How many beds have I slept in? How many heads have slept on this pillow and how many hearts have thumped beneath these sheets?

It's only facts you could remember. That you once had parents and now you no longer have them. You know your name. You know food preferences and aversions. You remember how to read and can do basic math—everything from the previous year at school. But what happened and everything before it was wiped clean from your memory. And you wish it would have stayed like that.

A year later at the Christian orphanage, the Hindi-Christian orphanage, since the identity of a people can never fully be taken from them, that's when it began. Lying on the floor next to sixty other children, all of them, like you, are alone. You, without your memory, begin to understand the way of life. Adult stuff. Other children, you see them, full of happiness or full of sadness. But know that one cannot exist without the other. That happiness and sadness always occur together. And that's how you think of the dream that begins to visit you. In the dream, you remember every detail. You remember their faces, and how their faces combine to make your face. And you wish there was a memory before it happened, five minutes even, so you could see the life behind the cheekbones and eyebrows. But the only memory you have of your parents is them lying motionless in the dirt as their blood spills from their bodies and into the earth.

Now, 40 years later, it only comes on through aggravation, by stress—until now. Every night for the last two years you've dreamed of it, and it feels fresh and new as if it's the first each time. So, what do you do now? You wake up more tired than when you fell asleep. Your work quality suffers, and you play it off with the interns as if you are testing them, but you don't know how much longer you will be able to keep it up. You go to your primary care physician who recommends a psychiatrist who you visit with for a few minutes and you tell them it's a chemical imbalance, and don't we have ways of chemically stabilizing the mind? You know them from Med school, a friend

He rips the top off the salt packet he took from the café lounge downstairs near the hotel lobby and pours half of it on his tongue, jamming the grains into the roof of his mouth and then lets the saliva pool in the corners. He thinks about the part of every person that makes them do the things they do. Makes them do the things without even thinking about it. About how if you stop and think for a half second before doing anything, you realize how absurd it is. How absurd living is, and the things we do to occupy our time and the small things we believe are meaningful.

[[[And then you see the watering hole, and the path behind you. And you wonder what would happen if you turned around, went away from the water and tried to find out where all of this started. And you wonder what it's like to not have a body to return to, and why you ever felt like you needed one in the first place. ]]]

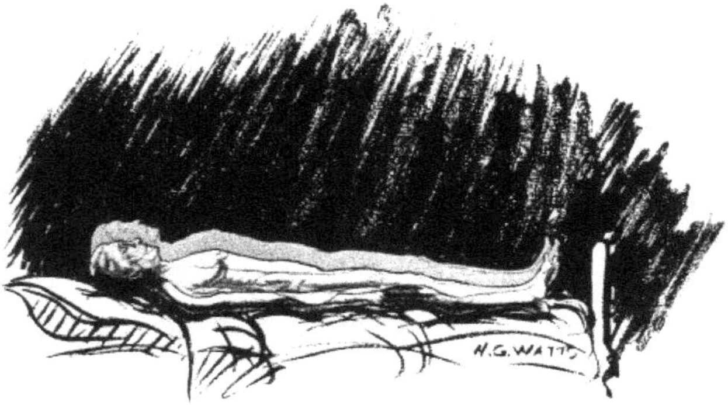

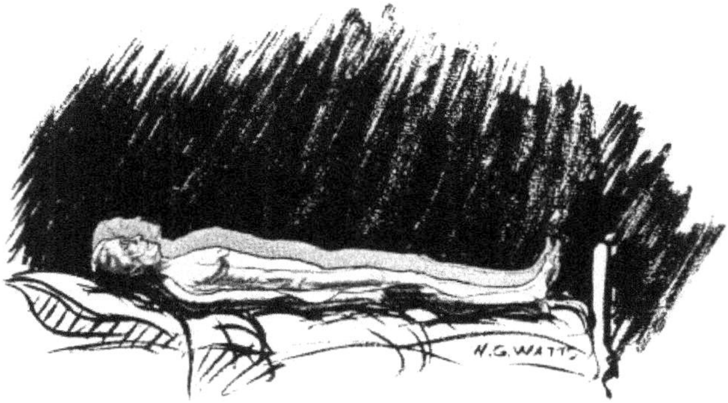


[[[You see a watering hole. Reprieve from the old dusty path.

It's like waking up from being blacked out, a short dizzy spell from standing too quickly, and then you lock in on details: sand, water, car.

You know you are dreaming, and it's *the* dream, and no matter how many times you've prepared for it, how many positive mantras you've programed yourself to recite, you never feel like you've done enough.

Shit, you think, मादरचोद. The hand thing. Do the hand thing. You see them, in fist balls. You tell yourself to relax.

You know dreams are only memories, and you can only remember because you've dreamed about it. After it happened, you had no memory and when people asked: "child, where are your parents? Your माता-पिता? The day is old and haven't you a home to return to?" No, no parents. No, no home.

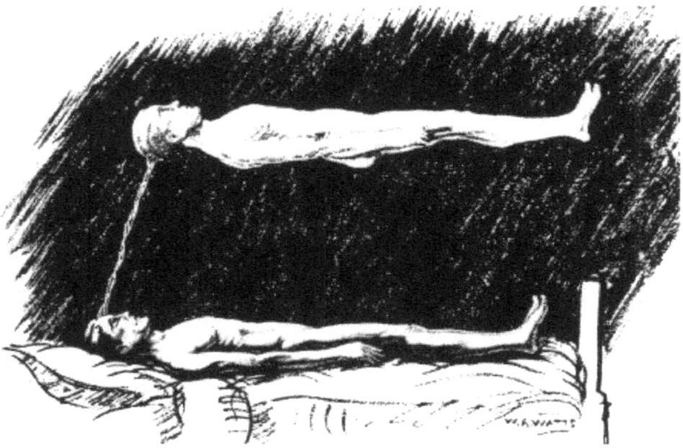

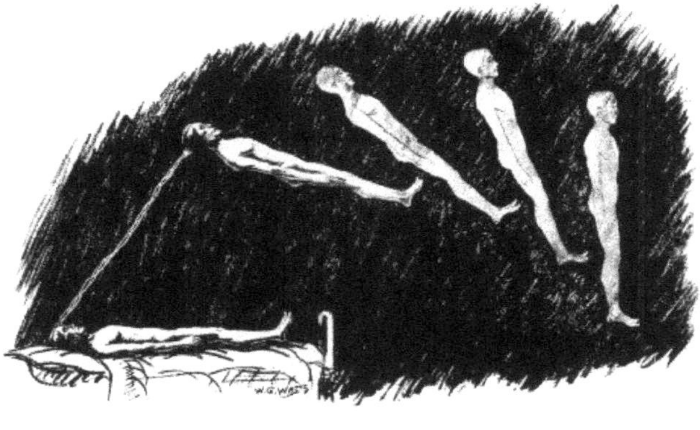

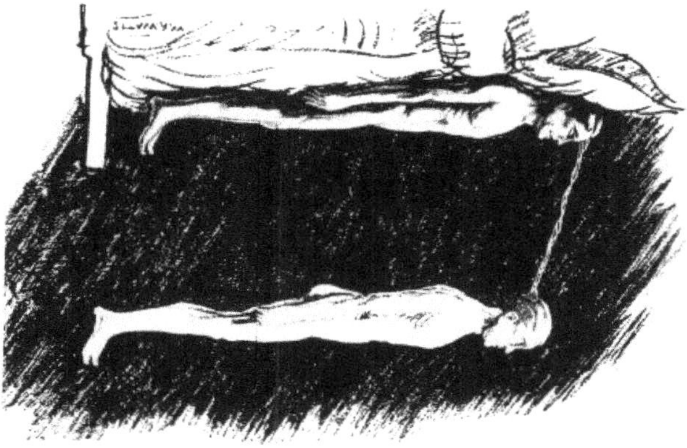

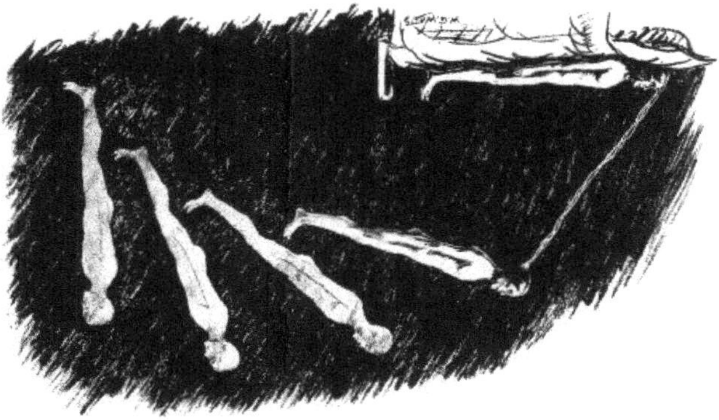

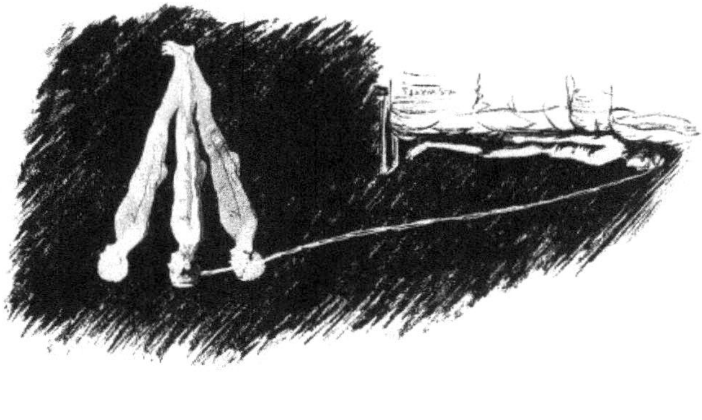

# ANDREW J. WILT

This chapter was written by Andrew J. Wilt. He writes self-help books like AGE OF AGILITY: THE NEW TOOLS FOR CAREER SUCCESS and is the Publisher & Co-Founder of 11:11 Press. When your number is called, he too will be waiting for you at the river. Until then.

ELEVEN
11:11
ELEVEN
PRESS

---

11:11 Press is an American independent literary publisher based in Minneapolis, MN. Founded in 2018, 11:11 publishes innovative literature of all forms and varieties. We believe in the freedom of artistic expression, the realization of creative potential, and the transcendental power of stories.

Lightning Source UK Ltd.
Milton Keynes UK
UKHW010741160322
400148UK00003B/402

9 781948 687249